FLANNERY O'CONNOR is widely regarded as one of the finest short story writers of our time. Her expert craftsmanship, her uncanny ability for characterization, the depth and intensity of her morality—combined in strict discipline—make her one of this generation's most respected authors. All of the qualities which have made her writing so outstanding are to be found in the collection, A GOOD MAN IS HARD TO FIND. Since its first publication, it has been highly acclaimed in critical circles. A sampling of the reviewers' comments follows below.

"Miss O'Connor is a regionalist in the best sense of the word: that is, she understands her country and its people so well that in her hands they become all humanity."

N.Y. *Herald Tribune Book Review*

"Miss O'Connor, with a direct, detached style, manages to preserve the complexity of the lives she takes up, and she has a musician's ear for the progress and qualities of sound that makes even the least of her tales a delight to read."

Commonweal

"Much savagery, compassion, farce, art and truth have gone into these stories. Miss O'Connor's characters are wholeheartedly horrible, and almost better than life. I find it hard to think of a funnier or more frightening writer."

ROBERT LOWELL

"Another talented Southern lady whose work is highly unladylike . . . Her instruments are a brutal irony, a slam-bang humor and a style of writing as balefully direct as a death sentence."

Time

"Most of the 10 stories have an underlying cruelty that is handled with the casualness that life itself takes toward human meanness. Yet withal there is besides an unsentimental compassion for even the cruelest and meanest of the people."

Best Sellers

FLANNERY O'CONNOR

A Good Man Is Hard to Find

AND OTHER STORIES

IMAGE BOOKS
A Division of Doubleday & Company, Inc.
Garden City, New York

Image Books edition 1970
by special arrangement with Harcourt, Brace & World, Inc.
Image Books edition published September 1970

FOR SALLY AND ROBERT FITZGERALD

Other Books by Flannery O'Connor

WISE BLOOD
THE VIOLENT BEAR IT AWAY
EVERYTHING THAT RISES MUST CONVERGE
THREE (contains: WISE BLOOD,
    THE VIOLENT BEAR IT AWAY, and
    A GOOD MAN IS HARD TO FIND)

CONTENTS

A GOOD MAN
IS HARD TO FIND

A GOOD MAN IS HARD TO FIND

The grandmother didn't want to go to Florida. She wanted to visit some of her connections in east Tennessee and she was seizing at every chance to change Bailey's mind. Bailey was the son she lived with, her only boy. He was sitting on the edge of his chair at the table, bent over the orange sports section of the *Journal*. "Now look here, Bailey," she said, "see here, read this," and she stood with one hand on her thin hip and the other rattling the newspaper at his bald head. "Here this fellow that calls himself The Misfit is aloose from the Federal Pen and headed toward Florida and you read here what it says he did to these people. Just you read it. I wouldn't take my children in any direction with a criminal like that aloose in it. I couldn't answer to my conscience if I did."

Bailey didn't look up from his reading so she wheeled around then and faced the children's mother, a young woman in slacks, whose face was as broad and innocent as a cabbage and was tied around with a green headkerchief that had two points on the top like rabbit's ears. She was sitting on the sofa, feeding the baby his apricots out of a jar. "The children have been to Florida before," the old lady said. "You all ought to take them somewhere else for a change so they would see different parts of the world and be broad. They never have been to east Tennessee."

The children's mother didn't seem to hear her but the eight-year-old boy, John Wesley, a stocky child with glasses, said, "If you don't want to go to Florida, why dontcha stay at home?" He and the little girl, June Star, were reading the funny papers on the floor.

"She wouldn't stay at home to be queen for a day," June Star said without raising her yellow head.

"Yes and what would you do if this fellow, The Misfit, caught you?" the grandmother asked.

"I'd smack his face," John Wesley said.

"She wouldn't stay at home for a million bucks," June Star said. "Afraid she'd miss something. She has to go everywhere we go."

"All right, Miss," the grandmother said. "Just remember that the next time you want me to curl your hair."

June Star said her hair was naturally curly.

The next morning the grandmother was the first one in the car, ready to go. She had her big black valise that looked like the head of a hippopotamus in one corner, and underneath it she was hiding a basket with Pitty Sing, the cat, in it. She didn't intend for the cat to be left alone in the house for three days because he would miss her too much and she was afraid he might brush against one of the gas burners and accidentally asphyxiate himself. Her son, Bailey, didn't like to arrive at a motel with a cat.

She sat in the middle of the back seat with John Wesley and June Star on either side of her. Bailey and the children's mother and the baby sat in front and they left Atlanta at eight forty-five with the mileage on the car at 55890. The grandmother wrote this down because she thought it would be interesting to say how many miles they had been when they got back. It took them twenty minutes to reach the outskirts of the city.

The old lady settled herself comfortably, removing her white cotton gloves and putting them up with her purse on the shelf in front of the back window. The children's mother still had on slacks and still had her head tied up in a green kerchief, but the grandmother had on a navy blue straw sailor hat with a bunch of white violets on the brim and a navy blue dress with a small white dot in the print. Her collars and cuffs were white organdy trimmed with lace and at her neckline she had pinned a purple spray of cloth violets containing a sachet. In case of an accident, anyone seeing her dead on the highway would know at once that she was a lady.

She said she thought it was going to be a good day for driving, neither too hot nor too cold, and she cautioned Bailey that the speed limit was fifty-five miles an hour and that the patrolmen hid themselves behind billboards and small clumps of trees and sped out after you before you had a chance to slow down. She pointed out interesting details of the scenery: Stone Mountain; the blue granite that in some places came up to both sides of the highway; the brilliant red clay banks slightly streaked with purple; and the various crops that made rows of green lace-work on the ground. The trees were full of silver-white sunlight and the meanest of them sparkled. The children were reading comic magazines and their mother had gone back to sleep.

"Let's go through Georgia fast so we won't have to look at it much," John Wesley said.

"If I were a little boy," said the grandmother, "I wouldn't talk about my native state that way. Tennessee has the mountains and Georgia has the hills."

"Tennessee is just a hillbilly dumping ground," John Wesley said, "and Georgia is a lousy state too."

"You said it," June Star said.

"In my time," said the grandmother, folding her thin veined fingers, "children were more respectful of their native states and their parents and everything else. People did right then. Oh look at the cute little pickaninny!" she said and pointed to a Negro child standing in the door of a shack. "Wouldn't that make a picture, now?" she asked and they all turned and looked at the little Negro out of the back window. He waved.

"He didn't have any britches on," June Star said.

"He probably didn't have any," the grandmother explained. "Little niggers in the country don't have things like we do. If I could paint, I'd paint that picture," she said.

The children exchanged comic books.

The grandmother offered to hold the baby and the children's mother passed him over the front seat to her. She set him on her knee and bounced him and told him about the things they were passing. She rolled her eyes and screwed up her mouth and stuck her leathery thin face into his smooth bland one. Occasionally he gave her a faraway smile. They passed a large cotton field with five or six graves fenced in the middle of it, like a small island. "Look at the graveyard!" the grandmother said, pointing it out. "That was the old family burying ground. That belonged to the plantation."

"Where's the plantation?" John Wesley asked.

"Gone With the Wind," said the grandmother. "Ha. Ha."

When the children finished all the comic books they had brought, they opened the lunch and ate it. The grandmother ate a peanut butter sandwich and an olive and would not let the children throw the box and the paper napkins out the window. When there was nothing else to do they played a game by choosing a cloud and making the other two guess what shape it suggested. John Wesley took one the shape of a cow and June Star guessed a cow and John Wesley said, no, an automobile, and June Star said he didn't play fair, and they began to slap each other over the grandmother.

The grandmother said she would tell them a story if they would keep quiet. When she told a story, she rolled her eyes and waved her head and was very dramatic. She said once when she was a maiden lady she had been courted by a Mr. Edgar Atkins Teagarden from Jasper, Georgia. She said he was a very good-looking man and a gentleman and that he brought her a watermelon every Saturday afternoon with his initials cut in it, E. A. T. Well, one Saturday, she said, Mr. Teagarden brought the watermelon and there was nobody at home and he left it on the front porch and returned in his buggy to Jasper, but she never got the watermelon, she said, because a nigger boy ate it when he saw the initials, E. A. T.! This story tickled John Wesley's funny bone and he giggled and giggled but June Star didn't think it was any good. She said she wouldn't marry a man that just brought her a watermelon on Saturday. The grandmother said she would have done well to marry Mr. Teagarden because he was a gentleman and had bought Coca-Cola stock when it first came out and that he had died only a few years ago, a very wealthy man.

They stopped at The Tower for barbecued sandwiches. The Tower was a part stucco and part wood filling station and dance hall set in a clearing outside of Timothy. A fat man named Red Sammy Butts ran it and there were signs stuck here and there on the building and for miles up and down the highway saying, TRY RED SAMMY'S FAMOUS BARBECUE. NONE LIKE FAMOUS RED SAMMY'S! RED SAM! THE FAT BOY WITH THE HAPPY LAUGH. A VETERAN! RED SAMMY'S YOUR MAN!

Red Sammy was lying on the bare ground outside The Tower with his head under a truck while a gray monkey about a foot high, chained to a small chinaberry tree, chattered nearby. The monkey sprang back into the tree and got on the highest limb as soon as he saw the children jump out of the car and run toward him.

Inside, The Tower was a long dark room with a counter at one end and tables at the other and dancing space in the middle. They all sat down at a board table next to the nickelodeon and Red Sam's wife, a tall burnt-brown woman with hair and eyes lighter than her skin, came and took their order. The children's mother put a dime in the machine and played "The Tennessee Waltz," and the grandmother said that tune always made her want to dance. She asked Bailey if he would like to dance but he only glared at her. He didn't have a naturally sunny disposition like she did and trips made him nervous. The grandmother's brown eyes were very bright. She swayed her head from side to side and pretended she was dancing in her chair. June Star said play something she could tap to so the children's mother put in another dime and played a fast number and June Star stepped out onto the dance floor and did her tap routine.

"Ain't she cute?" Red Sam's wife said, leaning over the counter. "Would you like to come be my little girl?"

"No I certainly wouldn't," June Star said. "I wouldn't live in a broken-down place like this for a million bucks!" and she ran back to the table.

"Ain't she cute?" the woman repeated, stretching her mouth politely.

"Arn't you ashamed?" hissed the grandmother.

Red Sam came in and told his wife to quit lounging on the counter and hurry up with these people's order. His khaki trousers reached just to his hip bones and his stomach hung over them like a sack of meal swaying under his shirt. He came over and sat down at a table nearby and let out a combination sigh and yodel. "You can't win," he said. "You can't win," and he wiped his sweating red face off with a gray handkerchief. "These days you don't know who to trust," he said. "Ain't that the truth?"

"People are certainly not nice like they used to be," said the grandmother.

"Two fellers come in here last week," Red Sammy said, "driving a Chrysler. It was a old beat-up car but it was a good one and these boys looked all right to me. Said they worked at the mill and you know I let them fellers charge the gas they bought? Now why did I do that?"

"Because you're a good man!" the grandmother said at once.

"Yes'm, I suppose so," Red Sam said as if he were struck with this answer.

His wife brought the orders, carrying the five plates all

at once without a tray, two in each hand and one balanced on her arm. "It isn't a soul in this green world of God's that you can trust," she said. "And I don't count nobody out of that, not nobody," she repeated, looking at Red Sammy.

"Did you read about that criminal, The Misfit, that's escaped?" asked the grandmother.

"I wouldn't be a bit surprised if he didn't attact this place right here," said the woman. "If he hears about it being here, I wouldn't be none surprised to see him. If he hears it's two cent in the cash register, I wouldn't be a tall surprised if he . . ."

"That'll do," Red Sam said. "Go bring these people their Co'-Colas," and the woman went off to get the rest of the order.

"A good man is hard to find," Red Sammy said. "Everything is getting terrible. I remember the day you could go off and leave your screen door unlatched. Not no more."

He and the grandmother discussed better times. The old lady said that in her opinion Europe was entirely to blame for the way things were now. She said the way Europe acted you would think we were made of money and Red Sam said it was no use talking about it, she was exactly right. The children ran outside into the white sunlight and looked at the monkey in the lacy chinaberry tree. He was busy catching fleas on himself and biting each one carefully between his teeth as if it were a delicacy.

They drove off again into the hot afternoon. The grandmother took cat naps and woke up every few minutes with her own snoring. Outside of Toombsboro she woke up and recalled an old plantation that she had visited in this neighborhood once when she was a young lady. She said the house had six white columns across the front and that there was an avenue of oaks leading up to it and two little wooden trellis arbors on either side in front where you sat down with your suitor after a stroll in the garden. She recalled exactly which road to turn off to get to it. She knew that Bailey would not be willing to lose any time looking at an old house, but the more she talked about it, the more she wanted to see it once again and find out if the little twin arbors were still standing. "There was a secret panel in this house," she said craftily, not telling the truth but wishing that she were, "and the story went that all the family silver was hidden in it when Sherman came through but it was never found . . ."

"Hey!" John Wesley said. "Let's go see it! We'll find it! We'll poke all the woodwork and find it! Who lives there? Where do you turn off at? Hey Pop, can't we turn off there?"

"We never have seen a house with a secret panel!" June Star shrieked. "Let's go to the house with the secret panel! Hey Pop, can't we go see the house with the secret panel!"

"It's not far from here, I know," the grandmother said. "It wouldn't take over twenty minutes."

Bailey was looking straight ahead. His jaw was as rigid as a horseshoe. "No," he said.

The children began to yell and scream that they wanted to see the house with the secret panel. John Wesley kicked the back of the front seat and June Star hung over her mother's shoulder and whined desperately into her ear that they never had any fun even on their vacation, that they could never do what THEY wanted to do. The baby began to scream and John Wesley kicked the back of the seat so hard that his father could feel the blows in his kidney.

"All right!" he shouted and drew the car to a stop at the side of the road. "Will you all shut up? Will you all just shut up for one second? If you don't shut up, we won't go anywhere."

"It would be very educational for them," the grandmother murmured.

"All right," Bailey said, "but get this: this is the only time we're going to stop for anything like this. This is the one and only time."

"The dirt road that you have to turn down is about a mile back," the grandmother directed. "I marked it when we passed."

"A dirt road," Bailey groaned.

After they had turned around and were headed toward the dirt road, the grandmother recalled other points about the house, the beautiful glass over the front doorway and the candle-lamp in the hall. John Wesley said that the secret panel was probably in the fireplace.

"You can't go inside this house," Bailey said. "You don't know who lives there."

"While you all talk to the people in front, I'll run around behind and get in a window," John Wesley suggested.

"We'll all stay in the car," his mother said.

They turned onto the dirt road and the car raced roughly along in a swirl of pink dust. The grandmother recalled the times when there were no paved roads and thirty miles was a day's journey. The dirt road was hilly and there were sudden washes in it and sharp curves on dangerous embankments. All at once they would be on a hill, looking down over the blue tops of trees for miles around, then the next minute, they would be in a red depression with the dust-coated trees looking down on them.

"This place had better turn up in a minute," Bailey said, "or I'm going to turn around."

The road looked as if no one had traveled on it in months.

"It's not much farther," the grandmother said and just as she said it, a horrible thought came to her. The thought was so embarrassing that she turned red in the face and her eyes dilated and her feet jumped up, upsetting her valise in the corner. The instant the valise moved, the newspaper top she had over the basket under it rose with a snarl and Pitty Sing, the cat, sprang onto Bailey's shoulder.

The children were thrown to the floor and their mother,

clutching the baby, was thrown out the door onto the ground; the old lady was thrown into the front seat. The car turned over once and landed right-side-up in a gulch off the side of the road. Bailey remained in the driver's seat with the cat—gray-striped with a broad white face and an orange nose—clinging to his neck like a caterpillar.

As soon as the children saw they could move their arms and legs, they scrambled out of the car, shouting, "We've had an ACCIDENT!" The grandmother was curled up under the dashboard, hoping she was injured so that Bailey's wrath would not come down on her all at once. The horrible thought she had had before the accident was that the house she had remembered so vividly was not in Georgia but in Tennessee.

Bailey removed the cat from his neck with both hands and flung it out the window against the side of a pine tree. Then he got out of the car and started looking for the children's mother. She was sitting against the side of the red gutted ditch, holding the screaming baby, but she only had a cut down her face and a broken shoulder. "We've had an ACCIDENT!" the children screamed in a frenzy of delight.

"But nobody's killed," June Star said with disappointment as the grandmother limped out of the car, her hat still pinned to her head but the broken front brim standing up at a jaunty angle and the violet spray hanging off the side. They all sat down in the ditch, except the children, to recover from the shock. They were all shaking.

"Maybe a car will come along," said the children's mother hoarsely.

"I believe I have injured an organ," said the grandmother, pressing her side, but no one answered her. Bailey's teeth were clattering. He had on a yellow sport shirt with bright blue parrots designed in it and his face was as yellow as the shirt. The grandmother decided that she would not mention that the house was in Tennessee.

The road was about ten feet above and they could see

only the tops of the trees on the other side of it. Behind the ditch they were sitting in there were more woods, tall and dark and deep. In a few minutes they saw a car some distance away on top of a hill, coming slowly as if the occupants were watching them. The grandmother stood up and waved both arms dramatically to attract their attention. The car continued to come on slowly, disappeared around a bend and appeared again, moving even slower, on top of the hill they had gone over. It was a big black battered hearse-like automobile. There were three men in it.

It came to a stop just over them and for some minutes, the driver looked down with a steady expressionless gaze to where they were sitting, and didn't speak. Then he turned his head and muttered something to the other two and they got out. One was a fat boy in black trousers and a red sweat shirt with a silver stallion embossed on the front of it. He moved around on the right side of them and stood staring, his mouth partly open in a kind of loose grin. The other had on khaki pants and a blue striped coat and a gray hat pulled down very low, hiding most of his face. He came around slowly on the left side. Neither spoke.

The driver got out of the car and stood by the side of it, looking down at them. He was an older man than the other two. His hair was just beginning to gray and he wore silver-rimmed spectacles that gave him a scholarly look. He had a long creased face and didn't have on any shirt or undershirt. He had on blue jeans that were too tight for him and was holding a black hat and a gun. The two boys also had guns.

"We've had an ACCIDENT!" the children screamed.

The grandmother had the peculiar feeling that the bespectacled man was someone she knew. His face was as familiar to her as if she had known him all her life but she could not recall who he was. He moved away from the car and began to come down the embankment, placing his feet carefully so that he wouldn't slip. He had on tan and white shoes and no socks, and his ankles were red and thin. "Good afternoon," he said. "I see you all had you a little spill."

"We turned over twice!" said the grandmother.

"Oncet," he corrected. "We seen it happen. Try their car and see will it run, Hiram," he said quietly to the boy with the gray hat.

"What you got that gun for?" John Wesley asked. "Whatcha gonna do with that gun?"

"Lady," the man said to the children's mother, "would you mind calling them children to sit down by you? Children make me nervous. I want all you all to sit down right together there where you're at."

"What are you telling US what to do for?" June Star asked.

Behind them the line of woods gaped like a dark open mouth. "Come here," said their mother.

"Look here now," Bailey began suddenly, "we're in a predicament! We're in . . ."

The grandmother shrieked. She scrambled to her feet and stood staring. "You're The Misfit!" she said. "I recognized you at once!"

"Yes'm," the man said, smiling slightly as if he were pleased in spite of himself to be known, "but it would have been better for all of you, lady, if you hadn't of reckernized me."

Bailey turned his head sharply and said something to his mother that shocked even the children. The old lady began to cry and The Misfit reddened.

"Lady," he said, "don't you get upset. Sometimes a man says things he don't mean. I don't reckon he meant to talk to you thataway."

"You wouldn't shoot a lady, would you?" the grandmother said and removed a clean handkerchief from her cuff and began to slap at her eyes with it.

The Misfit pointed the toe of his shoe into the ground

and made a little hole and then covered it up again. "I would hate to have to," he said.

"Listen," the grandmother almost screamed, "I know you're a good man. You don't look a bit like you have common blood. I know you must come from nice people!"

"Yes mam," he said, "finest people in the world." When he smiled he showed a row of strong white teeth. "God never made a finer woman than my mother and my daddy's heart was pure gold," he said. The boy with the red sweat shirt had come around behind them and was standing with his gun at his hip. The Misfit squatted down on the ground. "Watch them children, Bobby Lee," he said. "You know they make me nervous." He looked at the six of them huddled together in front of him and he seemed to be embarrassed as if he couldn't think of anything to say. "Ain't a cloud in the sky," he remarked, looking up at it. "Don't see no sun but don't see no cloud neither."

"Yes, it's a beautiful day," said the grandmother. "Listen," she said, "you shouldn't call yourself The Misfit because I know you're a good man at heart. I can just look at you and tell."

"Hush!" Bailey yelled. "Hush! Everybody shut up and let me handle this!" He was squatting in the position of a runner about to sprint forward but he didn't move.

"I pre-chate that, lady," The Misfit said and drew a little circle in the ground with the butt of his gun.

"It'll take a half a hour to fix this here car," Hiram called, looking over the raised hood of it.

"Well, first you and Bobby Lee get him and that little boy to step over yonder with you," The Misfit said, pointing to Bailey and John Wesley. "The boys want to ast you something," he said to Bailey. "Would you mind stepping back in them woods there with them?"

"Listen," Bailey began, "we're in a terrible predicament! Nobody realizes what this is," and his voice cracked. His eyes were as blue and intense as the parrots in his shirt and he remained perfectly still.

The grandmother reached up to adjust her hat brim as if she were going to the woods with him but it came off in her hand. She stood staring at it and after a second she let it fall on the ground. Hiram pulled Bailey up by the arm as if he were assisting an old man. John Wesley caught hold of his father's hand and Bobby Lee followed. They went off toward the woods and just as they reached the dark edge, Bailey turned and supporting himself against a gray naked pine trunk, he shouted, "I'll be back in a minute, Mamma, wait on me!"

"Come back this instant!" his mother shrilled but they all disappeared into the woods.

"Bailey Boy!" the grandmother called in a tragic voice but she found she was looking at The Misfit squatting on the ground in front of her. "I just know you're a good man," she said desperately. "You're not a bit common!"

"Nome, I ain't a good man," The Misfit said after a second as if he had considered her statement carefully, "but I ain't the worst in the world neither. My daddy said I was a different breed of dog from my brothers and sisters. 'You know,' Daddy said, 'it's some that can live their whole life out without asking about it and it's others has to know why it is, and this boy is one of the latters. He's going to be into everything!'" He put on his black hat and looked up suddenly and then away deep into the woods as if he were embarrassed again. "I'm sorry I don't have on a shirt before you ladies," he said, hunching his shoulders slightly. "We buried our clothes that we had on when we escaped and we're just making do until we can get better. We borrowed these from some folks we met," he explained.

"That's perfectly all right," the grandmother said. "Maybe Bailey has an extra shirt in his suitcase."

"I'll look and see terrectly," The Misfit said.

"Where are they taking him?" the children's mother screamed.

"Daddy was a card himself," The Misfit said. "You

couldn't put anything over on him. He never got in trouble with the Authorities though. Just had the knack of handling them."

"You could be honest too if you'd only try," said the grandmother. "Think how wonderful it would be to settle down and live a comfortable life and not have to think about somebody chasing you all the time."

The Misfit kept scratching in the ground with the butt of his gun as if he were thinking about it. "Yes'm, somebody is always after you," he murmured.

The grandmother noticed how thin his shoulder blades were just behind his hat because she was standing up looking down on him. "Do you ever pray?" she asked.

He shook his head. All she saw was the black hat wiggle between his shoulder blades. "Nome," he said.

There was a pistol shot from the woods, followed closely by another. Then silence. The old lady's head jerked around. She could hear the wind move through the tree tops like a long satisfied insuck of breath. "Bailey Boy!" she called.

"I was a gospel singer for a while," The Misfit said. "I been most everything. Been in the arm service, both land and sea, at home and abroad, been twict married, been an undertaker, been with the railroads, plowed Mother Earth, been in a tornado, seen a man burnt alive oncet," and he looked up at the children's mother and the little girl who were sitting close together, their faces white and their eyes glassy; "I even seen a woman flogged," he said.

"Pray, pray," the grandmother began, "pray, pray . . ."

"I never was a bad boy that I remember of," The Misfit said in an almost dreamy voice, "but somewheres along the line I done something wrong and got sent to the penitentiary. I was buried alive," and he looked up and held her attention to him by a steady stare.

"That's when you should have started to pray," she said. "What did you do to get sent to the penitentiary that first time?"

"Turn to the right, it was a wall," The Misfit said, looking up again at the cloudless sky. "Turn to the left, it was a wall. Look up it was a ceiling, look down it was a floor. I forget what I done, lady. I set there and set there, trying to remember what it was I done and I ain't recalled it to this day. Oncet in a while, I would think it was coming to me, but it never come."

"Maybe they put you in by mistake," the old lady said vaguely.

"Nome," he said. "It wasn't no mistake. They had the papers on me."

"You must have stolen something," she said.

The Misfit sneered slightly. "Nobody had nothing I wanted," he said. "It was a head-doctor at the penitentiary said what I had done was kill my daddy but I known that for a lie. My daddy died in nineteen ought nineteen of the epidemic flu and I never had a thing to do with it. He was buried in the Mount Hopewell Baptist churchyard and you can go there and see for yourself."

"If you would pray," the old lady said, "Jesus would help you."

"That's right," The Misfit said.

"Well then, why don't you pray?" she asked trembling with delight suddenly.

"I don't want no hep," he said. "I'm doing all right by myself."

Bobby Lee and Hiram came ambling back from the woods. Bobby Lee was dragging a yellow shirt with bright blue parrots in it.

"Thow me that shirt, Bobby Lee," The Misfit said. The shirt came flying at him and landed on his shoulder and he put it on. The grandmother couldn't name what the shirt reminded her of. "No, lady," The Misfit said while he was buttoning it up, "I found out the crime don't matter. You can do one thing or you can do another, kill a man or take a tire off his car, because sooner or later you're going to forget what it was you done and just be punished for it."

The children's mother had begun to make heaving noises as if she couldn't get her breath. "Lady," he asked, "would you and that little girl like to step off yonder with Bobby Lee and Hiram and join your husband?"

"Yes, thank you," the mother said faintly. Her left arm dangled helplessly and she was holding the baby, who had gone to sleep, in the other. "Hep that lady up, Hiram," The Misfit said as she struggled to climb out of the ditch, "and Bobby Lee, you hold onto that little girl's hand."

"I don't want to hold hands with him," June Star said. "He reminds me of a pig."

The fat boy blushed and laughed and caught her by the arm and pulled her off into the woods after Hiram and her mother.

Alone with The Misfit, the grandmother found that she had lost her voice. There was not a cloud in the sky nor any sun. There was nothing around her but woods. She wanted to tell him that he must pray. She opened and closed her mouth several times before anything came out. Finally she found herself saying, "Jesus. Jesus," meaning, Jesus will help you, but the way she was saying it, it sounded as if she might be cursing.

"Yes'm," The Misfit said as if he agreed. "Jesus thown everything off balance. It was the same case with Him as with me except He hadn't committed any crime and they could prove I had committed one because they had the papers on me. Of course," he said, "they never shown me my papers. That's why I sign myself now. I said long ago, you get you a signature and sign everything you do and keep a copy of it. Then you'll know what you done and you can hold up the crime to the punishment and see do they match and in the end you'll have something to prove you ain't been treated right. I call myself The Misfit," he said, "because I can't make what all I done wrong fit what all I gone through in punishment."

There was a piercing scream from the woods, followed closely by a pistol report. "Does it seem right to you, lady, that one is punished a heap and another ain't punished at all?"

"Jesus!" the old lady cried. "You've got good blood! I know you wouldn't shoot a lady! I know you come from nice people! Pray! Jesus, you ought not to shoot a lady. I'll give you all the money I've got!"

"Lady," The Misfit said, looking beyond her far into the woods, "there never was a body that give the undertaker a tip."

There were two more pistol reports and the grandmother raised her head like a parched old turkey hen crying for water and called, "Bailey Boy, Bailey Boy!" as if her heart would break.

"Jesus was the only One that ever raised the dead," The Misfit continued, "and He shouldn't have done it. He thown everything off balance. If He did what He said, then it's nothing for you to do but thow away everything and follow Him, and if He didn't, then it's nothing for you to do but enjoy the few minutes you got left the best way you can—by killing somebody or burning down his house or doing some other meanness to him. No pleasure but meanness," he said and his voice had become almost a snarl.

"Maybe He didn't raise the dead," the old lady mumbled, not knowing what she was saying and feeling so dizzy that she sank down in the ditch with her legs twisted under her.

"I wasn't there so I can't say He didn't," The Misfit said. "I wisht I had of been there," he said, hitting the ground with his fist. "It ain't right I wasn't there because if I had of been there I would of known. Listen lady," he said in a high voice, "if I had of been there I would of known and I wouldn't be like I am now." His voice seemed about to crack and the grandmother's head cleared for an instant. She saw the man's face twisted close to her own as if he were going to cry and she murmured, "Why you're one of my babies. You're one of my own children!" She reached out and touched him on the shoulder. The Misfit sprang back as if a snake had bitten him and shot her three times through the chest. Then he put his gun down on the ground and took off his glasses and began to clean them.

Hiram and Bobby Lee returned from the woods and stood over the ditch, looking down at the grandmother who half sat and half lay in a puddle of blood with her legs crossed under her like a child's and her face smiling up at the cloudless sky.

Without his glasses, The Misfit's eyes were red-rimmed and pale and defenseless-looking. "Take her off and thow her where you thown the others," he said, picking up the cat that was rubbing itself against his leg.

"She was a talker, wasn't she?" Bobby Lee said, sliding down the ditch with a yodel.

"She would of been a good woman," The Misfit said, "if it had been somebody there to shoot her every minute of her life."

"Some fun!" Bobby Lee said.

"Shut up, Bobby Lee," The Misfit said. "It's no real pleasure in life."

THE RIVER

The child stood glum and limp in the middle of the dark living room while his father pulled him into a plaid coat. His right arm was hung in the sleeve but the father buttoned the coat anyway and pushed him forward toward a pale spotted hand that stuck through the half-open door.

"He ain't fixed right," a loud voice said from the hall.

"Well then for Christ's sake fix him," the father muttered. "It's six o'clock in the morning." He was in his bathrobe and barefooted. When he got the child to the door and tried to shut it, he found her looming in it, a speckled skeleton in a long pea-green coat and felt helmet.

"And his and my carfare," she said. "It'll be twict we have to ride the car."

He went in the bedroom again to get the money and when he came back, she and the boy were both standing in the middle of the room. She was taking stock. "I couldn't smell those dead cigarette butts long if I was ever to come sit with you," she said, shaking him down in his coat.

"Here's the change," the father said. He went to the door and opened it wide and waited.

After she had counted the money she slipped it somewhere inside her coat and walked over to a watercolor hanging near the phonograph. "I know what time it is," she said, peering closely at the black lines crossing into broken planes of violent color. "I ought to. My shift goes on at 10 P.M. and don't get off till 5 and it takes me one hour to ride the Vine Street car."

"Oh, I see," he said; "well, we'll expect him back tonight, about eight or nine?"

"Maybe later," she said. "We're going to the river to a healing. This particular preacher don't get around this way often. I wouldn't have paid for that," she said, nodding at the painting, "I would have drew it myself."

"All right, Mrs. Connin, we'll see you then," he said, drumming on the door.

A toneless voice called from the bedroom, "Bring me an icepack."

"Too bad his mamma's sick," Mrs. Connin said. "What's her trouble?"

"We don't know," he muttered.

"We'll ask the preacher to pray for her. He's healed a lot of folks. The Reverend Bevel Summers. Maybe she ought to see him sometime."

"Maybe so," he said. "We'll see you tonight," and he disappeared into the bedroom and left them to go.

The little boy stared at her silently, his nose and eyes running. He was four or five. He had a long face and bulging chin and half-shut eyes set far apart. He seemed mute and patient, like an old sheep waiting to be let out.

"You'll like this preacher," she said. "The Reverend Bevel Summers. You ought to hear him sing."

The bedroom door opened suddenly and the father stuck his head out and said, "Good-by, old man. Have a good time."

"Good-by," the little boy said and jumped as if he had been shot.

Mrs. Connin gave the watercolor another look. Then they went out into the hall and rang for the elevator. "I wouldn't have drew it," she said.

Outside the gray morning was blocked off on either side by the unlit empty buildings. "It's going to fair up later," she said, "but this is the last time we'll be able to have any preaching at the river this year. Wipe your nose, Sugar Boy."

He began rubbing his sleeve across it but she stopped him. "That ain't nice," she said. "Where's your handkerchief?"

He put his hands in his pockets and pretended to look

for it while she waited. "Some people don't care how they send one off," she murmured to her reflection in the coffee shop window. "You pervide." She took a red and blue flowered handkerchief out of her pocket and stooped down and began to work on his nose. "Now blow," she said and he blew. "You can borry it. Put it in your pocket."

He folded it up and put it in his pocket carefully and they walked on to the corner and leaned against the side of a closed drugstore to wait for the car. Mrs. Connin turned up her coat collar so that it met her hat in the back. Her eyelids began to droop and she looked as if she might go to sleep against the wall. The little boy put a slight pressure on her hand.

"What's your name?" she asked in a drowsy voice. "I don't know but only your last name. I should have found out your first name."

His name was Harry Ashfield and he had never thought at any time before of changing it. "Bevel," he said.

Mrs. Connin raised herself from the wall. "Why ain't that a coincident!" she said. "I told you that's the name of this preacher!"

"Bevel," he repeated.

She stood looking down at him as if he had become a marvel to her. "I'll have to see you meet him today," she said. "He's no ordinary preacher. He's a healer. He couldn't do nothing for Mr. Connin though. Mr. Connin didn't have the faith but he said he would try anything once. He had this griping in his gut."

The trolley appeared as a yellow spot at the end of the deserted street.

"He's gone to the government hospital now," she said, "and they taken one-third of his stomach. I tell him he better thank Jesus for what he's got left but he says he ain't thanking nobody. Well I declare," she murmured, "Bevel!"

They walked out to the tracks to wait. "Will he heal me?" Bevel asked.

"What you got?"

"I'm hungry," he decided finally.

"Didn't you have your breakfast?"

"I didn't have time to be hungry yet then," he said.

"Well when we get home we'll both have us something," she said. "I'm ready myself."

They got on the car and sat down a few seats behind the driver and Mrs. Connin took Bevel on her knees. "Now you be a good boy," she said, "and let me get some sleep. Just don't get off my lap." She lay her head back and as he watched, gradually her eyes closed and her mouth fell open to show a few long scattered teeth, some gold and some darker than her face; she began to whistle and blow like a musical skeleton. There was no one in the car but themselves and the driver and when he saw she was asleep, he took out the flowered handkerchief and unfolded it and examined it carefully. Then he folded it up again and unzipped a place in the innerlining of his coat and hid it in there and shortly he went to sleep himself.

Her house was a half-mile from the end of the car line, set back a little from the road. It was tan paper brick with a porch across the front of it and a tin top. On the porch there were three little boys of different sizes with identical speckled faces and one tall girl who had her hair up in so many aluminum curlers that it glared like the roof. The three boys followed them inside and closed in on Bevel. They looked at him silently, not smiling.

"That's Bevel," Mrs. Connin said, taking off her coat. "It's a coincident he's named the same as the preacher. These boys are J. C., Spivey, and Sinclair, and that's Sarah Mildred on the porch. Take off that coat and hang it on the bed post, Bevel."

The three boys watched him while he unbuttoned the coat and took it off. Then they watched him hang it on the bed post and then they stood, watching the coat. They turned abruptly and went out the door and had a conference on the porch.

Bevel stood looking around him at the room. It was part kitchen and part bedroom. The entire house was two rooms and two porches. Close to his foot the tail of a light-colored dog moved up and down between two floor boards as he scratched his back on the underside of the house. Bevel jumped on it but the hound was experienced and had already withdrawn when his feet hit the spot.

The walls were filled with pictures and calendars. There were two round photographs of an old man and woman with collapsed mouths and another picture of a man whose eyebrows dashed out of two bushes of hair and clashed in a heap on the bridge of his nose; the rest of his face stuck out like a bare cliff to fall from. "That's Mr. Connin," Mrs. Connin said, standing back from the stove for a second to admire the face with him, "but it don't favor him any more." Bevel turned from Mr. Connin to a colored picture over the bed of a man wearing a white sheet. He had long hair and a gold circle around his head and he was sawing on a board while some children stood watching him. He was going to ask who that was when the three boys came in again and motioned for him to follow them. He thought of crawling under the bed and hanging onto one of the legs but the three boys only stood there, speckled and silent, waiting, and after a second he followed them at a little distance out on the porch and around the corner of the house. They started off through a field of rough yellow weeds to the hog pen, a five-foot boarded square full of shoats, which they intended to ease him over into. When they reached it, they turned and waited silently, leaning against the side.

He was coming very slowly, deliberately bumping his feet together as if he had trouble walking. Once he had been beaten up in the park by some strange boys when his sitter forgot him, but he hadn't known anything was going to happen that time until it was over. He began to smell a strong odor of garbage and to hear the noises of a wild animal. He stopped a few feet from the pen and waited, pale but dogged.

The three boys didn't move. Something seemed to have happened to them. They stared over his head as if they saw something coming behind him but he was afraid to turn his own head and look. Their speckles were pale and their eyes were still and gray as glass. Only their ears twitched slightly. Nothing happened. Finally, the one in the middle said, "She'd kill us," and turned, dejected and hacked, and climbed up on the pen and hung over, staring in.

Bevel sat down on the ground, dazed with relief, and grinned up at them.

The one sitting on the pen glanced at him severely. "Hey you," he said after a second, "if you can't climb up and see these pigs you can lift that bottom board off and look in thataway." He appeared to offer this as a kindness.

Bevel had never seen a real pig but he had seen a pig in a book and knew they were small fat pink animals with curly tails and round grinning faces and bow ties. He leaned forward and pulled eagerly at the board.

"Pull harder," the littlest boy said. "It's nice and rotten. Just life out thet nail."

He eased a long reddish nail out of the soft wood.

"Now you can lift up the board and put your face to the . . ." a quiet voice began.

He had already done it and another face, gray, wet and sour, was pushing into his, knocking him down and back as it scraped out under the plank. Something snorted over him and charged back again, rolling him over and pushing him up from behind and then sending him forward, screaming through the yellow field, while it bounded behind.

The three Connins watched from where they were. The one sitting on the pen held the loose board back with his dangling foot. Their stern faces didn't brighten any but they seemed to become less taut, as if some great need had been partly satisfied. "Maw ain't going to like him lettin out thet hawg," the smallest one said.

Mrs. Connin was on the back porch and caught Bevel up as he reached the steps. The hog ran under the house and subsided, panting, but the child screamed for five minutes. When she had finally calmed him down, she gave him his breakfast and let him sit on her lap while he ate it. The shoat climbed the two steps onto the back porch and stood outside the screen door, looking in with his head lowered sullenly. He was long-legged and hump-backed and part of one of his ears had been bitten off.

"Git away!" Mrs. Connin shouted. "That one yonder favors Mr. Paradise that has the gas station," she said. "You'll see him today at the healing. He's got the cancer over his ear. He always comes to show he ain't been healed."

The shoat stood squinting a few seconds longer and then moved off slowly. "I don't want to see him," Bevel said.

They walked to the river, Mrs. Connin in front with him and the three boys strung out behind and Sarah Mildred, the tall girl, at the end to holler if one of them ran out on the road. They looked like the skeleton of an old boat with two pointed ends, sailing slowly on the edge of the highway. The white Sunday sun followed at a little distance, climbing fast through a scum of gray cloud as if it meant to overtake them. Bevel walked on the outside edge, holding Mrs. Connin's hand and looking down into the orange and purple gulley that dropped off from the concrete.

It occurred to him that he was lucky this time that they had found Mrs. Connin who would take you away for the day instead of an ordinary sitter who only sat where you lived or went to the park. You found out more when you left where you lived. He had found out already this morning that he had been made by a carpenter named

Jesus Christ. Before he had thought it had been a doctor named Sladewall, a fat man with a yellow mustache who gave him shots and thought his name was Herbert, but this must have been a joke. They joked a lot where he lived. If he had thought about it before, he would have thought Jesus Christ was a word like "oh" or "damm" or "God," or maybe somebody who had cheated them out of something sometime. When he had asked Mrs. Connin who the man in the sheet in the picture over her bed was, she had looked at him a while with her mouth open. Then she had said, "That's Jesus," and she had kept on looking at him.

In a few minutes she had got up and got a book out of the other room. "See here," she said, turning over the cover, "this belonged to my great grandmamma. I wouldn't part with it for nothing on earth." She ran her finger under some brown writing on a spotted page. "Emma Stevens Oakley, 1832," she said. "Ain't that something to have? And every word of it the gospel truth." She turned the next page and read him the name: "The Life of Jesus Christ for Readers Under Twelve." Then she read him the book.

It was a small book, pale brown on the outside with gold edges and a smell like old putty. It was full of pictures, one of the carpenter driving a crowd of pigs out of a man. They were real pigs, gray and sour-looking, and Mrs. Connin said Jesus had driven them all out of this one man. When she finished reading, she let him sit on the floor and look at the pictures again.

Just before they left for the healing, he had managed to get the book inside his innerlining without her seeing him. Now it made his coat hang down a little farther on one side than the other. His mind was dreamy and serene as they walked along and when they turned off the highway onto a long red clay road winding between banks of honeysuckle, he began to make wild leaps and pull forward on her hand as if he wanted to dash off and snatch the sun which was rolling away ahead of them now.

They walked on the dirt road for a while and then they crossed a field stippled with purple weeds and entered the shadows of a wood where the ground was covered with thick pine needles. He had never been in woods before and he walked carefully, looking from side to side as if he were entering a strange country. They moved along a bridle path that twisted downhill through crackling red leaves, and once, catching at a branch to keep himself from slipping, he looked into two frozen green-gold eyes enclosed in the darkness of a tree hole. At the bottom of the hill, the woods opened suddenly onto a pasture dotted here and there with black and white cows and sloping down, tier after tier, to a broad orange stream where the reflection of the sun was set like a diamond.

There were people standing on the near bank in a group, singing. Long tables were set up behind them and a few cars and trucks were parked in a road that came up by the river. They crossed the pasture, hurrying, because Mrs. Connin, using her hand for a shed over her eyes, saw the preacher already standing out in the water. She dropped her basket on one of the tables and pushed the three boys in front of her into the knot of people so that they wouldn't linger by the food. She kept Bevel by the hand and eased her way up to the front.

The preacher was standing about ten feet out in the stream where the water came up to his knees. He was a tall youth in khaki trousers that he had rolled up higher than the water. He had on a blue shirt and a red scarf around his neck but no hat and his light-colored hair was cut in sideburns that curved into the hollows of his cheeks. His face was all bone and red light reflected from the river. He looked as if he might have been nineteen years old. He was singing in a high twangy voice, above the singing on the bank, and he kept his hands behind him and his head tilted back.

He ended the hymn on a high note and stood silent, looking down at the water and shifting his feet in it. Then he looked up at the people on the bank. They stood close together, waiting; their faces were solemn but expectant and every eye was on him. He shifted his feet again.

"Maybe I know why you come," he said in the twangy voice, "maybe I don't.

"If you ain't come for Jesus, you ain't come for me. If you just come to see can you leave your pain in the river, you ain't come for Jesus. You can't leave your pain in the river," he said. "I never told nobody that." He stopped and looked down at his knees.

"I seen you cure a woman oncet!" a sudden high voice shouted from the hump of people. "Seen that woman git up and walk out straight where she had limped in!"

The preacher lifted one foot and then the other. He seemed almost but not quite to smile. "You might as well go home if that's what you come for," he said.

Then he lifted his head and arms and shouted, "Listen to what I got to say, you people! There ain't but one river and that's the River of Life, made out of Jesus' Blood. That's the river you have to lay your pain in, in the River of Faith, in the River of Life, in the River of Love, in the rich red river of Jesus' Blood, you people!"

His voice grew soft and musical. "All the rivers come from that one River and go back to it like it was the ocean sea and if you believe, you can lay your pain in that River and get rid of it because that's the River that was made to carry sin. It's a River full of pain itself, pain itself, moving toward the Kingdom of Christ, to be washed away, slow, you people, slow as this here old red water river round my feet.

"Listen," he sang, "I read in Mark about an unclean man, I read in Luke about a blind man, I read in John about a dead man! Oh you people hear! The same blood that makes this River red, made that leper clean, made that blind man stare, made that dead man leap! You people with trouble," he cried, "lay it in that River of Blood, lay it in that River of Pain, and watch it move away toward the Kingdom of Christ."

While he preached, Bevel's eyes followed drowsily the slow circles of two silent birds revolving high in the air. Across the river there was a low red and gold grove of sassafras with hills of dark blue trees behind it and an occasional pine jutting over the skyline. Behind, in the distance, the city rose like a cluster of warts on the side of the mountain. The birds revolved downward and dropped lightly in the top of the highest pine and sat hunch-shouldered as if they were supporting the sky.

"If it's this River of Life you want to lay your pain in, then come up," the preacher said, "and lay your sorrow here. But don't be thinking this is the last of it because this old red river don't end here. This old red suffering stream goes on, you people, slow to the Kingdom of Christ. This old red river is good to Baptize in, good to lay your faith in, good to lay your pain in, but it ain't this muddy water here that saves you. I been all up and down this river this week," he said. "Tuesday I was in Fortune Lake, next day in Ideal, Friday me and my wife drove to Lulawillow to see a sick man there. Them people didn't see no healing," he said and his face burned redder for a second. "I never said they would."

While he was talking a fluttering figure had begun to move forward with a kind of butterfly movement—an old woman with flapping arms whose head wobbled as if it might fall off any second. She managed to lower herself at the edge of the bank and let her arms churn in the water. Then she bent farther and pushed her face down in it and raised herself up finally, streaming wet; and still flapping, she turned a time or two in a blind circle until someone reached out and pulled her back into the group.

"She's been that way for thirteen years," a rough voice

shouted. "Pass the hat and give this kid his money. That's what he's here for." The shout, directed out to the boy in the river, came from a huge old man who sat like a humped stone on the bumper of a long ancient gray automobile. He had on a gray hat that was turned down over one ear and up over the other to expose a purple bulge on his left temple. He sat bent forward with his hands hanging between his knees and his small eyes half closed.

Bevel stared at him once and then moved into the folds of Mrs. Connin's coat and hid himself.

The boy in the river glanced at the old man quickly and raised his fist. "Believe Jesus or the devil!" he cried. "Testify to one or the other!"

"I know from my own self-experience," a woman's mysterious voice called from the knot of people, "I know from it that this preacher can heal. My eyes have been opened! I testify to Jesus!"

The preacher lifted his arms quickly and began to repeat all that he had said before about the River and the Kingdom of Christ and the old man sat on the bumper, fixing him with a narrow squint. From time to time Bevel stared at him again from around Mrs. Connin.

A man in overalls and a brown coat leaned forward and dipped his hand in the water quickly and shook it and leaned back, and a woman held a baby over the edge of the bank and splashed its feet with water. One man moved a little distance away and sat down on the bank and took off his shoes and waded out into the stream; he stood there for a few minutes with his face tilted as far back as it would go, then he waded back and put on his shoes. All this time, the preacher sang and did not appear to watch what went on.

As soon as he stopped singing, Mrs. Connin lifted Bevel up and said, "Listen here, preacher, I got a boy from town today that I'm keeping. His mamma's sick and he wants you to pray for her. And this is a coincident—his name is Bevel! Bevel," she said, turning to look at the people behind her, "same as his. Ain't that a coincident, though?"

There were some murmurs and Bevel turned and grinned over her shoulder at the faces looking at him. "Bevel," he said in a loud jaunty voice.

"Listen," Mrs. Connin said, "have you ever been Baptized, Bevel?"

He only grinned.

"I suspect he ain't ever been Baptized," Mrs. Connin said, raising her eyebrows at the preacher.

"Swang him over here," the preacher said and took a stride forward and caught him.

He held him in the crook of his arm and looked at the grinning face. Bevel rolled his eyes in a comical way and thrust his face forward, close to the preacher's. "My name is Bevvvuuuuul," he said in a loud deep voice and let the tip of his tongue slide across his mouth.

The preacher didn't smile. His bony face was rigid and his narrow gray eyes reflected the almost colorless sky. There was a loud laugh from the old man sitting on the car bumper and Bevel grasped the back of the preacher's collar and held it tightly. The grin had already disappeared from his face. He had the sudden feeling that this was not a joke. Where he lived everything was a joke. From the preacher's face, he knew immediately that nothing the preacher said or did was a joke. "My mother named me that," he said quickly.

"Have you ever been Baptized?" the preacher asked.

"What's that?" he murmured.

"If I Baptize you," the preacher said, "you'll be able to go to the Kingdom of Christ. You'll be washed in the river of suffering, son, and you'll go by the deep river of life. Do you want that?"

"Yes," the child said, and thought, I won't go back to the apartment then, I'll go under the river.

"You won't be the same again," the preacher said. "You'll count." Then he turned his face to the people and began to preach and Bevel looked over his shoulder at the pieces of the white sun scattered in the river. Suddenly the preacher said, "All right, I'm going to Baptize you now," and without more warning, he tightened his hold and swung him upside down and plunged his head into the water. He held him under while he said the words of Baptism and then he jerked him up again and looked sternly at the gasping child. Bevel's eyes were dark and dilated. "You count now," the preacher said. "You didn't even count before."

The little boy was too shocked to cry. He spit out the muddy water and rubbed his wet sleeve into his eyes and over his face.

"Don't forget his mamma," Mrs. Connin called. "He wants you to pray for his mamma. She's sick."

"Lord," the preacher said, "we pray for somebody in affliction who isn't here to testify. Is your mother sick in the hospital?" he asked. "Is she in pain?"

The child stared at him. "She hasn't got up yet," he said in a high dazed voice. "She has a hangover." The air was so quiet he could hear the broken pieces of the sun knocking in the water.

The preacher looked angry and startled. The red drained out of his face and the sky appeared to darken in his eyes. There was a loud guffaw from the bank and Mr. Paradise shouted, "Haw! Cure the afflicted woman with the hangover!" and began to beat his knee with his fist.

"He's had a long day," Mrs. Connin said, standing with him in the door of the apartment and looking sharply into the room where the party was going on. "I reckon it's past his regular bedtime." One of Bevel's eyes was closed and the other half closed; his nose was running and he kept his mouth open and breathed through it. The damp plaid coat dragged down on one side.

That would be her, Mrs. Connin decided, in the black britches—long black satin britches and barefoot sandals and red toenails. She was lying on half the sofa, with her knees crossed in the air and her head propped on the arm. She didn't get up.

"Hello Harry," she said. "Did you have a big day?" She had a long pale face, smooth and blank, and straight sweet-potato-colored hair, pulled back.

The father went off to get the money. There were two other couples. One of the men, blond with little violet-blue eyes, leaned out of his chair and said, "Well Harry, old man, have a big day?"

"His name ain't Harry. It's Bevel," Mrs. Connin said.

"His name is Harry," *she* said from the sofa. "Whoever heard of anybody named Bevel?"

The little boy had seemed to be going to sleep on his feet, his head drooping farther and farther forward; he pulled it back suddenly and opened one eye; the other was stuck.

"He told me this morning his name was Bevel," Mrs. Connin said in a shocked voice. "The same as our preacher. We been all day at a preaching and healing at the river. He said his name was Bevel, the same as the preacher's. That's what he told me."

"Bevel!" his mother said. "My God! what a name."

"This preacher is name Bevel and there's no better preacher around," Mrs. Connin said. "And furthermore," she added in a defiant tone, "he Baptized this child this morning!"

His mother sat straight up. "Well the nerve!" she muttered.

"Furthermore," Mrs. Connin said, "he's a healer and he prayed for you to be healed."

"Healed!" she almost shouted. "Healed of what for Christ's sake?"

"Of your affliction," Mrs. Connin said icily.

The father had returned with the money and was standing near Mrs. Connin waiting to give it to her. His eyes were lined with red threads. "Go on, go on," he said, "I want to hear more about her affliction. The exact nature of it has escaped . . ." He waved the bill and his voice trailed off. "Healing by prayer is mighty inexpensive," he murmured.

Mrs. Connin stood a second, staring into the room, with a skeleton's appearance of seeing everything. Then, without taking the money, she turned and shut the door behind her. The father swung around, smiling vaguely, and shrugged. The rest of them were looking at Harry. The little boy began to shamble toward the bedroom.

"Come here, Harry," his mother said. He automatically shifted his direction toward her without opening his eye any farther. "Tell me what happened today," she said when he reached her. She began to pull off his coat.

"I don't know," he muttered.

"Yes you do know," she said, feeling the coat heavier on one side. She unzipped the innerlining and caught the book and a dirty handkerchief as they fell out. "Where did you get these?"

"I don't know," he said and grabbed for them. "They're mine. She gave them to me."

She threw the handkerchief down and held the book too high for him to reach and began to read it, her face after a second assuming an exaggerated comical expression. The others moved around and looked at it over her shoulder. "My God," somebody said.

One of the men peered at it sharply from behind a thick pair of glasses. "That's valuable," he said. "That's a collector's item," and he took it away from the rest of them and retired to another chair.

"Don't let George go off with that," his girl said.

"I tell you it's valuable," George said. "1832."

Bevel shifted his direction again toward the room where he slept. He shut the door behind him and moved slowly in the darkness to the bed and sat down and took off his shoes and got under the cover. After a minute a shaft of light let in the tall silhouette of his mother. She tiptoed lightly across the room and sat down on the edge of his bed. "What did that dolt of a preacher say about me?" she whispered. "What lies have you been telling today, honey?"

He shut his eye and heard her voice from a long way away, as if he were under the river and she on top of it. She shook his shoulder. "Harry," she said, leaning down and putting her mouth to his ear, "tell me what he said." She pulled him into a sitting position and he felt as if he had been drawn up from under the river. "Tell me," she whispered and her bitter breath covered his face.

He saw the pale oval close to him in the dark. "He said I'm not the same now," he muttered. "I count."

After a second, she lowered him by his shirt front onto the pillow. She hung over him an instant and brushed her lips against his forehead. Then she got up and moved away, swaying her hips lightly through the shaft of light.

He didn't wake up early but the apartment was still dark and close when he did. For a while he lay there, picking his nose and eyes. Then he sat up in bed and looked out the window. The sun came in palely, stained gray by the glass. Across the street at the Empire Hotel, a colored cleaning woman was looking down from an upper window, resting her face on her folded arms. He got up and put on his shoes and went to the bathroom and then into the front room. He ate two crackers spread with anchovy paste, that he found on the coffee table, and drank some ginger ale left in a bottle and looked around for his book but it was not there.

The apartment was silent except for the faint humming of the refrigerator. He went into the kitchen and found some raisin bread heels and spread a half jar of peanut butter between them and climbed up on the tall kitchen stool and sat chewing the sandwich slowly, wiping his nose every now and then on his shoulder. When he finished he found some chocolate milk and drank that. He would rather have had the ginger ale he saw but they left the bottle openers where he couldn't reach them. He studied what was left in the refrigerator for a while—some shriveled vegetables that she had forgot were there and a lot of brown oranges that she bought and didn't squeeze; there were three or four kinds of cheese and something fishy in a paper bag; the rest was a pork bone. He left the refrigerator door open and wandered back into the dark living room and sat down on the sofa.

He decided they would be out cold until one o'clock and that they would all have to go to a restaurant for lunch. He wasn't high enough for the table yet and the waiter would bring a highchair and he was too big for a highchair. He sat in the middle of the sofa, kicking it with his heels. Then he got up and wandered around the room, looking into the ashtrays at the butts as if this might be a habit. In his own room he had picture books and blocks but they were for the most part torn up; he found the way to get new ones was to tear up the ones he had. There was very little to do at any time but eat; however, he was not a fat boy.

He decided he would empty a few of the ashtrays on the floor. If he only emptied a few, she would think they had fallen. He emptied two, rubbing the ashes carefully into the rug with his finger. Then he lay on the floor for a while, studying his feet which he held up in the air. His shoes were still damp and he began to think about the river.

Very slowly, his expression changed as if he were gradually seeing appear what he didn't know he'd been looking for. Then all of a sudden he knew what he wanted to do.

He got up and tiptoed into their bedroom and stood in the dim light there, looking for her pocketbook. His glance passed her long pale arm hanging off the edge of the bed down to the floor, and across the white mound his father made, and past the crowded bureau, until it rested on the pocketbook hung on the back of a chair. He took a car-token out of it and half a package of Life Savers. Then he left the apartment and caught the car at the corner. He hadn't taken a suitcase because there was nothing from there he wanted to keep.

He got off the car at the end of the line and started down the road he and Mrs. Connin had taken the day before. He knew there wouldn't be anybody at her house because the three boys and the girl went to school and Mrs. Connin had told him she went out to clean. He passed her yard and walked on the way they had gone to the river. The paper brick houses were far apart and after a while the dirt place to walk on ended and he had to walk on the edge of the highway. The sun was pale yellow and high and hot.

He passed a shack with an orange gas pump in front of it but he didn't see the old man looking out at nothing in particular from the doorway. Mr. Paradise was having an orange drink. He finished it slowly, squinting over the bottle at the small plaid-coated figure disappearing down the road. Then he set the empty bottle on a bench and, still squinting, wiped his sleeve over his mouth. He went in the shack and picked out a peppermint stick, a foot long and two inches thick, from the candy shelf, and stuck it in his hip pocket. Then he got in his car and drove slowly down the highway after the boy.

By the time Bevel came to the field speckled with purple weeds, he was dusty and sweating and he crossed it at a trot to get into the woods as fast as he could. Once inside, he wandered from tree to tree, trying to find the path they had taken yesterday. Finally he found a line worn in the pine needles and followed it until he saw the steep trail twisting down through the trees.

Mr. Paradise had left his automobile back some way on the road and had walked to the place where he was accustomed to sit almost every day, holding an unbaited fishline in the water while he stared at the river passing in front of him. Anyone looking at him from a distance would have seen an old boulder half hidden in the bushes.

Bevel didn't see him at all. He only saw the river, shimmering reddish yellow, and bounded into it with his shoes and his coat on and took a gulp. He swallowed some and spit the rest out and then he stood there in water up to his chest and looked around him. The sky was a clear pale blue, all in one piece—except for the hole the sun made—and fringed around the bottom with treetops. His coat floated to the surface and surrounded him like a strange gay lily pad and he stood grinning in the sun. He intended not to fool with preachers any more but to Baptize himself and to keep on going this time until he found the Kingdom of Christ in the river. He didn't mean to waste any more time. He put his head under the water at once and pushed forward.

In a second he began to gasp and sputter and his head reappeared on the surface; he started under again and the same thing happened. The river wouldn't have him. He tried again and came up, choking. This was the way it had been when the preacher held him under—he had had to fight with something that pushed him back in the face. He stopped and thought suddenly: it's another joke, it's just another joke! He thought how far he had come for nothing and he began to hit and splash and kick the filthy river. His feet were already treading on nothing. He gave one low cry of pain and indignation. Then he heard a shout and turned his head and saw something like a giant pig bounding after him, shaking a red and white club and shouting. He plunged under once and this time, the waiting current caught him like a long gentle hand and pulled him swiftly forward and down. For an instant he was overcome with surprise; then since he was moving quickly and knew that he was getting somewhere, all his fury and his fear left him.

Mr. Paradise's head appeared from time to time on the surface of the water. Finally, far downstream, the old man rose like some ancient water monster and stood empty-handed, staring with his dull eyes as far down the river line as he could see.

THE LIFE YOU SAVE MAY BE YOUR OWN

The old woman and her daughter were sitting on their porch when Mr. Shiftlet came up their road for the first time. The old woman slid to the edge of her chair and leaned forward, shading her eyes from the piercing sunset with her hand. The daughter could not see far in front of her and continued to play with her fingers. Although the old woman lived in this desolate spot with only her daughter and she had never seen Mr. Shiftlet before, she could tell, even from a distance, that he was a tramp and no one to be afraid of. His left coat sleeve was folded up to show there was only half an arm in it and his gaunt figure listed slightly to the side as if the breeze were pushing him. He had on a black town suit and a brown felt hat that was turned up in the front and down in the back and he carried a tin tool box by a handle. He came on, at an amble, up her road, his face turned toward the sun which appeared to be balancing itself on the peak of a small mountain.

The old woman didn't change her position until he was almost into her yard; then she rose with one hand fisted on her hip. The daughter, a large girl in a short blue organdy dress, saw him all at once and jumped up and began to stamp and point and make excited speechless sounds.

Mr. Shiftlet stopped just inside the yard and set his box on the ground and tipped his hat at her as if she were not in the least afflicted; then he turned toward the old woman and swung the hat all the way off. He had long black slick hair that hung flat from a part in the middle to beyond the tips of his ears on either side. His face descended in forehead for more than half its length and ended suddenly with his features just balanced over a jutting steel-trap jaw. He seemed to be a young man but he had a look of composed dissatisfaction as if he understood life thoroughly.

"Good evening," the old woman said. She was about the size of a cedar fence post and she had a man's gray hat pulled down low over her head.

The tramp stood looking at her and didn't answer. He turned his back and faced the sunset. He swung both his whole and his short arm up slowly so that they indicated an expanse of sky and his figure formed a crooked cross. The old woman watched him with her arms folded across her chest as if she were the owner of the sun, and the daughter watched, her head thrust forward and her fat helpless hands hanging at the wrists. She had long pink-gold hair and eyes as blue as a peacock's neck.

He held the pose for almost fifty seconds and then he picked up his box and came on to the porch and dropped down on the bottom step. "Lady," he said in a firm nasal voice, "I'd give a fortune to live where I could see me a sun do that every evening."

"Does it every evening," the old woman said and sat back down. The daughter sat down too and watched him with a cautious sly look as if he were a bird that had come up very close. He leaned to one side, rooting in his pants pocket, and in a second he brought out a package of chewing gum and offered her a piece. She took it and unpeeled it and began to chew without taking her eyes off him. He offered the old woman a piece but she only raised her upper lip to indicate she had no teeth.

Mr. Shiftlet's pale sharp glance had already passed over everything in the yard—the pump near the corner of the house and the big fig tree that three or four chickens were preparing to roost in—and had moved to a shed where he saw the square rusted back of an automobile. "You ladies drive?" he asked.

"That car ain't run in fifteen year," the old woman said. "The day my husband died, it quit running."

"Nothing is like it used to be, lady," he said. "The world is almost rotten."

"That's right," the old woman said. "You from around here?"

"Name Tom T. Shiftlet," he murmured, looking at the tires.

"I'm pleased to meet you," the old woman said. "Name Lucynell Crater and daughter Lucynell Crater. What you doing around here, Mr. Shiftlet?"

He judged the car to be about a 1928 or '29 Ford. "Lady," he said, and turned and gave her his full attention, "lemme tell you something. There's one of these doctors in Atlanta that's taken a knife and cut the human heart—the human heart," he repeated, leaning forward, "out of a man's chest and held it in his hand," and he held his hand out, palm up, as if it were slightly weighted with the human heart, "and studied it like it was a day-old chicken, and lady," he said, allowing a long significant pause in which his head slid forward and his clay-colored eyes brightened, "he don't know no more about it than you or me."

"That's right," the old woman said.

"Why, if he was to take that knife and cut into every corner of it, he still wouldn't know no more than you or me. What you want to bet?"

"Nothing," the old woman said wisely. "Where you come from, Mr. Shiftlet?"

He didn't answer. He reached into his pocket and brought out a sack of tobacco and a package of cigarette papers and rolled himself a cigarette, expertly with one hand, and attached it in a hanging position to his upper lip. Then he took a box of wooden matches from his pocket and struck one on his shoe. He held the burning match as if he were studying the mystery of flame while it traveled dangerously toward his skin. The daughter began to make loud noises and to point to his hand and shake her finger at him, but when the flame was just before touching him, he leaned down with his hand cupped over it as if he were going to set fire to his nose and lit the cigarette.

He flipped away the dead match and blew a stream of gray into the evening. A sly look came over his face. "Lady," he said, "nowadays, people'll do anything anyways. I can tell you my name is Tom T. Shiftlet and I come from Tarwater, Tennessee, but you never have seen me before: how you know I ain't lying? How you know my name ain't Aaron Sparks, lady, and I come from Singleberry, Georgia, or how you know it's not George Speeds and I come from Lucy, Alabama, or how you know I ain't Thompson Bright from Toolafalls, Mississippi?"

"I don't know nothing about you," the old woman muttered, irked.

"Lady," he said, "people don't care how they lie. Maybe the best I can tell you is, I'm a man; but listen lady," he said and paused and made his tone more ominous still, "what is a man?"

The old woman began to gum a seed. "What you carry in that tin box, Mr. Shiftlet?" she asked.

"Tools," he said, put back. "I'm a carpenter."

"Well, if you come out here to work, I'll be able to feed you and give you a place to sleep but I can't pay. I'll tell you that before you begin," she said.

There was no answer at once and no particular expression on his face. He leaned back against the two-by-four that helped support the porch roof. "Lady," he said slowly, "there's some men that some things mean more to them than money." The old woman rocked without comment and the daughter watched the trigger that moved up and down in his neck. He told the old woman then that all most people were interested in was money, but he asked what a man was made for. He asked her if a man was made for money, or what. He asked her what she thought she was made for but she didn't answer, she only sat rocking and wondered if a one-armed man could put a new roof on her garden house. He asked a lot of questions that she didn't answer. He told her that he was twenty-eight years old and had lived a varied life. He had been a gospel singer, a foreman on the railroad, an assistant in an undertaking parlor, and he had come over the radio for three months with Uncle Roy and his Red Creek Wranglers. He said he had fought and bled in the Arm Service of his country and visited every foreign land and that everywhere he had seen people that didn't care if they did a thing one way or another. He said he hadn't been raised thataway.

A fat yellow moon appeared in the branches of the fig tree as if it were going to roost there with the chickens. He said that a man had to escape to the country to see the world whole and that he wished he lived in a desolate place like this where he could see the sun go down every evening like God made it to do.

"Are you married or are you single?" the old woman asked.

There was a long silence. "Lady," he asked finally, "where would you find you an innocent woman today? I wouldn't have any of this trash I could just pick up."

The daughter was leaning very far down, hanging her head almost between her knees, watching him through a triangular door she had made in her overturned hair; and she suddenly fell in a heap on the floor and began to whimper. Mr. Shiftlet straightened her out and helped her get back in the chair.

"Is she your baby girl?" he asked.

"My only," the old woman said, "and she's the sweetest girl in the world. I wouldn't give her up for nothing on earth. She's smart too. She can sweep the floor, cook, wash, feed the chickens, and hoe. I wouldn't give her up for a casket of jewels."

"No," he said kindly, "don't ever let any man take her away from you."

"Any man come after her," the old woman said, "'ll have to stay around the place."

Mr. Shiftlet's eye in the darkness was focused on a part of the automobile bumper that glittered in the distance. "Lady," he said, jerking his short arm up as if he could point with it to her house and yard and pump, "there ain't a broken thing on this plantation that I couldn't fix for you, one-arm jackleg or not. I'm a man," he said with a sullen dignity, "even if I ain't a whole one. I got," he said, tapping his knuckles on the floor to emphasize the immensity of what he was going to say, "a moral intelligence!" and his face pierced out of the darkness into a shaft of doorlight and he stared at her as if he were astonished himself at this impossible truth.

The old woman was not impressed with the phrase. "I told you you could hang around and work for food," she said, "if you don't mind sleeping in that car yonder."

"Why listen, Lady," he said with a grin of delight, "the monks of old slept in their coffins!"

"They wasn't as advanced as we are," the old woman said.

The next morning he began on the roof of the garden house while Lucynell, the daughter, sat on a rock and watched him work. He had not been around a week before the change he had made in the place was apparent. He had patched the front and back steps, built a new hog pen, restored a fence, and taught Lucynell, who was completely deaf and had never said a word in her life, to say the word "bird." The big rosy-faced girl followed him everywhere, saying "Burrttddt ddbirrrttdt," and clapping her hands. The old woman watched from a distance, secretly pleased. She was ravenous for a son-in-law.

Mr. Shiftlet slept on the hard narrow back seat of the car with his feet out the side window. He had his razor and a can of water on a crate that served him as a bedside table and he put up a piece of mirror against the back glass and kept his coat neatly on a hanger that he hung over one of the windows.

In the evenings he sat on the steps and talked while the old woman and Lucynell rocked violently in their chairs on either side of him. The old woman's three mountains were black against the dark blue sky and were visited off and on by various planets and by the moon after it had left the chickens. Mr. Shiftlet pointed out that the reason he had improved this plantation was because he had taken a personal interest in it. He said he was even going to make the automobile run.

He had raised the hood and studied the mechanism and he said he could tell that the car had been built in the days when cars were really built. You take now, he said, one man puts in one bolt and another man puts in another bolt and another man puts in another bolt so that it's a man for a bolt. That's why you have to pay so much for a car: you're paying all those men. Now if you didn't have to pay but one man, you could get you a cheaper car and one that had had a personal interest taken in it, and it would be a better car. The old woman agreed with him that this was so.

Mr. Shiftlet said that the trouble with the world was that nobody cared, or stopped and took any trouble. He said he never would have been able to teach Lucynell to say a word if he hadn't cared and stopped long enough.

"Teach her to say something else," the old woman said.

"What you want her to say next?" Mr. Shiftlet asked.

The old woman's smile was broad and toothless and suggestive. "Teach her to say 'sugarpie,'" she said.

Mr. Shiftlet already knew what was on her mind.

The next day he began to tinker with the automobile and that evening he told her that if she would buy a fan belt, he would be able to make the car run.

The old woman said she would give him the money.

"You see that girl yonder?" she asked, pointing to Lucynell who was sitting on the floor a foot away, watching him, her eyes blue even in the dark. "If it was ever a man wanted to take her away, I would say, 'No man on earth is going to take that sweet girl of mine away from me!' but if he was to say, 'Lady, I don't want to take her away, I want her right here,' I would say, 'Mister, I don't blame you none. I wouldn't pass up a chance to live in a permanent place and get the sweetest girl in the world myself. You ain't no fool,' I would say."

"How old is she?" Mr. Shiftlet asked casually.

"Fifteen, sixteen," the old woman said. The girl was nearly thirty but because of her innocence it was impossible to guess.

"It would be a good idea to paint it too," Mr. Shiftlet remarked. "You don't want it to rust out."

"We'll see about that later," the old woman said.

The next day he walked into town and returned with the parts he needed and a can of gasoline. Late in the afternoon, terrible noises issued from the shed and the old woman rushed out of the house, thinking Lucynell was somewhere having a fit. Lucynell was sitting on a chicken crate, stamping her feet and screaming, "Burrddttt! bddurrddtttt!" but her fuss was drowned out by the car. With a volley of blasts it emerged from the shed, moving in a fierce and stately way. Mr. Shiftlet was in the driver's seat, sitting very erect. He had an expression of serious modesty on his face as if he had just raised the dead.

That night, rocking on the porch, the old woman began her business at once. "You want you an innocent woman, don't you?" she asked sympathetically. "You don't want none of this trash."

"No'm, I don't," Mr. Shiftlet said.

"One that can't talk," she continued, "can't sass you back or use foul language. That's the kind for you to have.

Right there," and she pointed to Lucynell sitting cross-legged in her chair, holding both feet in her hands.

"That's right," he admitted. "She wouldn't give me any trouble."

"Saturday," the old woman said, "you and her and me can drive into town and get married."

Mr. Shiftlet eased his position on the steps.

"I can't get married right now," he said. "Everything you want to do takes money and I ain't got any."

"What you need with money?" she asked.

"It takes money," he said. "Some people'll do anything anyhow these days, but the way I think, I wouldn't marry no woman that I couldn't take on a trip like she was somebody. I mean take her to a hotel and treat her. I wouldn't marry the Duchesser Windsor," he said firmly, "unless I could take her to a hotel and give her something good to eat.

"I was raised thataway and there ain't a thing I can do about it. My old mother taught me how to do."

"Lucynell don't even know what a hotel is," the old woman muttered. "Listen here, Mr. Shiftlet," she said, sliding forward in her chair, "you'd be getting a permanent house and a deep well and the most innocent girl in the world. You don't need no money. Lemme tell you something: there ain't any place in the world for a poor disabled friendless drifting man."

The ugly words settled in Mr. Shiftlet's head like a group of buzzards in the top of a tree. He didn't answer at once. He rolled himself a cigarette and lit it and then he said in an even voice, "Lady, a man is divided into two parts, body and spirit."

The old woman clamped her gums together.

"A body and a spirit," he repeated. "The body, lady, is like a house: it don't go anywhere; but the spirit, lady, is like a automobile: always on the move, always . . ."

"Listen, Mr. Shiftlet," she said, "my well never goes dry and my house is always warm in the winter and there's no mortgage on a thing about this place. You can go to the courthouse and see for yourself. And yonder under that shed is a fine automobile." She laid the bait carefully. "You can have it painted by Saturday. I'll pay for the paint."

In the darkness, Mr. Shiftlet's smile stretched like a weary snake waking up by a fire. After a second he recalled himself and said, "I'm only saying a man's spirit means more to him than anything else. I would have to take my wife off for the week end without no regards at all for cost. I got to follow where my spirit says to go."

"I'll give you fifteen dollars for a week-end trip," the old woman said in a crabbed voice. "That's the best I can do."

"That wouldn't hardly pay for more than the gas and the hotel," he said. "It wouldn't feed her."

"Seventeen-fifty," the old woman said. "That's all I got so it isn't any use you trying to milk me. You can take a lunch."

Mr. Shiftlet was deeply hurt by the word "milk." He didn't doubt that she had more money sewed up in her mattress but he had already told her he was not interested in her money. "I'll make that do," he said and rose and walked off without treating with her further.

On Saturday the three of them drove into town in the car that the paint had barely dried on and Mr. Shiftlet and Lucynell were married in the Ordinary's office while the old woman witnessed. As they came out of the courthouse, Mr. Shiftlet began twisting his neck in his collar. He looked morose and bitter as if he had been insulted while someone held him. "That didn't satisfy me none," he said. "That was just something a woman in an office did, nothing but paper work and blood tests. What do they know about my blood? If they was to take my heart and cut it out," he said, "they wouldn't know a thing about me. It didn't satisfy me at all."

"It satisfied the law," the old woman said sharply.

"The law," Mr. Shiftlet said and spit. "It's the law that don't satisfy me."

He had painted the car dark green with a yellow band around it just under the windows. The three of them climbed in the front seat and the old woman said, "Don't Lucynell look pretty? Looks like a baby doll." Lucynell was dressed up in a white dress that her mother had uprooted from a trunk and there was a Panama hat on her head with a bunch of red wooden cherries on the brim. Every now and then her placid expression was changed by a sly isolated little thought like a shoot of green in the desert. "You got a prize!" the old woman said.

Mr. Shiftlet didn't even look at her.

They drove back to the house to let the old woman off and pick up the lunch. When they were ready to leave, she stood staring in the window of the car, with her fingers clenched around the glass. Tears began to seep sideways out of her eyes and run along the dirty creases in her face. "I ain't ever been parted with her for two days before," she said.

Mr. Shiftlet started the motor.

"And I wouldn't let no man have her but you because I seen you would do right. Good-by, Sugarbaby," she said, clutching at the sleeve of the white dress. Lucynell looked straight at her and didn't seem to see her there at all. Mr. Shiftlet eased the car forward so that she had to move her hands.

The early afternoon was clear and open and surrounded by pale blue sky. Although the car would go only thirty miles an hour, Mr. Shiftlet imagined a terrific climb and dip and swerve that went entirely to his head so that he forgot his morning bitterness. He had always wanted an automobile but he had never been able to afford one before. He drove very fast because he wanted to make Mobile by nightfall.

Occasionally he stopped his thoughts long enough to look at Lucynell in the seat beside him. She had eaten the lunch as soon as they were out of the yard and now she was pulling the cherries off the hat one by one and throwing them out the window. He became depressed in spite of the car. He had driven about a hundred miles when he decided that she must be hungry again and at the next small town they came to, he stopped in front of an aluminum-painted eating place called The Hot Spot and took her in and ordered her a plate of ham and grits. The ride had made her sleepy and as soon as she got up on the stool, she rested her head on the counter and shut her eyes. There was no one in The Hot Spot but Mr. Shiftlet and the boy behind the counter, a pale youth with a greasy rag hung over his shoulder. Before he could dish up the food, she was snoring gently.

"Give it to her when she wakes up," Mr. Shiftlet said. "I'll pay for it now."

The boy bent over her and stared at the long pink-gold hair and the half-shut sleeping eyes. Then he looked up and stared at Mr. Shiftlet. "She looks like an angel of Gawd," he murmured.

"Hitch-hiker," Mr. Shiftlet explained. "I can't wait. I got to make Tuscaloosa."

The boy bent over again and very carefully touched his finger to a strand of the golden hair and Mr. Shiftlet left.

He was more depressed than ever as he drove on by himself. The late afternoon had grown hot and sultry and the country had flattened out. Deep in the sky a storm was preparing very slowly and without thunder as if it meant to drain every drop of air from the earth before it broke. There were times when Mr. Shiftlet preferred not to be alone. He felt too that a man with a car had a responsibility to others and he kept his eye out for a hitch-hiker. Occasionally he saw a sign that warned: "Drive carefully. The life you save may be your own."

The narrow road dropped off on either side into dry fields and here and there a shack or a filling station stood in a clearing. The sun began to set directly in front of the automobile. It was a reddening ball that through his windshield was slightly flat on the bottom and top. He saw a boy in overalls and a gray hat standing on the edge of the road and he slowed the car down and stopped in front of him. The boy didn't have his hand raised to thumb the ride, he was only standing there, but he had a small cardboard suitcase and his hat was set on his head in a way to indicate that he had left somewhere for good. "Son," Mr. Shiftlet said, "I see you want a ride."

The boy didn't say he did or he didn't but he opened the door of the car and got in, and Mr. Shiftlet started driving again. The child held the suitcase on his lap and folded his arms on top of it. He turned his head and looked out the window away from Mr. Shiftlet. Mr. Shiftlet felt oppressed. "Son," he said after a minute, "I got the best old mother in the world so I reckon you only got the second best."

The boy gave him a quick dark glance and then turned his face back out the window.

"It's nothing so sweet," Mr. Shiftlet continued, "as a boy's mother. She taught him his first prayers at her knee, she give him love when no other would, she told him what was right and what wasn't, and she seen that he done the right thing. Son," he said, "I never rued a day in my life like the one I rued when I left that old mother of mine."

The boy shifted in his seat but he didn't look at Mr. Shiftlet. He unfolded his arms and put one hand on the door handle.

"My mother was a angel of Gawd," Mr. Shiftlet said in a very strained voice. "He took her from heaven and giver to me and I left her." His eyes were instantly clouded over with a mist of tears. The car was barely moving.

The boy turned angrily in the seat. "You go to the devil!" he cried. "My old woman is a flea bag and yours is a stinking pole cat!" and with that he flung the door open and jumped out with his suitcase into the ditch.

Mr. Shiftlet was so shocked that for about a hundred

feet he drove along slowly with the door still open. A cloud, the exact color of the boy's hat and shaped like a turnip, had descended over the sun, and another, worse looking, crouched behind the car. Mr. Shiftlet felt that the rottenness of the world was about to engulf him. He raised his arm and let it fall again to his breast. "Oh Lord!" he prayed. "Break forth and wash the slime from this earth!"

The turnip continued slowly to descend. After a few minutes there was a guffawing peal of thunder from behind and fantastic raindrops, like tin-can tops, crashed over the rear of Mr. Shiftlet's car. Very quickly he stepped on the gas and with his stump sticking out the window he raced the galloping shower into Mobile.

A STROKE OF GOOD FORTUNE

Ruby came in the front door of the apartment building and lowered the paper sack with the four cans of number three beans in it onto the hall table. She was too tired to take her arms from around it or to straighten up and she hung there collapsed from the hips, her head balanced like a big florid vegetable at the top of the sack. She gazed with stony unrecognition at the face that confronted her in the dark yellow-spotted mirror over the table. Against her right cheek was a gritty collard leaf that had been stuck there half the way home. She gave it a vicious swipe with her arm and straightened up, muttering, "Collards, collards," in a voice of sultry subdued wrath. Standing up straight, she was a short woman, shaped nearly like a funeral urn. She had mulberry-colored hair stacked in sausage rolls around her head but some of these had come loose with the heat and the long walk from the grocery store and pointed frantically in various directions. "Collard greens!" she said, spitting the word from her mouth this time as if it were a poisonous seed.

She and Bill Hill hadn't eaten collard greens for five years and she wasn't going to start cooking them now. She had bought these on account of Rufus but she wasn't going to buy them but once. You would have thought that after two years in the armed forces Rufus would have come back ready to eat like somebody from somewhere; but no. When she asked him what he would like to have *special*, he had not had the gumption to think of one civilized dish—he had said collard greens. She had expected Rufus to have turned out into somebody with some get in him. Well, he had about as much get as a floor mop.

Rufus was her baby brother who had just come back from the European Theater. He had come to live with her because Pitman where they were raised was not there any more. All the people who had lived at Pitman had had the good sense to leave it, either by dying or by moving to the city. She had married Bill B. Hill, a Florida man who sold Miracle Products, and had come to live in the city. If Pitman had still been there Rufus would have been in Pitman. If one chicken had been left to walk across the road in Pitman, Rufus would have been there too to keep him company. She didn't like to admit it about her own kin, least about her own brother, but there he was—good for absolutely nothing. "I seen it after five minutes of him," she had told Bill Hill and Bill Hill, with no expression whatsoever, had said, "It taken me three." It was mortifying to let that kind of a husband see you had that kind of a brother.

She supposed there was no help for it. Rufus was like the other children. She was the only one in her family who had been different, who had had any get. She took a stub of pencil from her pocketbook and wrote on the side of the sack: Bill you bring this upstairs. Then she braced herself at the bottom of the steps for the climb to the fourth floor.

The steps were a thin black rent in the middle of the house, covered with a mole-colored carpet that looked as if it grew from the floor. They stuck straight up like steeple steps, it seemed to her. They reared up. The minute she stood at the bottom of them, they reared up and got steeper for her benefit. As she gazed up them, her mouth widened and turned down in a look of complete disgust. She was in no condition to go up anything. She was sick. Madam Zoleeda had told her but not before she knew it herself.

Madam Zoleeda was the palmist on Highway 87. She had said, "A long illness," but she had added, whispering, with a very I-already-know-but-I-won't-tell look, "it will bring you a stroke of good fortune!" and then had sat back grinning, a stout woman with green eyes that moved in their sockets as if they had been oiled. Ruby didn't need to be told. She had already figured out the good fortune. Moving. For two months she had had a distinct feeling that they were going to move. Bill Hill couldn't hold off much longer. He couldn't kill her. Where she wanted to be was in a subdivision—she started up the steps, leaning forward and holding onto the banisters—where you had your drugstores and grocery and a picture show right in your own neighborhood. As it was now, living downtown, she had to walk eight blocks to the main business streets and farther than that to get to a supermarket. She hadn't made any complaints for five years much but now with her health at stake as young as she was what did he think she was going to do, kill herself? She had her eye on a place in Meadowcrest Heights, a duplex bungalow with yellow awnings. She stopped on the fifth step to blow. As young as she was—thirty-four—you wouldn't think five steps would stew her. You better take it easy, baby, she told herself, you're too young to bust your gears.

Thirty-four wasn't old, wasn't any age at all. She remembered her mother at thirty-four—she had looked like a puckered-up old yellow apple, sour, she had always looked sour, she had always looked like she wasn't satisfied with anything. She compared herself at thirty-four with her mother at that age. Her mother's hair had been gray—hers wouldn't be gray now even if she hadn't touched it up. All those children were what did her mother in—eight of them: two born dead, one died the first year, one crushed under a mowing machine. Her mother had got deader with every one of them. And all of it for what? Because she hadn't known any better. Pure ignorance. The purest of downright ignorance!

And there her two sisters were, both married four years with four children apiece. She didn't see how they stood it, always going to the doctor to be jabbed at with instruments. She remembered when her mother had had Rufus. She was the only one of the children who couldn't stand it and she had walked all the way in to Melsy, in the hot sun ten miles, to the picture show to get clear of the screaming, and had sat through two westerns and a horror picture and a serial and then had walked all the way back and found it was just beginning, and she had had to listen all night. All that misery for Rufus! And him turned out now to have no more charge than a dish rag. She saw him waiting out nowhere before he was born, just waiting, waiting to make his mother, only thirty-four, into an old woman. She gripped the banister rail fiercely and heaved herself up another step, shaking her head. Lord, she was disappointed in him! After she had told all her friends her brother was back from the European Theater, here he comes—sounding like he'd never been out of a hog lot.

He looked old too. He looked older than she did and he was fourteen years younger. She was extremely young looking for her age. Not that thirty-four is any age and anyway she was married. She had to smile, thinking about that, because she had done so much better than her sisters—they had married from around. "This breathlessness," she muttered, stopping again. She decided she would have to sit down.

There were twenty-eight steps in each flight—twenty-eight.

She sat down and jumped quickly, feeling something under her. She caught her breath and then pulled the thing out: it was Hartley Gilfeet's pistol. Nine inches of treacherous tin! He was a six-year-old boy who lived on the fifth floor. If he had been hers, she'd have worn him out so hard so many times he wouldn't know how to leave his mess on a public stair. She could have fallen down those stairs as easy as not and ruined herself! But his stupid mother wasn't going to do anything to him even if she told her. All she did was scream at him and tell people how smart he was. "Little Mister Good Fortune!" she called him. "All his poor daddy left me!" His daddy had said on his death bed, "There's nothing but him I ever given you," and she had said, "Rodman, you given me a fortune!" and so she called him Little Mister Good Fortune. "I'd wear the seat of his good fortune out!" Ruby muttered.

The steps were going up and down like a seesaw with her in the middle of it. She did not want to get nauseated. Not that again. Now no. No. She was not. She sat tightly to the steps with her eyes shut until the dizziness stopped a little and the nausea subsided. No, I'm not going to no doctor, she said. No. No. She was not. They would have to carry her there knocked out before she would go. She had done all right doctoring herself all these years—no bad sick spells, no teeth out, no children, all that by herself. She would have had five children right now if she hadn't been careful.

She had wondered more than once if this breathlessness could be heart trouble. Once in a while, going up the steps, there'd be a pain in her chest along with it. That was what she wanted it to be—heart trouble. They couldn't very well remove your heart. They'd have to knock her in the head before they'd get her near a hospital, they'd have to—suppose she would die if they didn't?

She wouldn't.

Suppose she would?

She made herself stop this gory thinking. She was only thirty-four. There was nothing permanent wrong with her. She was fat and her color was good. She thought of herself again in comparison with her mother at thirty-four and she pinched her arm and smiled. Seeing that her mother or father neither had been much to look at, she had done very well. They had been the dried-up type, dried up and Pitman dried into them, them and Pitman shrunk down into something all dried and puckered up. And she had come out of that! A somebody as alive as her! She got up, gripping the banister rail but smiling to herself. She was warm and fat and beautiful and not too fat because Bill Hill liked her that way. She had gained some weight but he hadn't noticed except that he was maybe more happy lately and didn't know why. She felt the wholeness of herself, a whole thing climbing the stairs. She was up the first flight now and she looked back, pleased. As soon as Bill Hill fell down those steps once, maybe they would move. But they would move before that! Madam Zoleeda had known. She laughed aloud and moved on down the hall. Mr. Jerger's door grated and startled her. Oh Lord, she thought, *him*. He was a second-floor resident who was peculiar.

He peered at her coming down the hall. "Good morning!" he said, bowing the upper part of his body out the door. "Good morning to you!" He looked like a goat. He had little raisin eyes and a string beard and his jacket was a green that was almost black or a black that was almost green.

"Morning," she said. "Hower you?"

"Well!" he screamed. "Well indeed on this glorious day!" He was seventy-eight years old and his face looked as if it had mildew on it. In the mornings he studied and in the afternoons, he walked up and down the sidewalks, stopping children and asking them questions. Whenever he heard anyone in the hall, he opened his door and looked out.

"Yeah, it's a nice day," she said languidly.

"Do you know what great birthday this is?" he asked.

"Uh-uh," Ruby said. He always had a question like that. A history question that nobody knew; he would ask it and then make a speech on it. He used to teach in a high school.

"Guess," he urged her.

"Abraham Lincoln," she muttered.

"Hah! You are not trying," he said. "Try."

"George Washington," she said, starting up the stairs.

"Shame on you!" he cried. "And your husband from

there! Florida! Florida! Florida's birthday," he shouted. "Come in here." He disappeared into his room, beckoning a long finger at her.

She came down the two steps and said, "I gotta be going," and stuck her head inside the door. The room was the size of a large closet and the walls were completely covered with picture postcards of local buildings; this gave an illusion of space. A single transparent bulb hung down on Mr. Jerger and a small table.

"Now examine this," he said. He was bending over a book, running his finger under the lines: "'On Easter Sunday, April 3, 1516, he arrived on the tip of this continent.' Do you know who this *he* was?" he demanded.

"Yeah, Christopher Columbus," Ruby said.

"Ponce de Leon!" he screamed. "Ponce de Leon! You should know something about Florida," he said. "Your husband is from Florida."

"Yeah, he was born in Miami," Ruby said. "He's not from Tennessee."

"Florida is not a noble state," Mr. Jerger said, "but it is an important one."

"It's important alrighto," Ruby said.

"Do you know who Ponce de Leon was?"

"He was the founder of Florida," Ruby said brightly.

"He was a Spaniard," Mr. Jerger said. "Do you know what he was looking for?"

"Florida," Ruby said.

"Ponce de Leon was looking for the fountain of youth," Mr. Jerger said, closing his eyes.

"Oh," Ruby muttered.

"A certain spring," Mr. Jerger went on, "whose water gave perpetual youth to those who drank it. In other words," he said, "he was trying to be young always."

"Did he find it?" Ruby asked.

Mr. Jerger paused with his eyes still closed. After a minute he said, "Do you think he found it? Do you think he found it? Do you think nobody else would have got to it if he had found it? Do you think there would be one person living on this earth who hadn't drunk it?"

"I hadn't thought," Ruby said.

"Nobody thinks any more," Mr. Jerger complained.

"I got to be going."

"Yes, it's been found," Mr. Jerger said.

"Where at?" Ruby asked.

"I have drunk of it."

"Where'd you have to go to?" she asked. She leaned a little closer and got a whiff of him that was like putting her nose under a buzzard's wing.

"Into my heart," he said, placing his hand over it.

"Oh." Ruby moved back. "I gotta be going. I think my brother's home." She got over the door sill.

"Ask your husband if he knows what great birthday this is," Mr. Jerger said, looking at her coyly.

"Yeah, I will." She turned and waited until she heard his door click. She looked back to see that it was shut and then she blew out her breath and stood facing the dark remaining steep of steps. "God Almighty," she commented. They got darker and steeper as you went up.

By the time she had climbed five steps her breath was gone. She continued up a few more, blowing. Then she stopped. There was a pain in her stomach. It was a pain like a piece of something pushing something else. She had felt it before, a few days ago. It was the one that frightened her most. She had thought the word *cancer* once and dropped it instantly because no horror like that was coming to her because it couldn't. The word came back to her immediately with the pain but she slashed it in two with Madam Zoleeda. It will end in good fortune. She slashed it twice through and then again until there were only pieces of it that couldn't be recognized. She was going to stop on the next floor—God, if she ever got up there—and talk to Laverne Watts. Laverne Watts was a third-floor resident, the secretary to a chiropodist, and an especial friend of hers.

She got up there, gasping and feeling as if her knees were full of fizz, and knocked on Laverne's door with the butt of Hartley Gilfeet's gun. She leaned on the door frame to rest and suddenly the floor around her dropped on both sides. The walls turned black and she felt herself reeling, without breath, in the middle of the air, terrified at the drop that was coming. She saw the door open a great distance away and Laverne, about four inches high, standing in it.

Laverne, a tall straw-haired girl, let out a great guffaw and slapped her side as if she had just opened the door on the most comical sight she had yet seen. "That gun!" she yelled. "That gun! That look!" She staggered back to the sofa and fell on it, her legs rising higher than her hips and falling down again helplessly with a thud.

The floor came up to where Ruby could see it and remained, dipping a little. With a terrible stare of concentration, she stepped down to get on it. She scrutinized a chair across the room and then headed for it, putting her feet carefully one before the other.

"You should be in a wild-west show!" Laverne Watts said. "You're a howl!"

Ruby reached the chair and then edged herself onto it. "Shut up," she said hoarsely.

Laverne sat forward, pointing at her, and then fell back on the sofa, shaking again.

"Quit that!" Ruby yelled. "Quit that! I'm sick."

Laverne got up and took two or three long strides across the room. She leaned down in front of Ruby and looked into her face with one eye shut as if she were squinting through a keyhole. "You are sort of purple," she said.

"I'm damm sick," Ruby glowered.

Laverne stood looking at her and after a second she folded her arms and very pointedly stuck her stomach out and began to sway back and forth. "Well, what'd you come in here with that gun for? Where'd you get it?" she asked.

"Sat on it," Ruby muttered.

Laverne stood there, swaying with her stomach stuck out, and a very wise expression growing on her face. Ruby sat sprawled in the chair, looking at her feet. The room was getting still. She sat up and glared at her ankles. They were swollen! I'm not going to no doctor, she started, I'm not going to one. I'm not going. "Not going," she began to mumble, "to no doctor, not . . ."

"How long you think you can hold off?" Laverne murmured and began to giggle.

"Are my ankles swollen?" Ruby asked.

"They look like they've always looked to me," Laverne said, throwing herself down on the sofa again. "Kind of fat." She lifted her own ankles up on the end pillow and turned them slightly. "How do you like these shoes?" she asked. They were a grasshopper green with very high thin heels.

"I think they're swollen," Ruby said. "When I was coming up that last flight of stairs I had the awfulest feeling, all over me like . . ."

"You ought to go on to the doctor."

"I don't need to go to no doctor," Ruby muttered. "I can take care of myself. I haven't done bad at it all this time."

"Is Rufus at home?"

"I don't know. I kept myself away from doctors all my life. I kept—why?"

"Why what?"

"Why, is Rufus at home?"

"Rufus is cute," Laverne said. "I thought I'd ask him how he liked my shoes."

Ruby sat up with a fierce look, very pink and purple. "Why Rufus?" she growled. "He ain't but a baby." Laverne was thirty years old. "He don't care about women's shoes."

Laverne sat up and took off one of the shoes and peered inside it. "Nine B," she said. "I bet he'd like what's in it."

"That Rufus ain't but an enfant!" Ruby said. "He don't

have time to be looking at your feet. He ain't got that kind of time."

"Oh, he's got plenty of time," Laverne said.

"Yeah," Ruby muttered and saw him again, waiting, with plenty of time, out nowhere before he was born, just waiting to make his mother that much deader.

"I believe your ankles are swollen," Laverne said.

"Yeah," Ruby said, twisting them. "Yeah. They feel tight sort of. I had the awfulest feeling when I got up those steps, like sort of out of breath all over, sort of tight all over, sort of—awful."

"You ought to go on to the doctor."

"No."

"You ever been to one?"

"They carried me once when I was ten," Ruby said, "but I got away. Three of them holding me didn't do any good."

"What was it that time?"

"What you looking at me that way for?" Ruby muttered.

"What way?"

"That way," Ruby said, "—swagging out that stomach of yours that way."

"I just asked you what it was that time?"

"It was a boil. A nigger woman up the road told me what to do and I did it and it went away." She sat slumped on the edge of the chair, staring in front of her as if she were remembering an easier time.

Laverne began to do a kind of comic dance up and down the room. She took two or three slow steps in one direction with her knees bent and then she came back and kicked her leg slowly and painfully in the other. She began to sing in a loud guttural voice, rolling her eyes, "Put them all together, they spell MOTHER! MOTHER!" and stretching out her arms as if she were on the stage.

Ruby's mouth opened wordlessly and her fierce expression vanished. For a half-second she was motionless; then she sprang from the chair. "Not me!" she shouted. "Not me!"

Laverne stopped and only watched her with the wise look.

"Not me!" Ruby shouted. "Oh no not me! Bill Hill takes care of that. Bill Hill takes care of that! Bill Hill's been taking care of that for five years! That ain't going to happen to me!"

"Well old Bill Hill just slipped up about four or five months ago, my friend," Laverne said. "Just slipped up . . ."

"I don't reckon you know anything about it, you ain't even married, you ain't even . . ."

"I bet it's not one, I bet it's two," Laverne said. "You better go on to the doctor and find out how many it is."

"It is not!" Ruby shrilled. She thought she was so smart! She didn't know a sick woman when she saw one, all she could do was look at her feet and shoe em to Rufus, shoe em to Rufus and he was an enfant and she was thirty-four years old. "Rufus is an enfant!" she wailed.

"That will make two!" Laverne said.

"You shut up talking like that!" Ruby shouted. "You shut up this minute. I ain't going to have any baby!"

"Ha ha," Laverne said.

"I don't know how you think you know so much," Ruby said, "single as you are. If I was so single I wouldn't go around telling married people what their business is."

"Not just your ankles," Laverne said, "you're swollen all over."

"I ain't going to stay here and be insulted," Ruby said and walked carefully to the door, keeping herself erect and not looking down at her stomach the way she wanted to.

"Well I hope *all* of you feel better tomorrow," Laverne said.

"I think my heart will be better tomorrow," Ruby said. "But I hope we will be moving soon. I can't climb these steps with this heart trouble and," she added with a dignified glare, "Rufus don't care nothing about your big feet."

"You better put that gun up," Laverne said, "before you shoot somebody."

Ruby slammed the door shut and looked down at herself quickly. She was big there but she had always had a kind of big stomach. She did not stick out there different from the way she did any place else. It was natural when you took on some weight to take it on in the middle and Bill Hill didn't mind her being fat, he was just more happy and didn't know why. She saw Bill Hill's long happy face, grinning at her from the eyes downward in a way he had as if his look got happier as it neared his teeth. He would never slip up. She rubbed her hand across her skirt and felt the tightness of it but hadn't she felt that before? She had. It was the skirt—she had on the tight one that she didn't wear often, she had . . . she didn't have on the tight skirt. She had on the loose one. But it wasn't very loose. But that didn't make any difference, she was just fat.

She put her fingers on her stomach and pushed down and then took them off quickly. She began walking toward the stairs, slowly, as if the floor were going to move under her. She began the steps. The pain came back at once. It came back with the first step. "No," she whimpered, "no." It was just a little feeling, just a little feeling like a piece of her inside rolling over but it made her breath tighten in her throat. Nothing in her was supposed to roll over. "Just one step," she whispered, "just one step and it did it." It couldn't be cancer. Madam Zoleeda said it would end in good fortune. She began crying and saying, "Just one step and it did it," and going on up them absently as if she thought she were standing still. On the sixth one, she sat down suddenly, her hand slipping weakly down the banister spoke onto the floor.

"Noooo," she said and leaned her round red face between the two nearest poles. She looked down into the stairwell and gave a long hollow wail that widened and echoed as it went down. The stair cavern was dark green and mole-colored and the wail sounded at the very bottom like a voice answering her. She gasped and shut her eyes. No. No. It couldn't be any baby. She was not going to have something waiting in her to make her deader, she was not. Bill Hill couldn't have slipped up. He said it was guaranteed and it had worked all this time and it could not be that, it could not. She shuddered and held her hand tightly over her mouth. She felt her face drawn puckered: two born dead one died the first year and one run under like a dried yellow apple no she was only thirty-four years old, she was old. Madam Zoleeda said it would end in no drying up. Madam Zoleeda said oh but it will end in a stroke of good fortune! Moving. She had said it would end in a stroke of good moving.

She felt herself getting calmer. She felt herself, after a minute, getting almost calm and thought she got upset too easy; heck, it was gas. Madam Zoleeda hadn't been wrong about anything yet, she knew more than . . .

She jumped: there was a bang at the bottom of the stairwell and a rumble rattling up the steps, shaking them even up where she was. She looked through the banister poles and saw Hartley Gilfeet, with two pistols leveled, galloping up the stairs and heard a voice pierce down from the floor over her, "You Hartley, shut up that racket! You're shaking the house!" But he came on, thundering louder as he rounded the bend on the first floor and streaked up the hall. She saw Mr. Jerger's door fly open and him spring with clawed fingers and grasp a flying piece of shirt that whirled and shot off again with a high-pitched, "Leggo, you old goat teacher!" and came on nearer until the stairs rumbled directly under her and a charging chipmunk face crashed into her and rocketed through her head, smaller and smaller into a whirl of dark.

She sat on the step, clutching the banister spoke while the breath came back into her a thimbleful at a time and the stairs stopped seesawing. She opened her eyes and gazed down into the dark hole, down to the very bottom where she had started up so long ago. "Good Fortune," she said in a hollow voice that echoed along all the levels of the cavern, "Baby."

"Good Fortune, Baby," the three echoes leered.

Then she recognized the feeling again, a little roll. It was as if it were not in her stomach. It was as if it were out nowhere in nothing, out nowhere, resting and waiting, with plenty of time.

A TEMPLE OF THE HOLY GHOST

All week end the two girls were calling each other Temple One and Temple Two, shaking with laughter and getting so red and hot that they were positively ugly, particularly Joanne who had spots on her face anyway. They came in the brown convent uniforms they had to wear at Mount St. Scholastica but as soon as they opened their suitcases, they took off the uniforms and put on red skirts and loud blouses. They put on lipstick and their Sunday shoes and walked around in the high heels all over the house, always passing the long mirror in the hall slowly to get a look at their legs. None of their ways were lost on the child. If only one of them had come, that one would have played with her, but since there were two of them, she was out of it and watched them suspiciously from a distance.

They were fourteen—two years older than she was—but neither of them was bright, which was why they had been sent to the convent. If they had gone to a regular school, they wouldn't have done anything but think about boys; at the convent the sisters, her mother said, would keep a grip on their necks. The child decided, after observing them for a few hours, that they were practically morons and she was glad to think that they were only second cousins and she couldn't have inherited any of their stupidity. Susan called herself Su-zan. She was very skinny but she had a pretty pointed face and red hair. Joanne had yellow hair that was naturally curly but she talked through her nose and when she laughed, she turned purple in patches. Neither one of them could say an intelligent thing and all their sentences began, "You know this boy I know well one time he . . ."

They were to stay all week end and her mother said she didn't see how she would entertain them since she didn't know any boys their age. At this, the child, struck suddenly with genius, shouted, "There's Cheat! Get Cheat to come! Ask Miss Kirby to get Cheat to come show them around!" and she nearly choked on the food she had in her mouth. She doubled over laughing and hit the table with her fist and looked at the two bewildered girls while water started in her eyes and rolled down her fat cheeks and the braces she had in her mouth glared like tin. She had never thought of anything so funny before.

Her mother laughed in a guarded way and Miss Kirby blushed and carried her fork delicately to her mouth with one pea on it. She was a long-faced blonde schoolteacher who boarded with them and Mr. Cheatam was her admirer, a rich old farmer who arrived every Saturday afternoon in a fifteen-year-old baby-blue Pontiac powdered with red clay dust and black inside with Negroes that he charged ten cents apiece to bring into town on Saturday afternoons. After he dumped them he came to see Miss Kirby, always bringing a little gift—a bag of boiled peanuts or a watermelon or a stalk of sugar cane and once a wholesale box of Baby Ruth candy bars. He was bald-headed except for a little fringe of rust-colored hair and his face was nearly the same color as the unpaved roads and washed like them with ruts and gulleys. He wore a pale green shirt with a thin black stripe in it and blue galluses and his trousers cut across a protruding stomach that he pressed tenderly from time to time with his big flat thumb. All his teeth were backed with gold and he would roll his eyes at Miss Kirby in an impish way and say, "Haw haw," sitting in their porch swing with his legs spread apart and his hightopped shoes pointing in opposite directions on the floor.

"I don't think Cheat is going to be in town this week end," Miss Kirby said, not in the least understanding that this was a joke, and the child was convulsed afresh, threw herself backward in her chair, fell out of it, rolled on the floor and lay there heaving. Her mother told her if she didn't stop this foolishness she would have to leave the table.

Yesterday her mother had arranged with Alonzo Myers to drive them the forty-five miles to Mayville, where the convent was, to get the girls for the week end and Sunday afternoon he was hired to drive them back again. He was an eighteen-year-old boy who weighed two hundred and fifty pounds and worked for the taxi company and he was all you could get to drive you anywhere. He smoked or rather chewed a short black cigar and he had a round sweaty chest that showed through the yellow nylon shirt he wore. When he drove all the windows of the car had to be open.

"Well there's Alonzo!" the child roared from the floor. "Get Alonzo to show em around! Get Alonzo!"

The two girls, who had seen Alonzo, began to scream their indignation.

Her mother thought this was funny too but she said, "That'll be about enough out of you," and changed the subject. She asked them why they called each other Temple One and Temple Two and this sent them off into gales of giggles. Finally they managed to explain. Sister Perpetua, the oldest nun at the Sisters of Mercy in Mayville, had given them a lecture on what to do if a young man should—here they laughed so hard they were not able to go on without going back to the beginning—on what to do if a young man should—they put their heads in their laps—on what to do if—they finally managed to shout it out—if he should "behave in an ungentlemanly manner with them in the back of an automobile." Sister Perpetua said they were to say, "Stop sir! I am a Temple of the Holy Ghost!" and that would put an end to it. The child sat up off the floor with a blank face. She didn't see anything so funny in this. What was really funny was the idea of Mr. Cheatam or Alonzo Myers beauing them around. That killed her.

Her mother didn't laugh at what they had said. "I think you girls are pretty silly," she said. "After all, that's what you are–Temples of the Holy Ghost."

The two of them looked up at her, politely concealing their giggles, but with astonished faces as if they were beginning to realize that she was made of the same stuff as Sister Perpetua.

Miss Kirby preserved her set expression and the child thought, it's all over her head anyhow. I am a Temple of the Holy Ghost, she said to herself, and was pleased with the phrase. It made her feel as if somebody had given her a present.

After dinner, her mother collapsed on the bed and said, "Those girls are going to drive me crazy if I don't get some entertainment for them. They're awful."

"I bet I know who you could get," the child started.

"Now listen. I don't want to hear any more about Mr. Cheatam," her mother said. "You embarrass Miss Kirby. He's her only friend. Oh my Lord," and she sat up and looked mournfully out the window, "that poor soul is so lonesome she'll even ride in that car that smells like the last circle in hell."

And she's a Temple of the Holy Ghost too, the child reflected. "I wasn't thinking of him," she said. "I was thinking of those two Wilkinses, Wendell and Cory, that visit old lady Buchell out on her farm. They're her grandsons. They work for her."

"Now that's an idea," her mother murmured and gave her an appreciative look. But then she slumped again. "They're only farm boys. These girls would turn up their noses at them."

"Huh," the child said. "They wear pants. They're sixteen and they got a car. Somebody said they were both going to be Church of God preachers because you don't have to know nothing to be one."

"They would be perfectly safe with those boys all right," her mother said and in a minute she got up and called their grandmother on the telephone and after she had talked to the old woman a half an hour, it was arranged that Wendell and Cory would come to supper and afterwards take the girls to the fair.

Susan and Joanne were so pleased that they washed their hair and rolled it up on aluminum curlers. Hah, thought the child, sitting cross-legged on the bed to watch them undo the curlers, wait'll you get a load of Wendell and Cory! "You'll like these boys," she said. "Wendell is six feet tall ands got red hair. Cory is six feet six inches talls got black hair and wears a sport jacket and they gottem this car with a squirrel tail on the front."

"How does a child like you know so much about these men?" Susan asked and pushed her face up close to the mirror to watch the pupils in her eyes dilate.

The child lay back on the bed and began to count the narrow boards in the ceiling until she lost her place. I know them all right, she said to someone. We fought in the world war together. They were under me and I saved them five times from Japanese suicide divers and Wendell said I am going to marry that kid and the other said oh no you ain't I am and I said neither one of you is because I will court marshall you all before you can bat an eye. "I've seen them around is all," she said.

When they came the girls stared at them a second and then began to giggle and talk to each other about the convent. They sat in the swing together and Wendell and Cory sat on the banisters together. They sat like monkeys, their knees on a level with their shoulders and their arms hanging down between. They were short thin boys with red faces and high cheekbones and pale seed-like eyes. They had brought a harmonica and a guitar. One of them began to blow softly on the mouth organ, watching the girls over it, and the other started strumming the guitar and then began to sing, not watching them but keeping his head tilted upward as if he were only interested in hearing himself. He was singing a hillbilly song that sounded half like a love song and half like a hymn.

The child was standing on a barrel pushed into some bushes at the side of the house, her face on a level with the porch floor. The sun was going down and the sky was turning a bruised violet color that seemed to be connected with the sweet mournful sound of the music. Wendell began to smile as he sang and to look at the girls. He looked at Susan with a dog-like loving look and sang,

"I've found a friend in Jesus,
He's everything to me,
He's the lily of the valley,
He's the One who's set me free!"

Then he turned the same look on Joanne and sang,

"A wall of fire about me,
I've nothing now to fear,
He's the lily of the valley,
And I'll always have Him near!"

The girls looked at each other and held their lips stiff so as not to giggle but Susan let out one anyway and clapped her hand on her mouth. The singer frowned and for a few seconds only strummed the guitar. Then he began "The Old Rugged Cross" and they listened politely but when he had finished they said, "Let us sing one!" and before he could start another, they began to sing with their convent-trained voices,

"Tantum ergo Sacramentum
Veneremur Cernui:
Et antiquum documentum
Novo cedat ritui:"

The child watched the boys' solemn faces turn with perplexed frowning stares at each other as if they were uncertain whether they were being made fun of.

"Praestet fides supplementum
Sensuum defectui.
Genitori, Genitoque
Laus et jubilatio

Salus, honor, virtus quoque . . ."

The boys' faces were dark red in the gray-purple light. They looked fierce and startled.

"Sit et benedictio;
Procedenti ab utroque
Compar sit laudatio.
Amen."

The girls dragged out the Amen and then there was a silence.

"That must be Jew singing," Wendell said and began to tune the guitar.

The girls giggled idiotically but the child stamped her foot on the barrel. "You big dumb ox!" she shouted. "You big dumb Church of God ox!" she roared and fell off the barrel and scrambled up and shot around the corner of the house as they jumped from the banister to see who was shouting.

Her mother had arranged for them to have supper in the back yard and she had a table laid out there under some Japanese lanterns that she pulled out for garden parties. "I ain't eating with them," the child said and snatched her plate off the table and carried it to the kitchen and sat down with the thin blue-gummed cook and ate her supper.

"Howcome you be so ugly sometime?" the cook asked.

"Those stupid idiots," the child said.

The lanterns gilded the leaves of the trees orange on the level where they hung and above them was black-green and below them were different dim muted colors that made the girls sitting at the table look prettier than they were.

From time to time, the child turned her head and glared out the kitchen window at the scene below.

"God could strike you deaf dumb and blind," the cook said, "and then you wouldn't be as smart as you is."

"I would still be smarter than some," the child said.

After supper they left for the fair. She wanted to go to the fair but not with them so even if they had asked her she wouldn't have gone. She went upstairs and paced the long bedroom with her hands locked together behind her back and her head thrust forward and an expression, fierce and dreamy both, on her face. She didn't turn on the electric light but let the darkness collect and make the room smaller and more private. At regular intervals a light crossed the open window and threw shadows on the wall. She stopped and stood looking out over the dark slopes, past where the pond glinted silver, past the wall of woods to the speckled sky where a long finger of light was revolving up and around and away, searching the air as if it were hunting for the lost sun. It was the beacon light from the fair.

She could hear the distant sound of the calliope and she saw in her head all the tents raised up in a kind of gold sawdust light and the diamond ring of the ferris wheel going around and around up in the air and down again and the screeking merry-go-round going around and around on the ground. A fair lasted five or six days and there was a special afternoon for school children and a special night for niggers. She had gone last year on the afternoon for school children and had seen the monkeys and the fat man and had ridden on the ferris wheel. Certain tents were closed then because they contained things that would be known only to grown people but she had looked with interest at the advertising on the closed tents, at the faded-looking pictures on the canvas of people in tights, with stiff stretched composed faces like the faces of the martyrs waiting to have their tongues cut out by the Roman soldier. She had imagined that what was inside these tents concerned medicine and she had made up her mind to be a doctor when she grew up.

She had since changed and decided to be an engineer but as she looked out the window and followed the revolving searchlight as it widened and shortened and wheeled in its arc, she felt that she would have to be much more than just a doctor or an engineer. She would have to be a saint because that was the occupation that included everything you could know; and yet she knew she would never be a saint. She did not steal or murder but she was a born liar and slothful and she sassed her mother and was deliberately ugly to almost everybody. She was eaten up also with the sin of Pride, the worst one. She made fun of the Baptist preacher who came to the school at commencement to give the devotional. She would pull down her mouth and hold her forehead as if she were in agony and groan, "Fawther, we thank Thee," exactly the way he did and she had been told many times not to do it. She could never be a saint, but she thought she could be a martyr if they killed her quick.

She could stand to be shot but not to be burned in oil. She didn't know if she could stand to be torn to pieces by lions or not. She began to prepare her martyrdom, seeing herself in a pair of tights in a great arena, lit by the early Christians hanging in cages of fire, making a gold dusty light that fell on her and the lions. The first lion charged forward and fell at her feet, converted. A whole series of lions did the same. The lions liked her so much she even slept with them and finally the Romans were obliged to burn her but to their astonishment she would not burn down and finding she was so hard to kill, they finally cut off her head very quickly with a sword and she went immediately to heaven. She rehearsed this several times, returning each time at the entrance of Paradise to the lions.

Finally she got up from the window and got ready for bed and got in without saying her prayers. There were two heavy double beds in the room. The girls were occupying the other one and she tried to think of something cold and clammy that she could hide in their bed but her thought was fruitless. She didn't have anything she could think of, like a chicken carcass or a piece of beef liver. The sound of the calliope coming through the window kept her awake and she remembered that she hadn't said her prayers and got up and knelt down and began them. She took a running start and went through to the other side of the Apostle's Creed and then hung by her chin on the side of the bed, empty-minded. Her prayers, when she remembered to say them, were usually perfunctory but sometimes when she had done something wrong or heard music or lost something, or sometimes for no reason at all, she would be moved to fervor and would think of Christ on the long journey to Calvary, crushed three times under the rough cross. Her mind would stay on this a while and then get empty and when something roused her, she would find that she was thinking of a different thing entirely, of some dog or some girl or something she was going to do some day. Tonight, remembering Wendell and Cory, she was filled with thanksgiving and almost weeping with delight, she said, "Lord, Lord, thank You that I'm not in the Church of God, thank You Lord, thank You!" and got back in bed and kept repeating it until she went to sleep.

The girls came in at a quarter to twelve and waked her up with their giggling. They turned on the small blue-shaded lamp to see to get undressed by and their skinny shadows climbed up the wall and broke and continued moving about softly on the ceiling. The child sat up to hear what all they had seen at the fair. Susan had a plastic pistol full of cheap candy and Joanne a pasteboard cat with red polka dots in it. "Did you see the monkeys dance?" the child asked. "Did you see that fat man and those midgets?"

"All kinds of freaks," Joanne said. And then she said to Susan, "I enjoyed it all but the you-know-what," and her face assumed a peculiar expression as if she had bit into something that she didn't know if she liked or not.

The other stood still and shook her head once and nodded slightly at the child. "Little pitchers," she said in a low voice but the child heard it and her heart began to beat very fast.

She got out of her bed and climbed onto the footboard of theirs. They turned off the light and got in but she didn't move. She sat there, looking hard at them until their faces were well defined in the dark. "I'm not as old as you all," she said, "but I'm about a million times smarter."

"There are some things," Susan said, "that a child of your age doesn't know," and they both began to giggle.

"Go back to your own bed," Joanne said.

The child didn't move. "One time," she said, her voice hollow-sounding in the dark, "I saw this rabbit have rabbits."

There was a silence. Then Susan said, "How?" in an indifferent tone and she knew that she had them. She said she wouldn't tell until they told about the you-know-what. Actually she had never seen a rabbit have rabbits but she forgot this as they began to tell what they had seen in the tent.

It had been a freak with a particular name but they couldn't remember the name. The tent where it was had been divided into two parts by a black curtain, one side for men and one for women. The freak went from one side to the other, talking first to the men and then to the women, but everyone could hear. The stage ran all the way across the front. The girls heard the freak say to the men, "I'm going to show you this and if you laugh, God may strike you the same way." The freak had a country voice, slow and nasal and neither high nor low, just flat. "God made me thisaway and if you laugh He may strike you the same way. This is the way He wanted me to be and I ain't disputing His way. I'm showing you because I got to make the best of it. I expect you to act like ladies and gentlemen. I never done it to myself nor had a thing to do with it but I'm making the best of it. I don't dispute hit." Then there was a long silence on the other side of the tent and finally the freak left the men and came over onto the women's side and said the same thing.

The child felt every muscle strained as if she were hearing the answer to a riddle that was more puzzling than the riddle itself. "You mean it had two heads?" she said.

"No," Susan said, "it was a man and woman both. It pulled up its dress and showed us. It had on a blue dress."

The child wanted to ask how it could be a man and woman both without two heads but she did not. She wanted to get back into her own bed and think it out and she began to climb down off the footboard.

"What about the rabbit?" Joanne asked.

The child stopped and only her face appeared over the footboard, abstracted, absent. "It spit them out of its mouth," she said, "six of them."

She lay in bed trying to picture the tent with the freak walking from side to side but she was too sleepy to figure it out. She was better able to see the faces of the country people watching, the men more solemn than they were in church, and the women stern and polite, with painted-looking eyes, standing as if they were waiting for the first note of the piano to begin the hymn. She could hear the freak saying, "God made me thisaway and I don't dispute hit," and the people saying, "Amen. Amen."

"God done this to me and I praise Him."

"Amen. Amen."

"He could strike you thisaway."

"Amen. Amen."

"But he has not."

"Amen."

"Raise yourself up. A temple of the Holy Ghost. You! You are God's temple, don't you know? Don't you know? God's Spirit has a dwelling in you, don't you know?"

"Amen. Amen."

"If anybody desecrates the temple of God, God will bring him to ruin and if you laugh, He may strike you thisaway. A temple of God is a holy thing. Amen. Amen."

"I am a temple of the Holy Ghost."

"Amen."

The people began to slap their hands without making a loud noise and with a regular beat between the Amens, more and more softly, as if they knew there was a child near, half asleep.

The next afternoon the girls put on their brown convent uniforms again and the child and her mother took them back to Mount St. Scholastica. "Oh glory, oh Pete!" they said. "Back to the salt mines." Alonzo Myers drove them and the child sat in front with him and her mother sat in back between the two girls, telling them such things as how pleased she was to have had them and how they must come back again and then about the good times she and their mothers had had when they were girls at the convent. The child didn't listen to any of this twaddle but kept as close to the locked door as she could get and held her head out the window. They had thought Alonzo would smell better on Sunday but he did not. With her hair blowing over her face she could look directly into the ivory sun which was framed in the middle of the blue afternoon but when she pulled it away from her eyes she had to squint.

Mount St. Scholastica was a red brick house set back in a garden in the center of town. There was a filling station on one side of it and a firehouse on the other. It had a high black grillework fence around it and narrow bricked walks between old trees and japonica bushes that were heavy with blooms. A big moon-faced nun came bustling to the door to let them in and embraced her mother and would have done the same to her but that she stuck out her hand and preserved a frigid frown, looking just past the sister's shoes at the wainscoting. They had a tendency to kiss even homely children, but the nun shook her hand vigorously and even cracked her knuckles a little and said they must come to the chapel, that benediction was just beginning. You put your foot in their door and they got you praying, the child thought as they hurried down the polished corridor.

You'd think she had to catch a train, she continued in the same ugly vein as they entered the chapel where the sisters were kneeling on one side and the girls, all in brown uniforms, on the other. The chapel smelled of incense. It was light green and gold, a series of springing arches that ended with the one over the altar where the priest was kneeling in front of the monstrance, bowed low. A small boy in a surplice was standing behind him, swinging the censer. The child knelt down between her mother and the nun and they were well into the *"Tantum Ergo"* before her ugly thoughts stopped and she began to realize that she was in the presence of God. Hep me not to be so mean, she began mechanically. Hep me not to give her so much sass. Hep me not to talk like I do. Her mind began to get quiet and then empty but when the priest raised the monstrance with the Host shining ivory-colored in the center of it, she was thinking of the tent at the fair that had the freak in it. The freak was saying, "I don't dispute hit. This is the way He wanted me to be."

As they were leaving the convent door, the big nun swooped down on her mischievously and nearly smothered her in the black habit, mashing the side of her face into the crucifix hitched onto her belt and then holding her off and looking at her with little periwinkle eyes.

On the way home she and her mother sat in the back and Alonzo drove by himself in the front. The child observed three folds of fat in the back of his neck and noted that his ears were pointed almost like a pig's. Her mother, making conversation, asked him if he had gone to the fair.

"Gone," he said, "and never missed a thing and it was

good I gone when I did because they ain't going to have it next week like they said they was."

"Why?" asked her mother.

"They shut it on down," he said. "Some of the preachers from town gone out and inspected it and got the police to shut it on down."

Her mother let the conversation drop and the child's round face was lost in thought. She turned it toward the window and looked out over a stretch of pasture land that rose and fell with a gathering greenness until it touched the dark woods. The sun was a huge red ball like an elevated Host drenched in blood and when it sank out of sight, it left a line in the sky like a red clay road hanging over the trees.

THE ARTIFICIAL NIGGER

Mr. Head awakened to discover that the room was full of moonlight. He sat up and stared at the floor boards—the color of silver—and then at the ticking on his pillow, which might have been brocade, and after a second, he saw half of the moon five feet away in his shaving mirror, paused as if it were waiting for his permission to enter. It rolled forward and cast a dignifying light on everything. The straight chair against the wall looked stiff and attentive as if it were awaiting an order and Mr. Head's trousers, hanging to the back of it, had an almost noble air, like the garment some great man had just flung to his servant; but the face on the moon was a grave one. It gazed across the room and out the window where it floated over the horse stall and appeared to contemplate itself with the look of a young man who sees his old age before him.

Mr. Head could have said to it that age was a choice blessing and that only with years does a man enter into that calm understanding of life that makes him a suitable guide for the young. This, at least, had been his own experience.

He sat up and grasped the iron posts at the foot of his bed and raised himself until he could see the face on the alarm clock which sat on an overturned bucket beside the chair. The hour was two in the morning. The alarm on the clock did not work but he was not dependent on any mechanical means to awaken him. Sixty years had not dulled his responses; his physical reactions, like his moral ones, were guided by his will and strong character, and these could be seen plainly in his features. He had a long tube-like face with a long rounded open jaw and a long depressed nose. His eyes were alert but quiet, and in the miraculous moonlight they had a look of composure and of ancient wisdom as if they belonged to one of the great guides of men. He might have been Vergil summoned in the middle of the night to go to Dante, or better, Raphael, awakened by a blast of God's light to fly to the side of Tobias. The only dark spot in the room was Nelson's pallet, underneath the shadow of the window.

Nelson was hunched over on his side, his knees under his chin and his heels under his bottom. His new suit and hat were in the boxes that they had been sent in and these were on the floor at the foot of the pallet where he could get his hands on them as soon as he woke up. The slop jar, out of the shadow and made snow-white in the moonlight, appeared to stand guard over him like a small personal angel. Mr. Head lay back down, feeling entirely confident that he could carry out the moral mission of the coming day. He meant to be up before Nelson and to have the breakfast cooking by the time he awakened. The boy was always irked when Mr. Head was the first up. They would have to leave the house at four to get to the railroad junction by five-thirty. The train was to stop for them at five forty-five and they had to be there on time for this train was stopping merely to accommodate them.

This would be the boy's first trip to the city though he claimed it would be his second because he had been born there. Mr. Head had tried to point out to him that when he was born he didn't have the intelligence to determine his whereabouts but this had made no impression on the child at all and he continued to insist that this was to be his second trip. It would be Mr. Head's third trip. Nelson had said, "I will've already been there twict and I ain't but ten."

Mr. Head had contradicted him.

"If you ain't been there in fifteen years, how you know you'll be able to find your way about?" Nelson had asked. "How you know it hasn't changed some?"

"Have you ever," Mr. Head had asked, "seen me lost?"

Nelson certainly had not but he was a child who was

never satisfied until he had given an impudent answer and he replied, "It's nowhere around here to get lost at."

"The day is going to come," Mr. Head prophesied, "when you'll find you ain't as smart as you think you are." He had been thinking about this trip for several months but it was for the most part in moral terms that he conceived it. It was to be a lesson that the boy would never forget. He was to find out from it that he had no cause for pride merely because he had been born in a city. He was to find out that the city is not a great place. Mr. Head meant him to see everything there is to see in a city so that he would be content to stay at home for the rest of his life. He fell asleep thinking how the boy would at last find out that he was not as smart as he thought he was.

He was awakened at three-thirty by the smell of fatback frying and he leaped off his cot. The pallet was empty and the clothes boxes had been thrown open. He put on his trousers and ran into the other room. The boy had a corn pone on cooking and had fried the meat. He was sitting in the half-dark at the table, drinking cold coffee out of a can. He had on his new suit and his new gray hat pulled low over his eyes. It was too big for him but they had ordered it a size large because they expected his head to grow. He didn't say anything but his entire figure suggested satisfaction at having arisen before Mr. Head.

Mr. Head went to the stove and brought the meat to the table in the skillet. "It's no hurry," he said. "You'll get there soon enough and it's no guarantee you'll like it when you do neither," and he sat down across from the boy whose hat teetered back slowly to reveal a fiercely expressionless face, very much the same shape as the old man's. They were grandfather and grandson but they looked enough alike to be brothers and brothers not too far apart in age, for Mr. Head had a youthful expression by daylight, while the boy's look was ancient, as if he knew everything already and would be pleased to forget it.

Mr. Head had once had a wife and daughter and when

the wife died, the daughter ran away and returned after an interval with Nelson. Then one morning, without getting out of bed, she died and left Mr. Head with sole care of the year-old child. He had made the mistake of telling Nelson that he had been born in Atlanta. If he hadn't told him that, Nelson couldn't have insisted that this was going to be his second trip.

"You may not like it a bit," Mr. Head continued. "It'll be full of niggers."

The boy made a face as if he could handle a nigger.

"All right," Mr. Head said. "You ain't ever seen a nigger."

"You wasn't up very early," Nelson said.

"You ain't ever seen a nigger," Mr. Head repeated. "There hasn't been a nigger in this county since we run that one out twelve years ago and that was before you were born." He looked at the boy as if he were daring him to say he had ever seen a Negro.

"How you know I never saw a nigger when I lived there before?" Nelson asked. "I probably saw a lot of niggers."

"If you seen one you didn't know what he was," Mr. Head said, completely exasperated. "A six-month-old child don't know a nigger from anybody else."

"I reckon I'll know a nigger if I see one," the boy said and got up and straightened his slick sharply creased gray hat and went outside to the privy.

They reached the junction some time before the train was due to arrive and stood about two feet from the first set of tracks. Mr. Head carried a paper sack with some biscuits and a can of sardines in it for their lunch. A coarse-looking orange-colored sun coming up behind the east range of mountains was making the sky a dull red behind them, but in front of them it was still gray and they faced a gray transparent moon, hardly stronger than a thumbprint and completely without light. A small tin switch box and a black fuel tank were all there was to mark the place as a junction; the tracks were double and did not converge again until they were hidden behind the bends at either end of the clearing. Trains passing appeared to emerge from a tunnel of trees and, hit for a second by the cold sky, vanish terrified into the woods again. Mr. Head had had to make special arrangements with the ticket agent to have this train stop and he was secretly afraid it would not, in which case, he knew Nelson would say, "I never thought no train was going to stop for you." Under the useless morning moon the tracks looked white and fragile. Both the old man and the child stared ahead as if they were awaiting an apparition.

Then suddenly, before Mr. Head could make up his mind to turn back, there was a deep warning bleat and the train appeared, gliding very slowly, almost silently around the bend of trees about two hundred yards down the track, with one yellow front light shining. Mr. Head was still not certain it would stop and he felt it would make an even bigger idiot of him if it went by slowly. Both he and Nelson, however, were prepared to ignore the train if it passed them.

The engine charged by, filling their noses with the smell of hot metal and then the second coach came to a stop exactly where they were standing. A conductor with the face of an ancient bloated bulldog was on the step as if he expected them, though he did not look as if it mattered one way or the other to him if they got on or not. "To the right," he said.

Their entry took only a fraction of a second and the train was already speeding on as they entered the quiet car. Most of the travelers were still sleeping, some with their heads hanging off the chair arms, some stretched across two seats, and some sprawled out with their feet in the aisle. Mr. Head saw two unoccupied seats and pushed Nelson toward them. "Get in there by the winder," he said in his normal voice which was very loud at this hour of the morning. "Nobody cares if you sit there because it's nobody in it. Sit right there."

"I heard you," the boy muttered. "It's no use in you yelling," and he sat down and turned his head to the glass. There he saw a pale ghost-like face scowling at him beneath the brim of a pale ghost-like hat. His grandfather, looking quickly too, saw a different ghost, pale but grinning, under a black hat.

Mr. Head sat down and settled himself and took out his ticket and started reading aloud everything that was printed on it. People began to stir. Several woke up and stared at him. "Take off your hat," he said to Nelson and took off his own and put it on his knee. He had a small amount of white hair that had turned tobacco-colored over the years and this lay flat across the back of his head. The front of his head was bald and creased. Nelson took off his hat and put it on his knee and they waited for the conductor to come ask for their tickets.

The man across the aisle from them was spread out over two seats, his feet propped on the window and his head jutting into the aisle. He had on a light blue suit and a yellow shirt unbuttoned at the neck. His eyes had just opened and Mr. Head was ready to introduce himself when the conductor came up from behind and growled, "Tickets."

When the conductor had gone, Mr. Head gave Nelson the return half of his ticket and said, "Now put that in your pocket and don't lose it or you'll have to stay in the city."

"Maybe I will," Nelson said as if this were a reasonable suggestion.

Mr. Head ignored him. "First time this boy has ever been on a train," he explained to the man across the aisle, who was sitting up now on the edge of his seat with both feet on the floor.

Nelson jerked his hat on again and turned angrily to the window.

"He's never seen anything before," Mr. Head continued. "Ignorant as the day he was born, but I mean for him to get his fill once and for all."

The boy leaned forward, across his grandfather and toward the stranger. "I was born in the city," he said. "I was born there. This is my second trip." He said it in a high positive voice but the man across the aisle didn't look as if he understood. There were heavy purple circles under his eyes.

Mr. Head reached across the aisle and tapped him on the arm. "The thing to do with a boy," he said sagely, "is to show him all it is to show. Don't hold nothing back."

"Yeah," the man said. He gazed down at his swollen feet and lifted the left one about ten inches from the floor. After a minute he put it down and lifted the other. All through the car people began to get up and move about and yawn and stretch. Separate voices could be heard here and there and then a general hum. Suddenly Mr. Head's serene expression changed. His mouth almost closed and a light, fierce and cautious both, came into his eyes. He was looking down the length of the car. Without turning, he caught Nelson by the arm and pulled him forward. "Look," he said.

A huge coffee-colored man was coming slowly forward. He had on a light suit and a yellow satin tie with a ruby pin in it. One of his hands rested on his stomach which rode majestically under his buttoned coat, and in the other he held the head of a black walking stick that he picked up and set down with a deliberate outward motion each time he took a step. He was proceeding very slowly, his large brown eyes gazing over the heads of the passengers. He had a small white mustache and white crinkly hair. Behind him there were two young women, both coffee-colored, one in a yellow dress and one in a green. Their progress was kept at the rate of his and they chatted in low throaty voices as they followed him.

Mr. Head's grip was tightening insistently on Nelson's

arm. As the procession passed them, the light from a sapphire ring on the brown hand that picked up the cane reflected in Mr. Head's eye, but he did not look up nor did the tremendous man look at him. The group proceeded up the rest of the aisle and out of the car. Mr. Head's grip on Nelson's arm loosened. "What was that?" he asked.

"A man," the boy said and gave him an indignant look as if he were tired of having his intelligence insulted.

"What kind of a man?" Mr. Head persisted, his voice expressionless.

"A fat man," Nelson said. He was beginning to feel that he had better be cautious.

"You don't know what kind?" Mr. Head said in a final tone.

"An old man," the boy said and had a sudden foreboding that he was not going to enjoy the day.

"That was a nigger," Mr. Head said and sat back.

Nelson jumped up on the seat and stood looking backward to the end of the car but the Negro had gone.

"I'd of thought you'd know a nigger since you seen so many when you was in the city on your first visit," Mr. Head continued. "That's his first nigger," he said to the man across the aisle.

The boy slid down into the seat. "You said they were black," he said in an angry voice. "You never said they were tan. How do you expect me to know anything when you don't tell me right?"

"You're just ignorant is all," Mr. Head said and he got up and moved over in the vacant seat by the man across the aisle.

Nelson turned backward again and looked where the Negro had disappeared. He felt that the Negro had deliberately walked down the aisle in order to make a fool of him and he hated him with a fierce raw fresh hate; and also, he understood now why his grandfather disliked them. He looked toward the window and the face there seemed to suggest that he might be inadequate to the day's exactions. He wondered if he would even recognize the city when they came to it.

After he had told several stories, Mr. Head realized that the man he was talking to was asleep and he got up and suggested to Nelson that they walk over the train and see the parts of it. He particularly wanted the boy to see the toilet so they went first to the men's room and examined the plumbing. Mr. Head demonstrated the ice-water cooler as if he had invented it and showed Nelson the bowl with the single spigot where the travelers brushed their teeth. They went through several cars and came to the diner.

This was the most elegant car in the train. It was painted a rich egg-yellow and had a wine-colored carpet on the floor. There were wide windows over the tables and great spaces of the rolling view were caught in miniature in the sides of the coffee pots and in the glasses. Three very black Negroes in white suits and aprons were running up and down the aisle, swinging trays and bowing and bending over the travelers eating breakfast. One of them rushed up to Mr. Head and Nelson and said, holding up two fingers, "Space for two!" but Mr. Head replied in a loud voice, "We eaten before we left!"

The waiter wore large brown spectacles that increased the size of his eye whites. "Stan' aside then please," he said with an airy wave of the arm as if he were brushing aside flies.

Neither Nelson nor Mr. Head moved a fraction of an inch. "Look," Mr. Head said.

The near corner of the diner, containing two tables, was set off from the rest by a saffron-colored curtain. One table was set but empty but at the other, facing them, his back to the drape, sat the tremendous Negro. He was speaking in a soft voice to the two women while he buttered a muffin. He had a heavy sad face and his neck bulged over his white collar on either side. "They rope them off," Mr. Head explained. Then he said, "Let's go see the kitchen," and they walked the length of the diner but the black waiter was coming fast behind them.

"Passengers are not allowed in the kitchen!" he said in a haughty voice. "Passengers are NOT allowed in the kitchen!"

Mr. Head stopped where he was and turned. "And there's good reason for that," he shouted into the Negro's chest, "because the cockroaches would run the passengers out!"

All the travelers laughed and Mr. Head and Nelson walked out, grinning. Mr. Head was known at home for his quick wit and Nelson felt a sudden keen pride in him. He realized the old man would be his only support in the strange place they were approaching. He would be entirely alone in the world if he were ever lost from his grandfather. A terrible excitement shook him and he wanted to take hold of Mr. Head's coat and hold on like a child.

As they went back to their seats they could see through the passing windows that the countryside was becoming speckled with small houses and shacks and that a highway ran alongside the train. Cars sped by on it, very small and fast. Nelson felt that there was less breath in the air than there had been thirty minutes ago. The man across the aisle had left and there was no one near for Mr. Head to hold a conversation with so he looked out the window, through his own reflection, and read aloud the names of the buildings they were passing. "The Dixie Chemical Corp!" he announced. "Southern Maid Flour! Dixie Doors! Southern Belle Cotton Products! Patty's Peanut Butter! Southern Mammy Cane Syrup!"

"Hush up!" Nelson hissed.

All over the car people were beginning to get up and take their luggage off the overhead racks. Women were putting on their coats and hats. The conductor stuck his head in the car and snarled, "Firstoppppmry," and Nelson lunged out of his sitting position, trembling. Mr. Head pushed him down by the shoulder.

"Keep your seat," he said in dignified tones. "The first stop is on the edge of town. The second stop is at the main railroad station." He had come by this knowledge on his first trip when he had got off at the first stop and had had to pay a man fifteen cents to take him into the heart of town. Nelson sat back down, very pale. For the first time in his life, he understood that his grandfather was indispensable to him.

The train stopped and let off a few passengers and glided on as if it had never ceased moving. Outside, behind rows of brown rickety houses, a line of blue buildings stood up, and beyond them a pale rose-gray sky faded away to nothing. The train moved into the railroad yard. Looking down, Nelson saw lines and lines of silver tracks multiplying and criss-crossing. Then before he could start counting them, the face in the window started out at him, gray but distinct, and he looked the other way. The train was in the station. Both he and Mr. Head jumped up and ran to the door. Neither noticed that they had left the paper sack with the lunch in it on the seat.

They walked stiffly through the small station and came out of a heavy door into the squall of traffic. Crowds were hurrying to work. Nelson didn't know where to look. Mr. Head leaned against the side of the building and glared in front of him.

Finally Nelson said, "Well, how do you see what all it is to see?"

Mr. Head didn't answer. Then as if the sight of people passing had given him the clue, he said, "You walk," and started off down the street. Nelson followed, steadying his hat. So many sights and sounds were flooding in on him that for the first block he hardly knew what he was seeing. At the second corner, Mr. Head turned and looked behind him at the station they had left, a putty-colored terminal with a concrete dome on top. He thought that if he could keep the dome always in sight, he would be able to get back in the afternoon to catch the train again.

As they walked along, Nelson began to distinguish details and take note of the store windows, jammed with every kind of equipment—hardware, drygoods, chicken feed, liquor. They passed one that Mr. Head called his particular attention to where you walked in and sat on a chair with your feet upon two rests and let a Negro polish your shoes. They walked slowly and stopped and stood at the entrances so he could see what went on in each place but they did not go into any of them. Mr. Head was determined not to go into any city store because on his first trip here, he had got lost in a large one and had found his way out only after many people had insulted him.

They came in the middle of the next block to a store that had a weighing machine in front of it and they both in turn stepped up on it and put in a penny and received a ticket. Mr. Head's ticket said, "You weigh 120 pounds. You are upright and brave and all your friends admire you." He put the ticket in his pocket, surprised that the machine should have got his character correct but his weight wrong, for he had weighed on a grain scale not long before and knew he weighed 110. Nelson's ticket said, "You weigh 98 pounds. You have a great destiny ahead of you but beware of dark women." Nelson did not know any women and he weighed only 68 pounds but Mr. Head pointed out that the machine had probably printed the number upsidedown, meaning the 9 for a 6.

They walked on and at the end of five blocks the dome of the terminal sank out of sight and Mr. Head turned to the left. Nelson could have stood in front of every store window for an hour if there had not been another more interesting one next to it. Suddenly he said, "I was born here!" Mr. Head turned and looked at him with horror. There was a sweaty brightness about his face. "This is where I come from!" he said.

Mr. Head was appalled. He saw the moment had come

for drastic action. "Lemme show you one thing you ain't seen yet," he said and took him to the corner where there was a sewer entrance. "Squat down," he said, "and stick you head in there," and he held the back of the boy's coat while he got down and put his head in the sewer. He drew it back quickly, hearing a gurgling in the depths under the sidewalk. Then Mr. Head explained the sewer system, how the entire city was underlined with it, how it contained all the drainage and was full of rats and how a man could slide into it and be sucked along down endless pitchblack tunnels. At any minute any man in the city might be sucked into the sewer and never heard from again. He described it so well that Nelson was for some seconds shaken. He connected the sewer passages with the entrance to hell and understood for the first time how the world was put together in its lower parts. He drew away from the curb.

Then he said, "Yes, but you can stay away from the holes," and his face took on that stubborn look that was so exasperating to his grandfather. "This is where I come from!" he said.

Mr. Head was dismayed but he only muttered, "You'll get your fill," and they walked on. At the end of two more blocks he turned to the left, feeling that he was circling the dome; and he was correct for in a half-hour they passed in front of the railroad station again. At first Nelson did not notice that he was seeing the same stores twice but when they passed the one where you put your feet on the rests while the Negro polished your shoes, he perceived that they were walking in a circle.

"We done been here!" he shouted. "I don't believe you know where you're at!"

"The direction just slipped my mind for a minute," Mr. Head said and they turned down a different street. He still did not intend to let the dome get too far away and after two blocks in their new direction, he turned to the left. This street contained two- and three-story wooden dwellings. Anyone passing on the sidewalk could see into the rooms and Mr. Head, glancing through one window, saw a woman lying on an iron bed, looking out, with a sheet pulled over her. Her knowing expression shook him. A fierce-looking boy on a bicycle came driving down out of nowhere and he had to jump to the side to keep from being hit. "It's nothing to them if they knock you down," he said. "You better keep closer to me."

They walked on for some time on streets like this before he remembered to turn again. The houses they were passing now were all unpainted and the wood in them looked rotten; the street between was narrower. Nelson saw a colored man. Then another. Then another. "Niggers live in these houses," he observed.

"Well come on and we'll go somewheres else," Mr. Head said. "We didn't come to look at niggers," and they turned down another street but they continued to see Negroes everywhere. Nelson's skin began to prickle and they stepped along at a faster pace in order to leave the neighborhood as soon as possible. There were colored men in their undershirts standing in the doors and colored women rocking on the sagging porches. Colored children played in the gutters and stopped what they were doing to look at them. Before long they began to pass rows of stores with colored customers in them but they didn't pause at the entrances of these. Black eyes in black faces were watching them from every direction. "Yes," Mr. Head said, "this is where you were born—right here with all these niggers."

Nelson scowled. "I think you done got us lost," he said.

Mr. Head swung around sharply and looked for the dome. It was nowhere in sight. "I ain't got us lost either," he said. "You're just tired of walking."

"I ain't tired, I'm hungry," Nelson said. "Give me a biscuit."

They discovered then that they had lost the lunch.

"You were the one holding the sack," Nelson said. "I would have kepaholt of it."

"If you want to direct this trip, I'll go on by myself and leave you right here," Mr. Head said and was pleased to see the boy turn white. However, he realized they were lost and drifting farther every minute from the station. He was hungry himself and beginning to be thirsty and since they had been in the colored neighborhood, they had both begun to sweat. Nelson had on his shoes and he was unaccustomed to them. The concrete sidewalks were very hard. They both wanted to find a place to sit down but this was impossible and they kept on walking, the boy muttering under his breath, "First you lost the sack and then you lost the way," and Mr. Head growling from time to time, "Anybody wants to be from this nigger heaven can be from it!"

By now the sun was well forward in the sky. The odor of dinners cooking drifted out to them. The Negroes were all at their doors to see them pass. "Whyn't you ast one of these niggers the way?" Nelson said. "You got us lost."

"This is where you were born," Mr. Head said. "You can ast one yourself if you want to."

Nelson was afraid of the colored men and he didn't want to be laughed at by the colored children. Up ahead he saw a large colored woman leaning in a doorway that opened onto the sidewalk. Her hair stood straight out from her head for about four inches all around and she was resting on bare brown feet that turned pink at the sides. She had on a pink dress that showed her exact shape. As they came abreast of her, she lazily lifted one hand to her head and her fingers disappeared into her hair.

Nelson stopped. He felt his breath drawn up by the woman's dark eyes. "How do you get back to town?" he said in a voice that did not sound like his own.

After a minute she said, "You in town now," in a rich low tone that made Nelson feel as if a cool spray had been turned on him.

"How do you get back to the train?" he said in the same reed-like voice.

"You can catch you a car," she said.

He understood she was making fun of him but he was too paralyzed even to scowl. He stood drinking in every detail of her. His eyes traveled up from her great knees to her forehead and then made a triangular path from the glistening sweat on her neck down and across her tremendous bosom and over her bare arm back to where her fingers lay hidden in her hair. He suddenly wanted her to reach down and pick him up and draw him against her and then he wanted to feel her breath on his face. He wanted to look down and down into her eyes while she held him tighter and tighter. He had never had such a feeling before. He felt as if he were reeling down through a pitchblack tunnel.

"You can go a block down yonder and catch you a car take you to the railroad station, Sugarpie," she said.

Nelson would have collapsed at her feet if Mr. Head had not pulled him roughly away. "You act like you don't have any sense!" the old man growled.

They hurried down the street and Nelson did not look back at the woman. He pushed his hat sharply forward over his face which was already burning with shame. The sneering ghost he had seen in the train window and all the foreboding feelings he had on the way returned to him and he remembered that his ticket from the scale had said to beware of dark women and that his grandfather's had said he was upright and brave. He took hold of the old man's hand, a sign of dependence that he seldom showed.

They headed down the street toward the car tracks where a long yellow rattling trolley was coming. Mr. Head had never boarded a streetcar and he let that one pass. Nelson was silent. From time to time his mouth trembled slightly but his grandfather, occupied with his own problems, paid him no attention. They stood on the corner and neither looked at the Negroes who were passing, going about their business just as if they had been white, except that most of them stopped and eyed Mr. Head and Nelson. It occurred to Mr. Head that since the streetcar ran on tracks, they could simply follow the tracks. He gave Nelson a slight push and explained that they would follow the tracks on into the railroad station, walking, and they set off.

Presently to their great relief they began to see white people again and Nelson sat down on the sidewalk against the wall of a building. "I got to rest myself some," he said. "You lost the sack and the direction. You can just wait on me to rest myself."

"There's the tracks in front of us," Mr. Head said. "All we got to do is keep them in sight and you could have remembered the sack as good as me. This is where you were born. This is your old home town. This is your second trip. You ought to know how to do," and he squatted down and continued in this vein but the boy, easing his burning feet out of his shoes, did not answer.

"And standing there grinning like a chim-pan-zee while a nigger woman gives you directions. Great Gawd!" Mr. Head said.

"I never said I was nothing but born here," the boy said in a shaky voice. "I never said I would or wouldn't like it. I never said I wanted to come. I only said I was born here and I never had nothing to do with that. I want to go home. I never wanted to come in the first place. It was all your big idea. How you know you ain't following the tracks in the wrong direction?"

This last had occurred to Mr. Head too. "All these people are white," he said.

"We ain't passed here before," Nelson said. This was a neighborhood of brick buildings that might have been lived in or might not. A few empty automobiles were parked along the curb and there was an occasional passerby. The heat of the pavement came up through

Nelson's thin suit. His eyelids began to droop, and after a few minutes his head tilted forward. His shoulders twitched once or twice and then he fell over on his side and lay sprawled in an exhausted fit of sleep.

Mr. Head watched him silently. He was very tired himself but they could not both sleep at the same time and he could not have slept anyway because he did not know where he was. In a few minutes Nelson would wake up, refreshed by his sleep and very cocky, and would begin complaining that he had lost the sack and the way. You'd have a mighty sorry time if I wasn't here, Mr. Head thought; and then another idea occurred to him. He looked at the sprawled figure for several minutes; presently he stood up. He justified what he was going to do on the grounds that it is sometimes necessary to teach a child a lesson he won't forget, particularly when the child is always reasserting his position with some new impudence. He walked without a sound to the corner about twenty feet away and sat down on a covered garbage can in the alley where he could look out and watch Nelson wake up alone.

The boy was dozing fitfully, half conscious of vague noises and black forms moving up from some dark part of him into the light. His face worked in his sleep and he had pulled his knees up under his chin. The sun shed a dull dry light on the narrow street; everything looked like exactly what it was. After a while Mr. Head, hunched like an old monkey on the garbage can lid, decided that if Nelson didn't wake up soon, he would make a loud noise by bamming his foot against the can. He looked at his watch and discovered that it was two o'clock. Their train left at six and the possibility of missing it was too awful for him to think of. He kicked his foot backwards on the can and a hollow boom reverberated in the alley.

Nelson shot up onto his feet with a shout. He looked where his grandfather should have been and stared. He seemed to whirl several times and then, picking up his feet and throwing his head back, he dashed down the street like a wild maddened pony. Mr. Head jumped off the can and galloped after but the child was almost out of sight. He saw a streak of gray disappearing diagonally a block ahead. He ran as fast as he could, looking both ways down every intersection, but without sight of him again. Then as he passed the third intersection, completely winded, he saw about half a block down the street a scene that stopped him altogether. He crouched behind a trash box to watch and get his bearings.

Nelson was sitting with both legs spread out and by his side lay an elderly woman, screaming. Groceries were scattered about the sidewalk. A crowd of women had already gathered to see justice done and Mr. Head distinctly heard the old woman on the pavement shout, "You've broken my ankle and your daddy'll pay for it! Every nickel! Police! Police!" Several of the women were plucking at Nelson's shoulder but the boy seemed too dazed to get up.

Something forced Mr. Head from behind the trash box and forward, but only at a creeping pace. He had never in his life been accosted by a policeman. The women were milling around Nelson as if they might suddenly all dive on him at once and tear him to pieces, and the old woman continued to scream that her ankle was broken and to call for an officer. Mr. Head came on so slowly that he could have been taking a backward step after each forward one, but when he was about ten feet away, Nelson saw him and sprang. The child caught him around the hips and clung panting against him.

The women all turned on Mr. Head. The injured one sat up and shouted, "You sir! You'll pay every penny of my doctor's bill that your boy has caused. He's a juve-nile delinquent! Where is an officer? Somebody take this man's name and address!"

Mr. Head was trying to detach Nelson's fingers from the flesh in the back of his legs. The old man's head had lowered itself into his collar like a turtle's; his eyes were glazed with fear and caution.

"Your boy has broken my ankle!" the old woman shouted. "Police!"

Mr. Head sensed the approach of the policeman from behind. He stared straight ahead at the women who were massed in their fury like a solid wall to block his escape. "This is not my boy," he said. "I never seen him before."

He felt Nelson's fingers fall out of his flesh.

The women dropped back, staring at him with horror, as if they were so repulsed by a man who would deny his own image and likeness that they could not bear to lay hands on him. Mr. Head walked on, through a space they silently cleared, and left Nelson behind. Ahead of him he saw nothing but a hollow tunnel that had once been the street.

The boy remained standing where he was, his neck craned forward and his hands hanging by his sides. His hat was jammed on his head so that there were no longer any creases in it. The injured woman got up and shook her fist at him and the others gave him pitying looks, but he didn't notice any of them. There was no policeman in sight.

In a minute he began to move mechanically, making no effort to catch up with his grandfather but merely following at about twenty paces. They walked on for five blocks in this way. Mr. Head's shoulders were sagging and his neck hung forward at such an angle that it was not visible from behind. He was afraid to turn his head. Finally he cut a short hopeful glance over his shoulder. Twenty feet behind him, he saw two small eyes piercing into his back like pitchfork prongs.

The boy was not of a forgiving nature but this was the first time he had ever had anything to forgive. Mr. Head had never disgraced himself before. After two more blocks, he turned and called over his shoulder in a high desperately gay voice, "Let's us go get us a Co' Cola somewheres!"

Nelson, with a dignity he had never shown before, turned and stood with his back to his grandfather.

Mr. Head began to feel the depth of his denial. His face as they walked on became all hollows and bare ridges. He saw nothing they were passing but he perceived that they had lost the car tracks. There was no dome to be seen anywhere and the afternoon was advancing. He knew that if dark overtook them in the city, they would be beaten and robbed. The speed of God's justice was only what he expected for himself, but he could not stand to think that his sins would be visited upon Nelson and that even now, he was leading the boy to his doom.

They continued to walk on block after block through an endless section of small brick houses until Mr. Head almost fell over a water spigot sticking up about six inches off the edge of a grass plot. He had not had a drink of water since early morning but he felt he did not deserve it now. Then he thought that Nelson would be thirsty and they would both drink and be brought together. He squatted down and put his mouth to the nozzle and turned a cold stream of water into his throat. Then he called out in the high desperate voice, "Come on and getcher some water!"

This time the child stared through him for nearly sixty seconds. Mr. Head got up and walked on as if he had drunk poison. Nelson, though he had not had water since some he had drunk out of a paper cup on the train, passed by the spigot, disdaining to drink where his grandfather had. When Mr. Head realized this, he lost all hope. His face in the waning afternoon light looked ravaged and abandoned. He could feel the boy's steady hate, traveling at an even pace behind him and he knew that (if by some miracle they escaped being murdered in the city) it would continue just that way for the rest of his life. He knew that now he was wandering into a black strange place where nothing was like it had ever been before, a long old age without respect and an end that would be welcome because it would be the end.

As for Nelson, his mind had frozen around his grandfather's treachery as if he were trying to preserve it intact to present at the final judgment. He walked without looking to one side or the other, but every now and then his mouth would twitch and this was when he felt, from some remote place inside himself, a black mysterious form reach up as if it would melt his frozen vision in one hot grasp.

The sun dropped down behind a row of houses and hardly noticing, they passed into an elegant suburban section where mansions were set back from the road by lawns with birdbaths on them. Here everything was entirely deserted. For blocks they didn't pass even a dog. The big white houses were like partially submerged icebergs in the distance. There were no sidewalks, only drives, and these wound around and around in endless ridiculous circles. Nelson made no move to come nearer to Mr. Head. The old man felt that if he saw a sewer entrance he would drop down into it and let himself be carried away; and he could imagine the boy standing by, watching with only a slight interest, while he disappeared.

A loud bark jarred him to attention and he looked up to see a fat man approaching with two bulldogs. He waved both arms like someone shipwrecked on a desert island. "I'm lost!" he called. "I'm lost and can't find my way and me and this boy have got to catch this train and I can't find the station. Oh Gawd I'm lost! Oh hep me Gawd I'm lost!"

The man, who was bald-headed and had on golf knickers, asked him what train he was trying to catch and Mr. Head began to get out his tickets, trembling so violently he could hardly hold them. Nelson had come up to within fifteen feet and stood watching.

"Well," the fat man said, giving him back the tickets, "you won't have time to get back to town to make this but you can catch it at the suburb stop. That's three blocks from here," and he began explaining how to get there.

Mr. Head stared as if he were slowly returning from the dead and when the man had finished and gone off with the dogs jumping at his heels, he turned to Nelson and said breathlessly, "We're going to get home!"

The child was standing about ten feet away, his face bloodless under the gray hat. His eyes were triumphantly cold. There was no light in them, no feeling, no interest. He was merely there, a small figure, waiting. Home was nothing to him.

Mr. Head turned slowly. He felt he knew now what time would be like without seasons and what heat would be like without light and what man would be like without salvation. He didn't care if he never made the train and if it had not been for what suddenly caught his attention, like a cry out of the gathering dusk, he might have forgotten there was a station to go to.

He had not walked five hundred yards down the road when he saw, within reach of him, the plaster figure of a Negro sitting bent over on a low yellow brick fence that curved around a wide lawn. The Negro was about Nelson's size and he was pitched forward at an unsteady angle because the putty that held him to the wall had cracked. One of his eyes was entirely white and he held a piece of brown watermelon.

Mr. Head stood looking at him silently until Nelson stopped at a little distance. Then as the two of them stood there, Mr. Head breathed, "An artificial nigger!"

It was not possible to tell if the artificial Negro were meant to be young or old; he looked too miserable to be either. He was meant to look happy because his mouth was stretched up at the corners but the chipped eye and the angle he was cocked at gave him a wild look of misery instead.

"An artificial nigger!" Nelson repeated in Mr. Head's exact tone.

The two of them stood there with their necks forward at almost the same angle and their shoulders curved in almost exactly the same way and their hands trembling identically in their pockets. Mr. Head looked like an ancient child and Nelson like a miniature old man. They stood gazing at the artificial Negro as if they were faced with some great mystery, some monument to another's victory that brought them together in their common defeat. They could both feel it dissolving their differences like an action of mercy. Mr. Head had never known before what mercy felt like because he had been too good to deserve any, but he felt he knew now. He looked at Nelson and understood that he must say something to the child to show that he was still wise and in the look the boy returned he saw a hungry need for that assurance. Nelson's eyes seemed to implore him to explain once and for all the mystery of existence.

Mr. Head opened his lips to make a lofty statement and heard himself say, "They ain't got enough real ones here. They got to have an artificial one."

After a second, the boy nodded with a strange shivering about his mouth, and said, "Let's go home before we get ourselves lost again."

Their train glided into the suburb stop just as they reached the station and they boarded it together, and ten minutes before it was due to arrive at the junction, they went to the door and stood ready to jump off if it did not stop; but it did, just as the moon, restored to its full splendor, sprang from a cloud and flooded the clearing with light. As they stepped off, the sage grass was shivering gently in shades of silver and the clinkers under their feet glittered with a fresh black light. The treetops, fencing the junction like the protecting walls of a garden, were darker than the sky which was hung with gigantic white clouds illuminated like lanterns.

Mr. Head stood very still and felt the action of mercy touch him again but this time he knew that there were no words in the world that could name it. He understood that it grew out of agony, which is not denied to any man and which is given in strange ways to children. He understood it was all a man could carry into death to give his Maker and he suddenly burned with shame that he had so little of it to take with him. He stood appalled, judging himself with the thoroughness of God, while the action of mercy covered his pride like a flame and consumed it. He had never thought himself a great sinner before but he saw now that his true depravity had been hidden from him lest it cause him despair. He realized that he was forgiven for sins from the beginning of time, when he had conceived in his own heart the sin of Adam, until the present, when he had denied poor Nelson. He saw that no sin was too monstrous for him to claim as his own, and since God loved in proportion as He forgave, he felt ready at that instant to enter Paradise.

Nelson, composing his expression under the shadow of his hat brim, watched him with a mixture of fatigue and suspicion, but as the train glided past them and disappeared like a frightened serpent into the woods, even his face lightened and he muttered, "I'm glad I've went once, but I'll never go back again!"

A CIRCLE IN THE FIRE

Sometimes the last line of trees was a solid gray-blue wall a little darker than the sky but this afternoon it was almost black and behind it the sky was a livid glaring white. "You know that woman that had that baby in that iron lung?" Mrs. Pritchard said. She and the child's mother were underneath the window the child was looking down from. Mrs. Pritchard was leaning against the chimney, her arms folded on a shelf of stomach, one foot crossed and the toe pointed into the ground. She was a large woman with a small pointed face and steady ferreting eyes. Mrs. Cope was the opposite, very small and trim, with a large round face and black eyes that seemed to be enlarging all the time behind her glasses as if she were continually being astonished. She was squatting down pulling grass out of the border beds around the house. Both women had on sunhats that had once been identical but now Mrs. Pritchard's was faded and out of shape while Mrs. Cope's was still stiff and bright green.

"I read about her," she said.

"She was a Pritchard that married a Brookins and so's kin to me—about my seventh or eighth cousin by marriage."

"Well, well," Mrs. Cope muttered and threw a large clump of nut grass behind her. She worked at the weeds and nut grass as if they were an evil sent directly by the devil to destroy the place.

"Beinst she was kin to us, we gone to see the body," Mrs. Pritchard said. "Seen the little baby too."

Mrs. Cope didn't say anything. She was used to these calamitous stories; she said they wore her to a frazzle. Mrs. Pritchard would go thirty miles for the satisfaction of seeing anybody laid away. Mrs. Cope always changed the subject to something cheerful but the child had observed that this only put Mrs. Pritchard in a bad humor.

The child thought the blank sky looked as if it were pushing against the fortress wall, trying to break through. The trees across the near field were a patchwork of gray and yellow greens. Mrs. Cope was always worrying about fires in her woods. When the nights were very windy, she would say to the child, "Oh Lord, do pray there won't be any fires, it's so windy," and the child would grunt from behind her book or not answer at all because she heard it so often. In the evenings in the summer when they sat on the porch, Mrs. Cope would say to the child who was reading fast to catch the last light, "Get up and look at the sunset, it's gorgeous. You ought to get up and look at it," and the child would scowl and not answer or glare up once across the lawn and two front pastures to the gray-blue sentinel line of trees and then begin to read again with no change of expression, sometimes muttering for meanness, "It looks like a fire. You better get up and smell around and see if the woods ain't on fire."

"She had her arm around it in the coffin," Mrs. Pritchard went on, but her voice was drowned out by the sound of the tractor that the Negro, Culver, was driving up the road from the barn. The wagon was attached and another Negro was sitting in the back, bouncing, his feet jogging about a foot from the ground. The one on the tractor drove it past the gate that led into the field on the left.

Mrs. Cope turned her head and saw that he had not gone through the gate because he was too lazy to get off and open it. He was going the long way around at her expense. "Tell him to stop and come here!" she shouted.

Mrs. Pritchard heaved herself from the chimney and waved her arm in a fierce circle but he pretended not to hear. She stalked to the edge of the lawn and screamed, "Get off, I toljer! She wants you!"

He got off and started toward the chimney, pushing his head and shoulders forward at each step to give the appearance of hurrying. His head was thrust up to the top in a white cloth hat streaked with different shades of sweat. The brim was down and hid all but the lower parts of his reddish eyes.

Mrs. Cope was on her knees, pointing the trowel into the ground. "Why aren't you going through the gate there?" she asked and waited, her eyes shut and her mouth stretched flat as if she were prepared for any ridiculous answer.

"Got to raise the blade on the mower if we do," he said and his gaze bore just to the left of her. Her Negroes were as destructive and impersonal as the nut grass.

Her eyes, as she opened them, looked as if they would keep on enlarging until they turned her wrongsideout. "Raise it," she said and pointed across the road with the trowel.

He moved off.

"It's nothing to them," she said. "They don't have the responsibility. I thank the Lord all these things don't come at once. They'd destroy me."

"Yeah, they would," Mrs. Pritchard shouted against the sound of the tractor. He opened the gate and raised the blade and drove through and down into the field; the noise diminished as the wagon disappeared. "I don't see myself how she had it *in* it," she went on in her normal voice.

Mrs. Cope was bent over, digging fiercely at the nut grass again. "We have a lot to be thankful for," she said. "Every day you should say a prayer of thanksgiving. Do you do that?"

"Yes'm," Mrs. Pritchard said. "See she was in it four months before she even got thataway. Look like to me if I was in one of them, I would leave off . . . how you reckon they . . . ?"

"Every day I say a prayer of thanksgiving," Mrs. Cope said. "Think of all we have. Lord," she said and sighed, "we have everything," and she looked around at her rich pastures and hills heavy with timber and shook her head as if it might all be a burden she was trying to shake off her back.

Mrs. Pritchard studied the woods. "All I got is four abscess teeth," she remarked.

"Well, be thankful you don't have five," Mrs. Cope snapped and threw back a clump of grass. "We might all be destroyed by a hurricane. I can always find something to be thankful for."

Mrs. Pritchard took up a hoe resting against the side of the house and struck lightly at a weed that had come up between two bricks in the chimney. "I reckon *you* can," she said, her voice a little more nasal than usual with contempt.

"Why, think of all those poor Europeans," Mrs. Cope went on, "that they put in boxcars like cattle and rode them to Siberia. Lord," she said, "we ought to spend half our time on our knees."

"I know if I was in an iron lung there would be some things I wouldn't do," Mrs. Pritchard said, scratching her bare ankle with the end of the hoe.

"Even that poor woman had plenty to be thankful for," Mrs. Cope said.

"She could be thankful she wasn't dead."

"Certainly," Mrs. Cope said, and then she pointed the trowel up at Mrs. Pritchard and said, "I have the best kept place in the county and do you know why? Because I work. I've had to work to save this place and work to keep it." She emphasized each word with the trowel. "I don't let anything get ahead of me and I'm not always looking for trouble. I take it as it comes."

"If it all come at oncet sometime," Mrs. Pritchard began.

"It doesn't all come at once," Mrs. Cope said sharply.

The child could see over to where the dirt road joined the highway. She saw a pick-up truck stop at the gate and let off three boys who started walking up the pink dirt road. They walked single file, the middle one bent to the side carrying a black pig-shaped valise.

"Well, if it ever did," Mrs. Pritchard said, "it wouldn't be nothing you could do but fling up your hands."

Mrs. Cope didn't even answer this. Mrs. Pritchard folded her arms and gazed down the road as if she could easily enough see all these fine hills flattened to nothing. She saw the three boys who had almost reached the front walk by now. "Lookit yonder," she said. "Who you reckon they are?"

Mrs. Cope leaned back and supported herself with one hand behind her and looked. The three came toward them but as if they were going to walk on through the side of the house. The one with the suitcase was in front now. Finally about four feet from her, he stopped and set it down. The three boys looked something alike except that the middle-sized one wore silver-rimmed spectacles and carried the suitcase. One of his eyes had a slight cast to it so that his gaze seemed to be coming from two directions at once as if it had them surrounded. He had on a sweat shirt with a faded destroyer printed on it but his chest was so hollow that the destroyer was broken in the middle and seemed on the point of going under. His hair was stuck to his forehead with sweat. He looked to be about thirteen. All three boys had white penetrating stares. "I don't reckon you remember me, Mrs. Cope," he said.

"Your face is certainly familiar," she murmured, scrutinizing him. "Now let's see . . ."

"My daddy used to work here," he hinted.

"Boyd?" she said. "Your father was Mr. Boyd and you're J. C.?"

"Nome, I'm Powell, the secont one, only I've growed some since then and my daddy he's daid now. Done died."

"Dead. Well I declare," Mrs. Cope said as if death were always an unusual thing. "What was Mr. Boyd's trouble?"

One of Powell's eyes seemed to be making a circle of the place, examining the house and the white water tower behind it and the chicken houses and the pastures that rolled away on either side until they met the first line of woods. The other eye looked at her. "Died in Florda," he said and began kicking the valise.

"Well I declare," she murmured. After a second she said, "And how is your mother?"

"Mah'd again." He kept watching his foot kick the suitcase. The other two boys stared at her impatiently.

"And where do you all live now?" she asked.

"Atlanta," he said. "You know, out to one of them developments."

"Well I see," she said, "I see." After a second she said it again. Finally she asked, "And who are these other boys?" and smiled at them.

"Garfield Smith him, and W. T. Harper him," he said, nodding his head backward first in the direction of the large boy and then the small one.

"How do you boys do?" Mrs. Cope said. "This is Mrs. Pritchard. Mr. and Mrs. Pritchard work here now."

They ignored Mrs. Pritchard who watched them with steady beady eyes. The three seemed to hang there, waiting, watching Mrs. Cope.

"Well well," she said, glancing at the suitcase, "it's nice of you to stop and see me. I think that was real sweet of you."

Powell's stare seemed to pinch her like a pair of tongs. "Come back to see how you was doing," he said hoarsely.

"Listen here," the smallest boy said, "all the time we been knowing him he's been telling us about this here place. Said it was everything here. Said it was horses here. Said he had the best time of his entire life right here on this here place. Talks about it all the time."

"Never shuts his trap about this place," the big boy grunted, drawing his arm across his nose as if to muffle his words.

"Always talking about them horses he rid here," the

small one continued, "and said he would let us ride them too. Said it was one name Gene."

Mrs. Cope was always afraid someone would get hurt on her place and sue her for everything she had. "They aren't shod," she said quickly. "There was one named Gene but he's dead now but I'm afraid you boys can't ride the horses because you might get hurt. They're dangerous," she said, speaking very fast.

The large boy sat down on the ground with a noise of disgust and began to finger rocks out of his tennis shoe. The small one darted looks here and there and Powell fixed her with his stare and didn't say anything.

After a minute the little boy said, "Say, lady, you know what he said one time? He said when he died he wanted to come here!"

For a second Mrs. Cope looked blank; then she blushed; then a peculiar look of pain came over her face as she realized that these children were hungry. They were staring because they were hungry! She almost gasped in their faces and then she asked them quickly if they would have something to eat. They said they would but their expressions, composed and unsatisfied, didn't lighten any. They looked as if they were used to being hungry and it was no business of hers.

The child upstairs had grown red in the face with excitement. She was kneeling down by the window so that only her eyes and forehead showed over the sill. Mrs. Cope told the boys to come around on the other side of the house where the lawn chairs were and she led the way and Mrs. Pritchard followed. The child moved from the right bedroom across the hall and over into the left bedroom and looked down on the other side of the house where there were three white lawn chairs and a red hammock strung between two hazelnut trees. She was a pale fat girl of twelve with a frowning squint and a large mouth full of silver bands. She knelt down at the window.

The three boys came around the corner of the house

and the large one threw himself into the hammock and lit a stub of cigarette. The small boy tumbled down on the grass next to the black suitcase and rested his head on it and Powell sat down on the edge of one of the chairs and looked as if he were trying to enclose the whole place in one encircling stare. The child heard her mother and Mrs. Pritchard in a muted conference in the kitchen. She got up and went out into the hall and leaned over the banisters.

Mrs. Cope's and Mrs. Pritchard's legs were facing each other in the back hall. "Those poor children are hungry," Mrs. Cope said in a dead voice.

"You seen that suitcase?" Mrs. Pritchard asked. "What if they intend to spend the night with you?"

Mrs. Cope gave a slight shriek. "I can't have three boys in here with only me and Sally Virginia," she said. "I'm sure they'll go when I feed them."

"I only know they got a suitcase," Mrs. Pritchard said.

The child hurried back to the window. The large boy was stretched out in the hammock with his wrists crossed under his head and the cigarette stub in the center of his mouth. He spit it out in an arc just as Mrs. Cope came around the corner of the house with a plate of crackers. She stopped instantly as if a snake had been slung in her path. "Ashfield!" she said. "Please pick that up. I'm afraid of fires."

"Gawfield!" the little boy shouted indignantly. "Gawfield!"

The large boy raised himself without a word and lumbered for the butt. He picked it up and put it in his pocket and stood with his back to her, examining a tattooed heart on his forearm. Mrs. Pritchard came up holding three Coca-Colas by the necks in one hand and gave one to each of them.

"I remember everything about this place," Powell said, looking down the opening of his bottle.

"Where did you all go when you left here?" Mrs. Cope

asked and put the plate of crackers on the arm of his chair.

He looked at it but didn't take one. He said, "I remember it was one name Gene and it was one name George. We gone to Florda and my daddy he, you know, died, and then we gone to my sister's and then my mother she, you know, mah'd, and we been there ever since."

"There are some crackers," Mrs. Cope said and sat down in the chair across from him.

"He don't like it in Atlanta," the little boy said, sitting up and reaching indifferently for a cracker. "He ain't ever satisfied with where he's at except this place here. Lemme tell you what he'll do, lady. We'll be playing ball, see, on this here place in this development we got to play ball on, see, and he'll quit playing and say, 'Goddam, it was a horse down there name Gene and if I had him here I'd bust this concrete to hell riding him!'"

"I'm sure Powell doesn't use words like that, do you, Powell?" Mrs. Cope said.

"No, mam," Powell said. His head was turned completely to the side as if he were listening for the horses in the field.

"I don't like them kind of crackers," the little boy said and returned his to the plate and got up.

Mrs. Cope shifted in her chair. "So you boys live in one of those nice new developments," she said.

"The only way you can tell your own is by smell," the small boy volunteered. "They're four stories high and there's ten of them, one behind the other. Let's go see them horses," he said.

Powell turned his pinching look on Mrs. Cope. "We thought we would just spend the night in your barn," he said. "My uncle brought us this far on his pick-up truck and he's going to stop for us again in the morning."

There was a moment in which she didn't say a thing and the child in the window thought: she's going to fly out of that chair and hit the tree.

"Well, I'm afraid you can't do that," she said, getting up

suddenly. "The barn's full of hay and I'm afraid of fire from your cigarettes."

"We won't smoke," he said.

"I'm afraid you can't spend the night in there just the same," she repeated as if she were talking politely to a gangster.

"Well, we can camp out in the woods then," the little boy said. "We brought our own blankets anyways. That's what we got in thatere suitcase. Come on."

"In the woods!" she said. "Oh no! The woods are very dry now, I can't have people smoking in my woods. You'll have to camp out in the field, in this field here next to the house, where there aren't any trees."

"Where she can keep her eye on you," the child said under her breath.

"Her woods," the large boy muttered and got out of the hammock.

"We'll sleep in the field," Powell said but not particularly as if he were talking to her. "This afternoon I'm going to show them about this place." The other two were already walking away and he got up and bounded after them and the two women sat with the black suitcase between them.

"Not no thank you, not no nothing," Mrs. Pritchard remarked.

"They only played with what we gave them to eat," Mrs. Cope said in a hurt voice.

Mrs. Pritchard suggested that they might not like *soft* drinks.

"They certainly *looked* hungry," Mrs. Cope said.

About sunset they appeared out of the woods, dirty and sweating, and came to the back porch and asked for water. They did not ask for food but Mrs. Cope could tell that they wanted it. "All I have is some cold guinea," she said. "Would you boys like some guinea and some sandwiches?"

"I wouldn't eat nothing bald-headed like a guinea," the

little boy said. "I would eat a chicken or a turkey but not no guinea."

"Dog wouldn't eat one of them," the large boy said. He had taken off his shirt and stuck it in the back of his trousers like a tail. Mrs. Cope carefully avoided looking at him. The little boy had a cut on his arm.

"You boys haven't been riding the horses when I asked you not to, have you?" she asked suspiciously and they all said, "No mam!" at once in loud enthusiastic voices like the Amens are said in country churches.

She went into the house and made them sandwiches and, while she did it, she held a conversation with them from inside the kitchen, asking what their fathers did and how many brothers and sisters they had and where they went to school. They answered in short explosive sentences, pushing each other's shoulders and doubling up with laughter as if the questions had meanings she didn't know about. "And do you have men teachers or lady teachers at your school?" she asked.

"Some of both and some you can't tell which," the big boy hooted.

"And does your mother work, Powell?" she asked quickly.

"She ast you does your mother work!" the little boy yelled. "His mind's affected by them horses he only looked at," he said. "His mother she works at a factory and leaves him to mind the rest of them only he don't mind them much. Lemme tell you, lady, one time he locked his little brother in a box and set it on fire."

"I'm sure Powell wouldn't do a thing like that," she said, coming out with the plate of sandwiches and setting it down on the step. They emptied the plate at once and she picked it up and stood holding it, looking at the sun which was going down in front of them, almost on top of the tree line. It was swollen and flame-colored and hung in a net of ragged cloud as if it might burn through any second and fall into the woods. From the upstairs window the child saw her shiver and catch both arms to her sides. "We have so much to be thankful for," she said suddenly in a mournful marveling tone. "Do you boys thank God every night for all He's done for you? Do you thank Him for everything?"

This put an instant hush over them. They bit into the sandwiches as if they had lost all taste for food.

"Do you?" she persisted.

They were as silent as thieves hiding. They chewed without a sound.

"Well, I know I do," she said at length and turned and went back to the house and the child watched their shoulders drop. The large one stretched his legs out as if he were releasing himself from a trap. The sun burned so fast that it seemed to be trying to set everything in sight on fire. The white water tower was glazed pink and the grass was an unnatural green as if it were turning to glass. The child suddenly stuck her head far out the window and said, "Ugggghhrhh," in a loud voice, crossing her eyes and hanging her tongue out as far as possible as if she were going to vomit.

The large boy looked up and stared at her. "Jesus," he growled, "another woman."

She dropped back from the window and stood with her back against the wall, squinting fiercely as if she had been slapped in the face and couldn't see who had done it. As soon as they left the steps, she came down into the kitchen where Mrs. Cope was washing the dishes. "If I had that big boy down I'd beat the daylight out of him," she said.

"You keep away from those boys," Mrs. Cope said, turning sharply. "Ladies don't beat the daylight out of people. You keep out of their way. They'll be gone in the morning."

But in the morning they were not gone.

When she went out on the porch after breakfast, they were standing around the back door, kicking the steps. They were smelling the bacon she had had for her breakfast. "Why boys!" she said. "I thought you were going to meet your uncle." They had the same look of hardened hunger that had pained her yesterday but today she felt faintly provoked.

The big boy turned his back at once and the small one squatted down and began to scratch in the sand. "We ain't, though," Powell said.

The big boy turned his head just enough to take in a small section of her and said, "We ain't bothering nothing of yours."

He couldn't see the way her eyes enlarged but he could take note of the significant silence. After a minute she said in an altered voice, "Would you boys care for some breakfast?"

"We got plenty of our own food," the big boy said. "We don't want nothing of yours."

She kept her eyes on Powell. His thin white face seemed to confront but not actually to see her. "You boys know that I'm glad to have you," she said, "but I expect you to behave. I expect you to act like gentlemen."

They stood there, each looking in a different direction, as if they were waiting for her to leave. "After all," she said in a suddenly high voice, "this is my place."

The big boy made some ambiguous noise and they turned and walked off toward the barn, leaving her there with a shocked look as if she had had a searchlight thrown on her in the middle of the night.

In a little while Mrs. Pritchard came over and stood in the kitchen door with her cheek against the edge of it. "I reckon you know they rode them horses all yesterday afternoon," she said. "Stole a bridle out the saddle room and rode bareback because Hollis seen them. He runnum out the barn at nine o'clock last night and then he runnum out the milk room this morning and there was milk all over their mouths like they had been drinking out the cans."

"I cannot have this," Mrs. Cope said and stood at the sink with both fists knotted at her sides. "I cannot have this," and her expression was the same as when she tore at the nut grass.

"There ain't a thing you can do about it," Mrs. Pritchard said. "What I expect is you'll have them for a week or so until school begins. They just figure to have themselves a vacation in the country and there ain't nothing you can do but fold your hands."

"I do not fold my hands," Mrs. Cope said. "Tell Mr. Pritchard to put the horses up in the stalls."

"He's already did that. You take a boy thirteen year old is equal in meanness to a man twict his age. It's no telling what he'll think up to do. You never know where he'll strike next. This morning Hollis seen them behind the bull pen and that big one ast if it wasn't some place they could wash at and Hollis said no it wasn't and that you didn't want no boys dropping cigarette butts in your woods and he said, 'She don't own them woods,' and Hollis said, 'She does too,' and that there little one he said, 'Man, Gawd owns them woods and her too,' and that there one with the glasses said, 'I reckon she owns the sky over this place too,' and that there littlest one says, 'Owns the sky and can't no airplane go over here without she says so,' and then the big one says, 'I never seen a place with so many damm women on it, how do you stand it here?' and Hollis said he had done had enough of their big talk by then and he turned and walked off without giving no reply one way or the other."

"I'm going out there and tell those boys they can get a ride away from here on the milk truck," Mrs. Cope said and she went out the back door, leaving Mrs. Pritchard and the child together in the kitchen.

"Listen," the child said. "I could handle them quicker than that."

"Yeah?" Mrs. Pritchard murmured, giving her a long leering look. "How'd you handle them?"

The child gripped both hands together and made a contorted face as if she were strangling someone.

"They'd handle you," Mrs. Pritchard said with satisfaction.

The child retired to the upstairs window to get out of her way and looked down where her mother was walking off from the three boys who were squatting under the water tower, eating something out of a cracker box. She heard her come in the kitchen door and say, "They say they'll go on the milk truck, and no wonder they aren't hungry—they have that suitcase half full of food."

"Likely stole every bit of it too," Mrs. Pritchard said.

When the milk truck came, the three boys were nowhere in sight, but as soon as it left without them their three faces appeared, looking out of the opening in the top of the calf barn. "Can you beat this?" Mrs. Cope said, standing at one of the upstairs windows with her hands at her hips. "It's not that I wouldn't be glad to have them—it's their attitude."

"You never like nobody's attitude," the child said. "I'll go tell them they got five minutes to leave here in."

"You are not to go anywhere near those boys, do you hear me?" Mrs. Cope said.

"Why?" the child asked.

"I'm going out there and give them a piece of my mind," Mrs. Cope said.

The child took over the position in the window and in a few minutes she saw the stiff green hat catching the glint of the sun as her mother crossed the road toward the calf barn. The three faces immediately disappeared from the opening, and in a second the large boy dashed across the lot, followed an instant later by the other two. Mrs. Pritchard came out and the two women started for the grove of trees the boys had vanished into. Presently the two sunhats disappeared in the woods and the three boys came out at the left side of it and ambled across the field and into another patch of woods. By the time Mrs. Cope and Mrs. Pritchard reached the field, it was empty and there was nothing for them to do but come home again.

Mrs. Cope had not been inside long before Mrs. Pritchard came running toward the house, shouting something. "They've let out the bull!" she hollered. "Let out the bull!" And in a second she was followed by the bull himself, ambling, black and leisurely, with four geese hissing at his heels. He was not mean until hurried and it took Mr. Pritchard and the two Negroes a half-hour to ease him back to his pen. While the men were engaged in this, the boys let the oil out of the three tractors and then disappeared again into the woods.

Two blue veins had come out on either side of Mrs. Cope's forehead and Mrs. Pritchard observed them with satisfaction. "Like I toljer," she said, "there ain't a thing you can do about it."

Mrs. Cope ate her dinner hastily, not conscious that she had her sunhat on. Every time she heard a noise, she jumped up. Mrs. Pritchard came over immediately after dinner and said, "Well, you want to know where they are now?" and smiled in an omniscient rewarded way.

"I want to know at once," Mrs. Cope said, coming to an almost military attention.

"Down to the road, throwing rocks at your mailbox," Mrs. Pritchard said, leaning comfortably in the door. "Done already about knocked it off its stand."

"Get in the car," Mrs. Cope said.

The child got in too and the three of them drove down the road to the gate. The boys were sitting on the embankment on the other side of the highway, aiming rocks across the road at the mailbox. Mrs. Cope stopped the car almost directly beneath them and looked up out of her window. The three of them stared at her as if they had never seen her before, the large boy with a sullen glare, the small one glint-eyed and unsmiling, and Powell with his two-sided glassed gaze hanging vacantly over the crippled destroyer on his shirt.

"Powell," she said, "I'm sure your mother would be ashamed of you," and she stopped and waited for this to make its effect. His face seemed to twist slightly but he continued to look through her at nothing in particular.

"Now I've put up with this as long as I can," she said. "I've tried to be nice to you boys. Haven't I been nice to you boys?"

They might have been three statues except that the big one, barely opening his mouth, said, "We're not even on your side the road, lady."

"There ain't a thing you can do about it," Mrs. Pritchard hissed loudly. The child was sitting on the back seat close to the side. She had a furious outraged look on her face but she kept her head drawn back from the window so that they couldn't see her.

Mrs. Cope spoke slowly, emphasizing every word. "I think I have been very nice to you boys. I've fed you twice. Now I'm going into town and if you're still here when I come back, I'll call the sheriff," and with this, she drove off. The child, turning quickly so that she could see out the back window, observed that they had not moved; they had not even turned their heads.

"You done angered them now," Mrs. Pritchard said, "and it ain't any telling what they'll do."

"They'll be gone when we get back," Mrs. Cope said.

Mrs. Pritchard could not stand an anticlimax. She required the taste of blood from time to time to keep her equilibrium. "I known a man oncet that his wife was poisoned by a child she had adopted out of pure kindness," she said. When they returned from town, the boys were not on the embankment and she said, "I would rather to see them than not to see them. When you see them you know what they're doing."

"Ridiculous," Mrs. Cope muttered. "I've scared them and they've gone and now we can forget them."

"I ain't forgetting them," Mrs. Pritchard said. "I wouldn't be none surprised if they didn't have a gun in that there suitcase."

Mrs. Cope prided herself on the way she handled the

type of mind that Mrs. Pritchard had. When Mrs. Pritchard saw signs and omens, she exposed them calmly for the figments of imagination that they were, but this afternoon her nerves were taut and she said, "Now I've had about enough of this. Those boys are gone and that's that."

"Well, we'll wait and see," Mrs. Pritchard said.

Everything was quiet for the rest of the afternoon but at supper time, Mrs. Pritchard came over to say that she had heard a high vicious laugh pierce out of the bushes near the hog pen. It was an evil laugh, full of calculated meanness, and she had heard it come three times, herself, distinctly.

"I haven't heard a thing," Mrs. Cope said.

"I look for them to strike just after dark," Mrs. Pritchard said.

That night Mrs. Cope and the child sat on the porch until nearly ten o'clock and nothing happened. The only sounds came from tree frogs and from one whippoorwill who called faster and faster from the same spot of darkness. "They've gone," Mrs. Cope said, "poor things," and she began to tell the child how much they had to be thankful for, for she said they might have had to live in a development themselves or they might have been Negroes or they might have been in iron lungs or they might have been Europeans ridden in boxcars like cattle, and she began a litany of her blessings, in a stricken voice, that the child, straining her attention for a sudden shriek in the dark, didn't listen to.

There was no sign of them the next morning either. The fortress line of trees was a hard granite blue, the wind had risen overnight and the sun had come up a pale gold. The season was changing. Even a small change in the weather made Mrs. Cope thankful, but when the seasons changed she seemed almost frightened at her good fortune in escaping whatever it was that pursued her. As she sometimes did when one thing was finished and another about to begin, she turned her attention to the child who had put on a pair of overalls over her dress and had pulled a man's old felt hat down as far as it would go on her head and was arming herself with two pistols in a decorated holster that she had fastened around her waist. The hat was very tight and seemed to be squeezing the redness into her face. It came down almost to the tops of her glasses. Mrs. Cope watched her with a tragic look. "Why do you have to look like an idiot?" she asked. "Suppose company were to come? When are you going to grow up? What's going to become of you? I look at you and I want to cry! Sometimes you look like you might belong to Mrs. Pritchard!"

"Leave me be," the child said in a high irritated voice. "Leave me be. Just leave me be. I ain't you," and she went off to the woods as if she were stalking out an enemy, her head thrust forward and each hand gripped on a gun.

Mrs. Pritchard came over, sour-humored, because she didn't have anything calamitous to report. "I got the misery in my face today," she said, holding on to what she could salvage. "Theseyer teeth. They each one feel like an individual boil."

The child crashed through the woods, making the fallen leaves sound ominous under her feet. The sun had risen a little and was only a white hole like an opening for the wind to escape through in a sky a little darker than itself, and the tops of the trees were black against the glare. "I'm going to get you," she said. "I'm going to get you one by one and beat you black and blue. Line up. LINE UP!" she said and waved one of the pistols at a cluster of long bare-trunked pines, four times her height, as she passed them. She kept moving, muttering and growling to herself and occasionally hitting out with one of the guns at a branch that got in her way. From time to time she stopped to remove the thorn vine that caught in her shirt and she would say, "Leave me be, I told you. Leave me be," and give it a crack with the pistol and then stalk on.

Presently she sat down on a stump to cool off but she planted both feet carefully and firmly on the ground. She lifted them and put them down several times, grinding them fiercely into the dirt as if she were crushing something under her heels. Suddenly she heard a laugh.

She sat up, prickle-skinned. It came again. She heard the sound of splashing and she stood up, uncertain which way to run. She was not far from where this patch of woods ended and the back pasture began. She eased toward the pasture, careful not to make a sound, and coming suddenly to the edge of it, she saw the three boys, not twenty feet away, washing in the cow trough. Their clothes were piled against the black valise out of reach of the water that flowed over the side of the tank. The large boy was standing up and the small one was trying to climb onto his shoulders. Powell was sitting down looking straight ahead through glasses that were splashed with water. He was not paying any attention to the other two. The trees must have looked like green waterfalls through his wet glasses. The child stood partly hidden behind a pine trunk, the side of her face pressed into the bark.

"I wish I lived here!" the little boy shouted, balancing with his knees clutched around the big one's head.

"I'm goddam glad I don't," the big boy panted, and jumped up to dislodge him.

Powell sat without moving, without seeming to know that the other two were behind him, and looked straight ahead like a ghost sprung upright in his coffin. "If this place was not here any more," he said, "you would never have to think of it again."

"Listen," the big boy said, sitting down quietly in the water with the little one still moored to his shoulders, "it don't belong to nobody."

"It's ours," the little boy said.

The child behind the tree did not move.

Powell jumped out of the trough and began to run. He

ran all the way around the field as if something were after him and as he passed the tank again, the other two jumped out and raced with him, the sun glinting on their long wet bodies. The big one ran the fastest and was the leader. They dashed around the field twice and finally dropped down by their clothes and lay there with their ribs moving up and down. After a while, the big one said hoarsely, "Do you know what I would do with this place if I had the chance?"

"No, what?" the little boy said and sat up to give him his full attention.

"I'd build a big parking lot on it, or something," he muttered.

They began to dress. The sun made two white spots on Powell's glasses and blotted out his eyes. "I know what let's do," he said. He took something small from his pocket and showed it to them. For almost a minute they sat looking at what he had in his hand. Then without any more discussion, Powell picked up the suitcase and they got up and moved past the child and entered the woods not ten feet from where she was standing, slightly away from the tree now, with the imprint of the bark embossed red and white on the side of her face.

She watched with a dazed stare as they stopped and collected all the matches they had between them and began to set the brush on fire. They began to whoop and holler and beat their hands over their mouths and in a few seconds there was a narrow line of fire widening between her and them. While she watched, it reached up from the brush, snatching and biting at the lowest branches of the trees. The wind carried rags of it higher and the boys disappeared shrieking behind it.

She turned and tried to run across the field but her legs were too heavy and she stood there, weighted down with some new unplaced misery that she had never felt before. But finally she began to run.

Mrs. Cope and Mrs. Pritchard were in the field behind

the barn when Mrs. Cope saw smoke rising from the woods across the pasture. She shrieked and Mrs. Pritchard pointed up the road to where the child came loping heavily, screaming, "Mama, Mama, they're going to build a parking lot here!"

Mrs. Cope began to scream for the Negroes while Mrs. Pritchard, charged now, ran down the road shouting. Mr. Pritchard came out of the open end of the barn and the two Negroes stopped filling the manure spreader in the lot and started toward Mrs. Cope with their shovels. "Hurry, hurry!" she shouted. "Start throwing dirt on it!" They passed her almost without looking at her and headed off slowly across the field toward the smoke. She ran after them a little way, shrilling, "Hurry, hurry, don't you see it! Don't you see it!"

"It'll be there when we git there," Culver said and they thrust their shoulders forward a little and went on at the same pace.

The child came to a stop beside her mother and stared up at her face as if she had never seen it before. It was the face of the new misery she felt, but on her mother it looked old and it looked as if it might have belonged to anybody, a Negro or a European or to Powell himself. The child turned her head quickly, and past the Negroes' ambling figures she could see the column of smoke rising and widening unchecked inside the granite line of trees. She stood taut, listening, and could just catch in the distance a few wild high shrieks of joy as if the prophets were dancing in the fiery furnace, in the circle the angel had cleared for them.

A LATE ENCOUNTER WITH THE ENEMY

General Sash was a hundred and four years old. He lived with his granddaughter, Sally Poker Sash, who was sixty-two years old and who prayed every night on her knees that he would live until her graduation from college. The General didn't give two slaps for her graduation but he never doubted he would live for it. Living had got to be such a habit with him that he couldn't conceive of any other condition. A graduation exercise was not exactly his idea of a good time, even if, as she said, he would be expected to sit on the stage in his uniform. She said there would be a long procession of teachers and students in their robes but that there wouldn't be anything to equal *him* in his uniform. He knew this well enough without her telling him, and as for the damm procession, it could march to hell and back and not cause him a quiver. He liked parades with floats full of Miss Americas and Miss Daytona Beaches and Miss Queen Cotton Products. He didn't have any use for processions and a procession full of schoolteachers was about as deadly as the River Styx to his way of thinking. However, he was willing to sit on the stage in his uniform so that they could see him.

Sally Poker was not as sure as he was that he would live until her graduation. There had not been any perceptible change in him for the last five years, but she had the sense that she might be cheated out of her triumph because she so often was. She had been going to summer school every year for the past twenty because when she started teaching, there were no such things as degrees. In those times, she said, everything was normal but nothing had been normal since she was sixteen, and for the past twenty summers, when she should have been resting, she had had to take a trunk in the burning heat to the state teacher's college; and though when she returned in the fall, she always taught in the exact way she had been taught not to teach, this was a mild revenge that didn't satisfy her sense of justice. She wanted the General at her graduation because she wanted to show what she stood for, or, as she said, "what all was behind her," and was not behind them. This *them* was not anybody in particular. It was just all the upstarts who had turned the world on its head and unsettled the ways of decent living.

She meant to stand on that platform in August with the General sitting in his wheel chair on the stage behind her and she meant to hold her head very high as if she were saying, "See him! See him! My kin, all you upstarts! Glorious upright old man standing for the old traditions! Dignity! Honor! Courage! See him!" One night in her sleep she screamed, "See him! See him!" and turned her head and found him sitting in his wheel chair behind her with a terrible expression on his face and with all his clothes off except the general's hat and she had waked up and had not dared to go back to sleep again that night.

For his part, the General would not have consented even to attend her graduation if she had not promised to see to it that he sit on the stage. He liked to sit on any stage. He considered that he was still a very handsome man. When he had been able to stand up, he had measured five feet four inches of pure game cock. He had white hair that reached to his shoulders behind and he would not wear teeth because he thought his profile was more striking without them. When he put on his full-dress general's uniform, he knew well enough that there was nothing to match him anywhere.

This was not the same uniform he had worn in the War between the States. He had not actually been a general in that war. He had probably been a foot soldier; he didn't remember what he had been; in fact, he didn't remember that war at all. It was like his feet, which hung down now shriveled at the very end of him, without feeling, covered with a blue-gray afghan that Sally Poker had crocheted when she was a little girl. He didn't remember the Spanish-American War in which he had lost a son; he didn't even remember the son. He didn't have any use for history because he never expected to meet it again. To his mind, history was connected with processions and life with parades and he liked parades. People were always asking him if he remembered this or that—a dreary black procession of questions about the past. There was only one event in the past that had any significance for him and that he cared to talk about: that was twelve years ago when he had received the general's uniform and had been in the premiere.

"I was in that preemy they had in Atlanta," he would tell visitors sitting on his front porch. "Surrounded by beautiful guls. It wasn't a thing local about it. It was nothing local about it. Listen here. It was a nashnul event and they had me in it—up onto the stage. There was no bobtails at it. Every person at it had paid ten dollars to get in and had to wear his tuxseeder. I was in this uniform. A beautiful gul presented me with it that afternoon in a hotel room."

"It was in a suite in the hotel and I was in it too, Papa," Sally Poker would say, winking at the visitors. "You weren't alone with any young lady in a hotel room."

"Was, I'd a known what to do," the old General would say with a sharp look and the visitors would scream with laughter. "This was a Hollywood, California, gul," he'd continue. "She was from Hollywood, California, and didn't have any part in the pitcher. Out there they have so many beautiful guls that they don't need that they call them a extra and they don't use them for nothing but presenting people with things and having their pitchers taken. They took my pitcher with her. No, it was two of them. One on either side and me in the middle with my arms around each of them's waist and their waist ain't any bigger than a half a dollar."

Sally Poker would interrupt again. "It was Mr. Govisky that gave you the uniform, Papa, and he gave me the most exquisite corsage. Really, I wish you could have seen it. It was made with gladiola petals taken off and painted gold and put back together to look like a rose. It was exquisite. I wish you could have seen it, it was . . ."

"It was as big as her head," the General would snarl. "I was tellin it. They gimme this uniform and they gimme this soward and they say, 'Now General, we don't want you to start a war on us. All we want you to do is march right up on that stage when you're innerduced tonight and answer a few questions. Think you can do that?' 'Think I can do it!' I say. 'Listen here. I was doing things before you were born,' and they hollered."

"He was the hit of the show," Sally Poker would say, but she didn't much like to remember the premiere on account of what had happened to her feet at it. She had bought a new dress for the occasion—a long black crepe dinner dress with a rhinestone buckle and a bolero—and a pair of silver slippers to wear with it, because she was supposed to go up on the stage with him to keep him from falling. Everything was arranged for them. A real limousine came at ten minutes to eight and took them to the theater. It drew up under the marquee at exactly the right time, after the big stars and the director and the author and the governor and the mayor and some less important stars. The police kept traffic from jamming and there were ropes to keep the people off who couldn't go. All the people who couldn't go watched them step out of the limousine into the lights. Then they walked down the red and gold foyer and an usherette in a Confederate cap and little short skirt conducted them to their special seats. The audience was already there and a group of UDC members began to clap when they saw the General in his uniform and that started everybody to clap. A few more celebrities came after them and then the doors closed and the lights went down.

A young man with blond wavy hair who said he represented the motion-picture industry came out and began to introduce everybody and each one who was introduced walked up on the stage and said how really happy he was to be here for this great event. The General and his granddaughter were introduced sixteenth on the program. He was introduced as General Tennessee Flintrock Sash of the Confederacy, though Sally Poker had told Mr. Govisky that his name was George Poker Sash and that he had only been a major. She helped him up from his seat but her heart was beating so fast she didn't know whether she'd make it herself.

The old man walked up the aisle slowly with his fierce white head high and his hat held over his heart. The orchestra began to play the Confederate Battle Hymn very softly and the UDC members rose as a group and did not sit down again until the General was on the stage. When he reached the center of the stage with Sally Poker just behind him guiding his elbow, the orchestra burst out in a loud rendition of the Battle Hymn and the old man, with real stage presence, gave a vigorous trembling salute and stood at attention until the last blast had died away. Two of the usherettes in Confederate caps and short skirts held a Confederate and a Union flag crossed behind them.

The General stood in the exact center of the spotlight and it caught a weird moon-shaped slice of Sally Poker—the corsage, the rhinestone buckle and one hand clenched around a white glove and handkerchief. The young man with the blond wavy hair inserted himself into the circle of light and said he was *really* happy to have here tonight for this great event, one, he said, who had fought and bled in the battles they would soon see daringly re-acted on the screen, and "Tell me, General," he asked, "how old are you?"

"Niiiiiinnttty-two!" the General screamed.

The young man looked as if this were just about the most impressive thing that had been said all evening. "Ladies and gentlemen," he said, "let's give the General the biggest hand we've got!" and there was applause immediately and the young man indicated to Sally Poker with a motion of his thumb that she could take the old man back to his seat now so that the next person could be introduced; but the General had not finished. He stood immovable in the exact center of the spotlight, his neck thrust forward, his mouth slightly open, and his voracious gray eyes drinking in the glare and the applause. He elbowed his granddaughter roughly away. "How I keep so young," he screeched, "I kiss all the pretty guls!"

This was met with a great din of spontaneous applause and it was at just that instant that Sally Poker looked down at her feet and discovered that in the excitement of getting ready she had forgotten to change her shoes: two brown Girl Scout oxfords protruded from the bottom of her dress. She gave the General a yank and almost ran with him off the stage. He was very angry that he had not got to say how glad he was to be here for this event and on the way back to his seat, he kept saying as loud as he could, "I'm glad to be here at this preemy with all these beautiful guls!" but there was another celebrity going up the other aisle and nobody paid any attention to him. He slept through the picture, muttering fiercely every now and then in his sleep.

Since then, his life had not been very interesting. His feet were completely dead now, his knees worked like old hinges, his kidneys functioned when they would, but his heart persisted doggedly to beat. The past and the future were the same thing to him, one forgotten and the other not remembered; he had no more notion of dying than a cat. Every year on Confederate Memorial Day, he was bundled up and lent to the Capitol City Museum where he was displayed from one to four in a musty room full of old photographs, old uniforms, old artillery, and historic documents. All these were carefully preserved in glass cases so that children would not put their hands on them. He wore his general's uniform from the premiere and sat, with a fixed scowl, inside a small roped area. There was nothing about him to indicate that he was alive except an occasional movement in his milky gray eyes, but once when a bold child touched his sword, his arm shot forward and slapped the hand off in an instant. In the spring when the old homes were opened for pilgrimages, he was invited to wear his uniform and sit in some conspicuous spot and lend atmosphere to the scene. Some of these times he only snarled at the visitors but sometimes he told about the premiere and the beautiful girls.

If he had died before Sally Poker's graduation, she thought she would have died herself. At the beginning of the summer term, even before she knew if she would pass, she told the Dean that her grandfather, General Tennessee Flintrock Sash of the Confederacy, would attend her graduation and that he was a hundred and four years old and that his mind was still clear as a bell. Distinguished visitors were always welcome and could sit on the stage and be introduced. She made arrangements with her nephew, John Wesley Poker Sash, a Boy Scout, to come wheel the General's chair. She thought how sweet it would be to see the old man in his courageous gray and the young boy in his clean khaki—the old and the new, she thought appropriately—they would be behind her on the stage when she received her degree.

Everything went almost exactly as she had planned. In the summer while she was away at school, the General stayed with other relatives and they brought him and John Wesley, the Boy Scout, down to the graduation. A reporter came to the hotel where they stayed and took the General's picture with Sally Poker on one side of him and John Wesley on the other. The General, who had had his picture taken with beautiful girls, didn't think much of this. He had forgotten precisely what kind of event this was he was going to attend but he remembered that he was to wear his uniform and carry the sword.

On the morning of the graduation, Sally Poker had to line up in the academic procession with the B.S.'s in Elementary Education and she couldn't see to getting him on the stage herself—but John Wesley, a fat blond boy of ten with an executive expression, guaranteed to take care of everything. She came in her academic gown to the hotel and dressed the old man in his uniform. He was as frail as a dried spider. "Aren't you just thrilled, Papa?" she asked. "I'm just thrilled to death!"

"Put the soward acrost my lap, damm you," the old man said, "where it'll shine."

She put it there and then stood back looking at him. "You look just grand," she said.

"God damm it," the old man said in a slow monotonous certain tone as if he were saying it to the beating of his heart. "God damm every goddam thing to hell."

"Now, now," she said and left happily to join the procession.

The graduates were lined up behind the Science building and she found her place just as the line started to move. She had not slept much the night before and when she had, she had dreamed of the exercises, murmuring, "See him, see him?" in her sleep but waking up every time just before she turned her head to look at him behind her. The graduates had to walk three blocks in the hot sun in their black wool robes and as she plodded stolidly along she thought that if anyone considered this academic procession something impressive to behold, they need only wait until they saw that old General in his courageous gray and that clean young Boy Scout stoutly wheeling his chair across the stage with the sunlight catching the sword. She imagined that John Wesley had the old man ready now behind the stage.

The black procession wound its way up the two blocks and started on the main walk leading to the auditorium.

The visitors stood on the grass, picking out their graduates. Men were pushing back their hats and wiping their foreheads and women were lifting their dresses slightly from the shoulders to keep them from sticking to their backs. The graduates in their heavy robes looked as if the last beads of ignorance were being sweated out of them. The sun blazed off the fenders of automobiles and beat from the columns of the buildings and pulled the eye from one spot of glare to another. It pulled Sally Poker's toward the big red Coca-Cola machine that had been set up by the side of the auditorium. Here she saw the General parked, scowling and hatless in his chair in the blazing sun while John Wesley, his blouse loose behind, his hip and cheek pressed to the red machine, was drinking a Coca-Cola. She broke from the line and galloped to them and snatched the bottle away. She shook the boy and thrust in his blouse and put the hat on the old man's head. "Now get him in there!" she said, pointing one rigid finger to the side door of the building.

For his part the General felt as if there were a little hole beginning to widen in the top of his head. The boy wheeled him rapidly down a walk and up a ramp and into a building and bumped him over the stage entrance and into position where he had been told and the General glared in front of him at heads that all seemed to flow together and eyes that moved from one face to another. Several figures in black robes came and picked up his hand and shook it. A black procession was flowing up each aisle and forming to stately music in a pool in front of him. The music seemed to be entering his head through the little hole and he thought for a second that the procession would try to enter it too.

He didn't know what procession this was but there was something familiar about it. It must be familiar to him since it had come to meet him, but he didn't like a black procession. Any procession that came to meet him, he thought irritably, ought to have floats with beautiful guls on them like the floats before the preemy. It must be something connected with history like they were always having. He had no use for any of it. What happened then wasn't anything to a man living now and he was living now.

When all the procession had flowed into the black pool, a black figure began orating in front of it. The figure was telling something about history and the General made up his mind he wouldn't listen, but the words kept seeping in through the little hole in his head. He heard his own name mentioned and his chair was shuttled forward roughly and the Boy Scout took a big bow. They called his name and the fat brat bowed. Goddam you, the old man tried to say, get out of my way, I can stand up!—but he was jerked back again before he could get up and take the bow. He supposed the noise they made was for him. If he was over, he didn't intend to listen to any more of it. If it hadn't been for the little hole in the top of his head, none of the words would have got to him. He thought of putting his finger up there into the hole to block them but the hole was a little wider than his finger and it felt as if it were getting deeper.

Another black robe had taken the place of the first one and was talking now and he heard his name mentioned again but they were not talking about him, they were still talking about history. "If we forget our past," the speaker was saying, "we won't remember our future and it will be as well for we won't have one." The General heard some of these words gradually. He had forgotten history and he didn't intend to remember it again. He had forgotten the name and face of his wife and the names and faces of his children or even if he had a wife and children, and he had forgotten the names of places and the places themselves and what had happened at them.

He was considerably irked by the hole in his head. He had not expected to have a hole in his head at this event. It was the slow black music that had put it there and though most of the music had stopped outside, there was still a little of it in the hole, going deeper and moving around in his thoughts, letting the words he heard into the dark places of his brain. He heard the words, Chickamauga, Shiloh, Johnston, Lee, and he knew he was inspiring all these words that meant nothing to him. He wondered if he had been a general at Chickamauga or at Lee. Then he tried to see himself and the horse mounted in the middle of a float full of beautiful girls, being driven slowly through downtown Atlanta. Instead, the old words began to stir in his head as if they were trying to wrench themselves out of place and come to life.

The speaker was through with that war and had gone on to the next one and now he was approaching another and all his words, like the black procession, were vaguely familiar and irritating. There was a long finger of music in the General's head, probing various spots that were words, letting in a little light on the words and helping them to live. The words began to come toward him and he said, Dammit! I ain't going to have it! and he started edging backwards to get out of the way. Then he saw the figure in the black robe sit down and there was a noise and the black pool in front of him began to rumble and to flow toward him from either side to the black slow music, and he said, Stop dammit! I can't do but one thing at a time! He couldn't protect himself from the words and attend to the procession too and the words were coming at him fast. He felt that he was running backwards and the words were coming at him like musket fire, just escaping him but getting nearer and nearer. He turned around and began to run as fast as he could but he found himself running toward the words. He was running into a regular volley of them and meeting them with quick curses. As the music swelled toward him, the entire past opened up on him out of nowhere and he felt his body riddled in a hundred places with sharp stabs of pain and he fell down, returning a curse for every hit. He saw his wife's narrow face looking at him critically through her round gold-rimmed glasses; he saw one of his squinting bald-headed sons; and his mother ran toward him with an anxious look; then a succession of places—Chickamauga, Shiloh, Marthasville—rushed at him as if the past were the only future now and he had to endure it. Then suddenly he saw that the black procession was almost on him. He recognized it, for it had been dogging all his days. He made such a desperate effort to see over it and find out what comes after the past that his hand clenched the sword until the blade touched bone.

The graduates were crossing the stage in a long file to receive their scrolls and shake the president's hand. As Sally Poker, who was near the end, crossed, she glanced at the General and saw him sitting fixed and fierce, his eyes wide open, and she turned her head forward again and held it a perceptible degree higher and received her scroll. Once it was all over and she was out of the auditorium in the sun again, she located her kin and they waited together on a bench in the shade for John Wesley to wheel the old man out. That crafty scout had bumped him out the back way and rolled him at high speed down a flagstone path and was waiting now, with the corpse, in the long line at the Coca-Cola machine.

GOOD COUNTRY PEOPLE

Besides the neutral expression that she wore when she was alone, Mrs. Freeman had two others, forward and reverse, that she used for all her human dealings. Her forward expression was steady and driving like the advance of a heavy truck. Her eyes never swerved to left or right but turned as the story turned as if they followed a yellow line down the center of it. She seldom used the other expression because it was not often necessary for her to retract a statement, but when she did, her face came to a complete stop, there was an almost imperceptible movement of her black eyes, during which they seemed to be receding, and then the observer would see that Mrs. Freeman, though she might stand there as real as several grain sacks thrown on top of each other, was no longer there in spirit. As for getting anything across to her when this was the case, Mrs. Hopewell had given it up. She might talk her head off. Mrs. Freeman could never be brought to admit herself wrong on any point. She would stand there and if she could be brought to say anything, it was something like, "Well, I wouldn't of said it was and I wouldn't of said it wasn't," or letting her gaze range over the top kitchen shelf where there was an assortment of dusty bottles, she might remark, "I see you ain't ate many of them figs you put up last summer."

They carried on their most important business in the kitchen at breakfast. Every morning Mrs. Hopewell got up at seven o'clock and lit her gas heater and Joy's. Joy was her daughter, a large blonde girl who had an artificial leg. Mrs. Hopewell thought of her as a child though she was thirty-two years old and highly educated. Joy would get up while her mother was eating and lumber into the bathroom and slam the door, and before long, Mrs. Freeman would arrive at the back door. Joy would hear her mother call, "Come on in," and then they would talk for a while in low voices that were indistinguishable in the bathroom. By the time Joy came in, they had usually finished the weather report and were on one or the other of Mrs. Freeman's daughters, Glynese or Carramae. Joy called them Glycerin and Caramel. Glynese, a redhead, was eighteen and had many admirers; Carramae, a blonde, was only fifteen but already married and pregnant. She could not keep anything on her stomach. Every morning Mrs. Freeman told Mrs. Hopewell how many times she had vomited since the last report.

Mrs. Hopewell liked to tell people that Glynese and Carramae were two of the finest girls she knew and that Mrs. Freeman was a *lady* and that she was never ashamed to take her anywhere or introduce her to anybody they might meet. Then she would tell how she had happened to hire the Freemans in the first place and how they were a godsend to her and how she had had them four years. The reason for her keeping them so long was that they were not trash. They were good country people. She had telephoned the man whose name they had given as a reference and he had told her that Mr. Freeman was a good farmer but that his wife was the nosiest woman ever to walk the earth. "She's got to be into everything," the man said. "If she don't get there before the dust settles, you can bet she's dead, that's all. She'll want to know all your business. I can stand him real good," he had said, "but me nor my wife neither could have stood that woman one more minute on this place." That had put Mrs. Hopewell off for a few days.

She had hired them in the end because there were no other applicants but she had made up her mind beforehand exactly how she would handle the woman. Since she was the type who had to be into everything, then, Mrs. Hopewell had decided, she would not only let her be into everything, she would *see to it* that she was into everything—she would give her the responsibility of everything, she would put her in charge. Mrs. Hopewell had no bad qualities of her own but she was able to use other people's in such a constructive way that she never felt the lack. She had hired the Freemans and she had kept them four years.

Nothing is perfect. This was one of Mrs. Hopewell's favorite sayings. Another was: that is life! And still another, the most important, was: well, other people have their opinions too. She would make these statements, usually at the table, in a tone of gentle insistence as if no one held them but her, and the large hulking Joy, whose constant outrage had obliterated every expression from her face, would stare just a little to the side of her, her eyes icy blue, with the look of someone who has achieved blindness by an act of will and means to keep it.

When Mrs. Hopewell said to Mrs. Freeman that life was like that, Mrs. Freeman would say, "I always said so myself." Nothing had been arrived at by anyone that had not first been arrived at by her. She was quicker than Mr. Freeman. When Mrs. Hopewell said to her after they had been on the place a while, "You know, you're the wheel behind the wheel," and winked, Mrs. Freeman had said, "I know it. I've always been quick. It's some that are quicker than others."

"Everybody is different," Mrs. Hopewell said.

"Yes, most people is," Mrs. Freeman said.

"It takes all kinds to make the world."

"I always said it did myself."

The girl was used to this kind of dialogue for breakfast and more of it for dinner; sometimes they had it for supper too. When they had no guest they ate in the kitchen because that was easier. Mrs. Freeman always managed to arrive at some point during the meal and to watch them finish it. She would stand in the doorway if it were summer but in the winter she would stand with one elbow on top of the refrigerator and look down on them, or she would stand by the gas heater, lifting the back of her skirt slightly. Occasionally she would stand against the wall and roll her head from side to side. At no time was she in any hurry to leave. All this was very trying on Mrs. Hopewell but she was a woman of great patience. She realized that nothing is perfect and that in the Freemans she had good country people and that if, in this day and age, you get good country people, you had better hang onto them.

She had had plenty of experience with trash. Before the Freemans she had averaged one tenant family a year. The wives of these farmers were not the kind you would want to be around you for very long. Mrs. Hopewell, who had divorced her husband long ago, needed someone to walk over the fields with her; and when Joy had to be impressed for these services, her remarks were usually so ugly and her face so glum that Mrs. Hopewell would say, "If you can't come pleasantly, I don't want you at all," to which the girl, standing square and rigid-shouldered with her neck thrust slightly forward, would reply, "If you want me, here I am—LIKE I AM."

Mrs. Hopewell excused this attitude because of the leg (which had been shot off in a hunting accident when Joy was ten). It was hard for Mrs. Hopewell to realize that her child was thirty-two now and that for more than twenty years she had had only one leg. She thought of her still as a child because it tore her heart to think instead of the poor stout girl in her thirties who had never danced a step or had any *normal* good times. Her name was really Joy but as soon as she was twenty-one and away from home, she had had it legally changed. Mrs. Hopewell was certain that she had thought and thought until she had hit upon the ugliest name in any language. Then she had gone and had the beautiful name, Joy, changed without telling her mother until after she had done it. Her legal name was Hulga.

When Mrs. Hopewell thought the name, Hulga, she thought of the broad blank hull of a battleship. She would not use it. She continued to call her Joy to which the girl responded but in a purely mechanical way.

Hulga had learned to tolerate Mrs. Freeman who saved her from taking walks with her mother. Even Glynese and Carramae were useful when they occupied attention that might otherwise have been directed at her. At first she had thought she could not stand Mrs. Freeman for she had found that it was not possible to be rude to her. Mrs. Freeman would take on strange resentments and for days together she would be sullen but the source of her displeasure was always obscure; a direct attack, a positive leer, blatant ugliness to her face—these never touched her. And without warning one day, she began calling her Hulga.

She did not call her that in front of Mrs. Hopewell who would have been incensed but when she and the girl happened to be out of the house together, she would say something and add the name Hulga to the end of it, and the big spectacled Joy-Hulga would scowl and redden as if her privacy had been intruded upon. She considered the name her personal affair. She had arrived at it first purely on the basis of its ugly sound and then the full genius of its fitness had struck her. She had a vision of the name working like the ugly sweating Vulcan who stayed in the furnace and to whom, presumably, the goddess had to come when called. She saw it as the name of her highest creative act. One of her major triumphs was that her mother had not been able to turn her dust into Joy, but the greater one was that she had been able to turn it herself into Hulga. However, Mrs. Freeman's relish for using the name only irritated her. It was as if Mrs. Freeman's beady steel-pointed eyes had penetrated far enough behind her face to reach some secret fact. Something about her seemed to fascinate Mrs. Freeman and then one day Hulga realized that it was the artificial leg. Mrs. Freeman had a special fondness for the details of secret infections, hidden deformities, assaults upon children. Of diseases, she preferred the lingering or incurable. Hulga had heard Mrs. Hopewell give her the details of the hunting accident, how the leg had been literally blasted off, how she had never lost consciousness. Mrs. Freeman could listen to it any time as if it had happened an hour ago.

When Hulga stumped into the kitchen in the morning (she could walk without making the awful noise but she made it—Mrs. Hopewell was certain—because it was ugly-sounding), she glanced at them and did not speak. Mrs. Hopewell would be in her red kimono with her hair tied around her head in rags. She would be sitting at the table, finishing her breakfast and Mrs. Freeman would be hanging by her elbow outward from the refrigerator, looking down at the table. Hulga always put her eggs on the stove to boil and then stood over them with her arms folded, and Mrs. Hopewell would look at her—a kind of indirect gaze divided between her and Mrs. Freeman—and would think that if she would only keep herself up a little, she wouldn't be so bad looking. There was nothing wrong with her face that a pleasant expression wouldn't help. Mrs. Hopewell said that people who looked on the bright side of things would be beautiful even if they were not.

Whenever she looked at Joy this way, she could not help but feel that it would have been better if the child had not taken the Ph.D. It had certainly not brought her out any and now that she had it, there was no more excuse for her to go to school again. Mrs. Hopewell thought it was nice for girls to go to school to have a good time but Joy had "gone through." Anyhow, she would not have been strong enough to go again. The doctors had told Mrs. Hopewell that with the best of care, Joy might see forty-five. She had a weak heart. Joy had made it plain that if it had not been for this condition, she would be far from these red hills and good country people. She would be in a university lecturing to people who knew what she was talking about. And Mrs. Hopewell could very well picture her there, looking like a scarecrow and lecturing to more of the same. Here she went about all day in a six-year-old skirt and a yellow sweat shirt with a faded cowboy on a horse embossed on it. She thought this was funny; Mrs. Hopewell thought it was idiotic and showed simply that she was still a child. She was brilliant but she didn't have a grain of sense. It seemed to Mrs. Hopewell that every year she grew less like other people and more like herself—bloated, rude, and squint-eyed. And she said such strange things! To her own mother she had said—without warning, without excuse, standing up in the middle of a meal with her face purple and her mouth half full—"Woman! do you ever look inside? Do you ever look inside and see what you are *not?* God!" she had cried sinking down again and staring at her plate, "Malebranche was right: we are not our own light. We are not our own light!" Mrs. Hopewell had no idea to this day what brought that on. She had only made the remark, hoping Joy would take it in, that a smile never hurt anyone.

The girl had taken the Ph.D. in philosophy and this left Mrs. Hopewell at a complete loss. You could say, "My daughter is a nurse," or "My daughter is a school teacher," or even, "My daughter is a chemical engineer." You could not say, "My daughter is a philosopher." That was something that had ended with the Greeks and Romans. All day Joy sat on her neck in a deep chair, reading. Sometimes she went for walks but she didn't like dogs or cats or birds or flowers or nature or nice young men. She looked at nice young men as if she could smell their stupidity.

One day Mrs. Hopewell had picked up one of the books the girl had just put down and opening it at random, she read, "Science, on the other hand, has to assert its soberness and seriousness afresh and declare that it is concerned solely with what-is. Nothing—how can it be for science anything but a horror and a phantasm? If science is right, then one thing stands firm: science wishes to know nothing of nothing. Such is after all the strictly scientific approach to Nothing. We know it by wishing to know nothing of Nothing." These words had been underlined with a blue pencil and they worked on Mrs. Hopewell like some evil incantation in gibberish. She shut the book quickly and went out of the room as if she were having a chill.

This morning when the girl came in, Mrs. Freeman was on Carramae. "She thrown up four times after supper," she said, "and was up twict in the night after three o'clock. Yesterday she didn't do nothing but ramble in the bureau drawer. All she did. Stand up there and see what she could run up on."

"She's got to eat," Mrs. Hopewell muttered, sipping her coffee, while she watched Joy's back at the stove. She was wondering what the child had said to the Bible salesman. She could not imagine what kind of a conversation she could possibly have had with him.

He was a tall gaunt hatless youth who had called yesterday to sell them a Bible. He had appeared at the door, carrying a large black suitcase that weighted him so heavily on one side that he had to brace himself against the door facing. He seemed on the point of collapse but he said in a cheerful voice, "Good morning, Mrs. Cedars!" and set the suitcase down on the mat. He was not a bad-looking young man though he had on a bright blue suit and yellow socks that were not pulled up far enough. He had prominent face bones and a streak of sticky-looking brown hair falling across his forehead.

"I'm Mrs. Hopewell," she said.

"Oh!" he said, pretending to look puzzled but with his eyes sparkling, "I saw it said 'The Cedars,' on the mailbox so I thought you was Mrs. Cedars!" and he burst out in a pleasant laugh. He picked up the satchel and under cover of a pant, he fell forward into her hall. It was rather as if the suitcase had moved first, jerking him after it. "Mrs. Hopewell!" he said and grabbed her hand. "I hope you are well!" and he laughed again and then all at once his face sobered completely. He paused and gave her a straight earnest look and said, "Lady, I've come to speak of serious things."

"Well, come in," she muttered, none too pleased because her dinner was almost ready. He came into the parlor and sat down on the edge of a straight chair and put the suitcase between his feet and glanced around the room as if he were sizing her up by it. Her silver gleamed on the two sideboards; she decided he had never been in a room as elegant as this.

"Mrs. Hopewell," he began, using her name in a way that sounded almost intimate, "I know you believe in Chrustian service."

"Well yes," she murmured.

"I know," he said and paused, looking very wise with his head cocked on one side, "that you're a good woman. Friends have told me."

Mrs. Hopewell never liked to be taken for a fool. "What are you selling?" she asked.

"Bibles," the young man said and his eye raced around the room before he added, "I see you have no family Bible in your parlor, I see that is the one lack you got!"

Mrs. Hopewell could not say, "My daughter is an atheist and won't let me keep the Bible in the parlor." She said, stiffening slightly, "I keep my Bible by my bedside." This was not the truth. It was in the attic somewhere.

"Lady," he said, "the word of God ought to be in the parlor."

"Well, I think that's a matter of taste," she began. "I think . . ."

"Lady," he said, "for a Chrustian, the word of God ought to be in every room in the house besides in his heart. I know you're a Chrustian because I can see it in every line of your face."

She stood up and said, "Well, young man, I don't want to buy a Bible and I smell my dinner burning."

He didn't get up. He began to twist his hands and looking down at them, he said softly, "Well lady, I'll tell you the truth—not many people want to buy one nowadays and besides, I know I'm real simple. I don't know how to say a thing but to say it. I'm just a country boy." He glanced up into her unfriendly face. "People like you don't like to fool with country people like me!"

"Why!" she cried, "good country people are the salt of the earth! Besides, we all have different ways of doing, it takes all kinds to make the world go 'round. That's life!"

"You said a mouthful," he said.

"Why, I think there aren't enough good country people in the world!" she said, stirred. "I think that's what's wrong with it!"

His face had brightened. "I didn't inraduce myself," he said. "I'm Manley Pointer from out in the country around Willohobie, not even from a place, just from near a place."

"You wait a minute," she said. "I have to see about my dinner." She went out to the kitchen and found Joy standing near the door where she had been listening.

"Get rid of the salt of the earth," she said, "and let's eat."

Mrs. Hopewell gave her a pained look and turned the heat down under the vegetables. "*I* can't be rude to anybody," she murmured and went back into the parlor.

He had opened the suitcase and was sitting with a Bible on each knee.

"You might as well put those up," she told him. "I don't want one."

"I appreciate your honesty," he said. "You don't see any more real honest people unless you go way out in the country."

"I know," she said, "real genuine folks!" Through the crack in the door she heard a groan.

"I guess a lot of boys come telling you they're working their way through college," he said, "but I'm not going to tell you that. Somehow," he said, "I don't want to go to college. I want to devote my life to Chrustian service. See," he said, lowering his voice, "I got this heart condition. I may not live long. When you know it's something wrong with you and you may not live long, well then, lady . . ." He paused, with his mouth open, and stared at her.

He and Joy had the same condition! She knew that her eyes were filling with tears but she collected herself quickly and murmured, "Won't you stay for dinner? We'd love to have you!" and was sorry the instant she heard herself say it.

"Yes mam," he said in an abashed voice, "I would sher love to do that!"

Joy had given him one look on being introduced to him and then throughout the meal had not glanced at him again. He had addressed several remarks to her, which she had pretended not to hear. Mrs. Hopewell could not understand deliberate rudeness, although she lived with it, and she felt she had always to overflow with hospitality to make up for Joy's lack of courtesy. She urged him to talk about himself and he did. He said he was the seventh child of twelve and that his father had been crushed under a tree when he himself was eight year old. He had been crushed very badly, in fact, almost cut in two and was practically not recognizable. His mother had got along the best she could by hard working and she had always seen that her children went to Sunday School and that they read the Bible every evening. He was now nineteen year old and he had been selling Bibles for four months. In that time he had sold seventy-seven Bibles and had the promise of two more sales. He wanted to become a missionary because he thought that was the way you could do most for people. "He who losest his life shall find it," he said simply and he was so sincere, so genuine and earnest that Mrs. Hopewell would not for the world have smiled. He prevented his peas from sliding onto the table by blocking them with a piece of bread which he later cleaned his plate with. She could see Joy observing sidewise how he handled his knife and fork and she saw too that every few minutes, the boy would dart a keen appraising glance at the girl as if he were trying to attract her attention.

After dinner Joy cleared the dishes off the table and disappeared and Mrs. Hopewell was left to talk with him. He told her again about his childhood and his father's accident and about various things that had happened to him. Every five minutes or so she would stifle a yawn. He sat for two hours until finally she told him she must go because she had an appointment in town. He packed his Bibles and thanked her and prepared to leave, but in the doorway he stopped and wrung her hand and said that not on any of his trips had he met a lady as nice as her and he asked if he could come again. She had said she would always be happy to see him.

Joy had been standing in the road, apparently looking at something in the distance, when he came down the steps toward her, bent to the side with his heavy valise. He stopped where she was standing and confronted her directly. Mrs. Hopewell could not hear what he said but she trembled to think what Joy would say to him. She could see that after a minute Joy said something and that then the boy began to speak again, making an excited gesture with his free hand. After a minute Joy said something else at which the boy began to speak once more. Then to her amazement, Mrs. Hopewell saw the two of them walk off together, toward the gate. Joy had walked all the way to the gate with him and Mrs. Hopewell could not imagine what they had said to each other, and she had not yet dared to ask.

Mrs. Freeman was insisting upon her attention. She had moved from the refrigerator to the heater so that Mrs. Hopewell had to turn and face her in order to seem to be listening. "Glynese gone out with Harvey Hill again last night," she said. "She had this sty."

"Hill," Mrs. Hopewell said absently, "is that the one who works in the garage?"

"Nome, he's the one that goes to chiropracter school,"

Mrs. Freeman said. "She had this sty. Been had it two days. So she says when he brought her in the other night he says, 'Lemme get rid of that sty for you,' and she says, 'How?' and he says, 'You just lay yourself down acrost the seat of that car and I'll show you.' So she done it and he popped her neck. Kept on a-popping it several times until she made him quit. This morning," Mrs. Freeman said, "she ain't got no sty. She ain't got no traces of a sty."

"I never heard of that before," Mrs. Hopewell said.

"He ast her to marry him before the Ordinary," Mrs. Freeman went on, "and she told him she wasn't going to be married in no *office*."

"Well, Glynese is a fine girl," Mrs. Hopewell said. "Glynese and Carramae are both fine girls."

"Carramae said when her and Lyman was married Lyman said it sure felt sacred to him. She said he said he wouldn't take five hundred dollars for being married by a preacher."

"How much would he take?" the girl asked from the stove.

"He said he wouldn't take five hundred dollars," Mrs. Freeman repeated.

"Well we all have work to do," Mrs. Hopewell said.

"Lyman said it just felt more sacred to him," Mrs. Freeman said. "The doctor wants Carramae to eat prunes. Says instead of medicine. Says them cramps is coming from pressure. You know where I think it is?"

"She'll be better in a few weeks," Mrs. Hopewell said.

"In the tube," Mrs. Freeman said. "Else she wouldn't be as sick as she is."

Hulga had cracked her two eggs into a saucer and was bringing them to the table along with a cup of coffee that she had filled too full. She sat down carefully and began to eat, meaning to keep Mrs. Freeman there by questions if for any reason she showed an inclination to leave. She could perceive her mother's eye on her. The first roundabout question would be about the Bible salesman and she did not wish to bring it on. "How did he pop her neck?" she asked.

Mrs. Freeman went into a description of how he had popped her neck. She said he owned a '55 Mercury but that Glynese said she would rather marry a man with only a '36 Plymouth who would be married by a preacher. The girl asked what if he had a '32 Plymouth and Mrs. Freeman said what Glynese had said was a '36 Plymouth.

Mrs. Hopewell said there were not many girls with Glynese's common sense. She said what she admired in those girls was their common sense. She said that reminded her that they had had a nice visitor yesterday, a young man selling Bibles. "Lord," she said, "he bored me to death but he was so sincere and genuine I couldn't be rude to him. He was just good country people, you know," she said, "–just the salt of the earth."

"I seen him walk up," Mrs. Freeman said, "and then later–I seen him walk off," and Hulga could feel the slight shift in her voice, the slight insinuation, that he had not walked off alone, had he? Her face remained expressionless but the color rose into her neck and she seemed to swallow it down with the next spoonful of egg. Mrs. Freeman was looking at her as if they had a secret together.

"Well, it takes all kinds of people to make the world go 'round," Mrs. Hopewell said. "It's very good we aren't all alike."

"Some people are more alike than others," Mrs. Freeman said.

Hulga got up and stumped, with about twice the noise that was necessary, into her room and locked the door. She was to meet the Bible salesman at ten o'clock at the gate. She had thought about it half the night. She had started thinking of it as a great joke and then she had begun to see profound implications in it. She had lain in bed imagining dialogues for them that were insane on the surface but that reached below to depths that no Bible salesman would be aware of. Their conversation yesterday had been of this kind.

He had stopped in front of her and had simply stood there. His face was bony and sweaty and bright, with a little pointed nose in the center of it, and his look was different from what it had been at the dinner table. He was gazing at her with open curiosity, with fascination, like a child watching a new fantastic animal at the zoo, and he was breathing as if he had run a great distance to reach her. His gaze seemed somehow familiar but she could not think where she had been regarded with it before. For almost a minute he didn't say anything. Then on what seemed an insuck of breath, he whispered, "You ever ate a chicken that was two days old?"

The girl looked at him stonily. He might have just put this question up for consideration at the meeting of a philosophical association. "Yes," she presently replied as if she had considered it from all angles.

"It must have been mighty small!" he said triumphantly and shook all over with little nervous giggles, getting very red in the face, and subsiding finally into his gaze of complete admiration, while the girl's expression remained exactly the same.

"How old are you?" he asked softly.

She waited some time before she answered. Then in a flat voice she said, "Seventeen."

His smiles came in succession like waves breaking on the surface of a little lake. "I see you got a wooden leg," he said. "I think you're real brave. I think you're real sweet."

The girl stood blank and solid and silent.

"Walk to the gate with me," he said. "You're a brave sweet little thing and I liked you the minute I seen you walk in the door."

Hulga began to move forward.

"What's your name?" he asked, smiling down on the top of her head.

"Hulga," she said.

"Hulga," he murmured, "Hulga. Hulga. I never heard of anybody name Hulga before. You're shy, aren't you, Hulga?" he asked.

She nodded, watching his large red hand on the handle of the giant valise.

"I like girls that wear glasses," he said. "I think a lot. I'm not like these people that a serious thought don't ever enter their heads. It's because I may die."

"I may die too," she said suddenly and looked up at him. His eyes were very small and brown, glittering feverishly.

"Listen," he said, "don't you think some people was meant to meet on account of what all they got in common and all? Like they both think serious thoughts and all?" He shifted the valise to his other hand so that the hand nearest her was free. He caught hold of her elbow and shook it a little. "I don't work on Saturday," he said. "I like to walk in the woods and see what Mother Nature is wearing. O'er the hills and far away. Pic-nics and things. Couldn't we go on a pic-nic tomorrow? Say yes, Hulga," he said and gave her a dying look as if he felt his insides about to drop out of him. He had even seemed to sway slightly toward her.

During the night she had imagined that she seduced him. She imagined that the two of them walked on the place until they came to the storage barn beyond the two back fields and there, she imagined, that things came to such a pass that she very easily seduced him and that then, of course, she had to reckon with his remorse. True genius can get an idea across even to an inferior mind. She imagined that she took his remorse in hand and changed it into a deeper understanding of life. She took all his shame away and turned it into something useful.

She set off for the gate at exactly ten o'clock, escaping without drawing Mrs. Hopewell's attention. She didn't take anything to eat, forgetting that food is usually taken on a picnic. She wore a pair of slacks and a dirty white shirt, and as an afterthought, she had put some Vapex on the collar of it since she did not own any perfume. When she reached the gate no one was there.

She looked up and down the empty highway and had the furious feeling that she had been tricked, that he had only meant to make her walk to the gate after the idea of him. Then suddenly he stood up, very tall, from behind a bush on the opposite embankment. Smiling, he lifted his hat which was new and wide-brimmed. He had not worn it yesterday and she wondered if he had bought it for the occasion. It was toast-colored with a red and white band around it and was slightly too large for him. He stepped from behind the bush still carrying the black valise. He had on the same suit and the same yellow socks sucked down in his shoes from walking. He crossed the highway and said, "I knew you'd come!"

The girl wondered acidly how he had known this. She pointed to the valise and asked, "Why did you bring your Bibles?"

He took her elbow, smiling down on her as if he could not stop. "You can never tell when you'll need the word of God, Hulga," he said. She had a moment in which she doubted that this was actually happening and then they began to climb the embankment. They went down into the pasture toward the woods. The boy walked lightly by her side, bouncing on his toes. The valise did not seem to be heavy today; he even swung it. They crossed half the pasture without saying anything and then, putting his hand easily on the small of her back, he asked softly, "Where does your wooden leg join on?"

She turned an ugly red and glared at him and for an instant the boy looked abashed. "I didn't mean you no harm," he said. "I only meant you're so brave and all. I guess God takes care of you."

"No," she said, looking forward and walking fast, "I don't even believe in God."

At this he stopped and whistled. "No!" he exclaimed as if he were too astonished to say anything else.

She walked on and in a second he was bouncing at her side, fanning with his hat. "That's very unusual for a girl," he remarked, watching her out of the corner of his eye. When they reached the edge of the wood, he put his hand on her back again and drew her against him without a word and kissed her heavily.

The kiss, which had more pressure than feeling behind it, produced that extra surge of adrenalin in the girl that enables one to carry a packed trunk out of a burning house, but in her, the power went at once to the brain. Even before he released her, her mind, clear and detached and ironic anyway, was regarding him from a great distance, with amusement but with pity. She had never been kissed before and she was pleased to discover that it was an unexceptional experience and all a matter of the mind's control. Some people might enjoy drain water if they were told it was vodka. When the boy, looking expectant but uncertain, pushed her gently away, she turned and walked on, saying nothing as if such business, for her, were common enough.

He came along panting at her side, trying to help her when he saw a root that she might trip over. He caught and held back the long swaying blades of thorn vine until she had passed beyond them. She led the way and he came breathing heavily behind her. Then they came out on a sunlit hillside, sloping softly into another one a little smaller. Beyond, they could see the rusted top of the old barn where the extra hay was stored.

The hill was sprinkled with small pink weeds. "Then you ain't saved?" he asked suddenly, stopping.

The girl smiled. It was the first time she had smiled at him at all. "In my economy," she said, "I'm saved and you are damned but I told you I didn't believe in God."

Nothing seemed to destroy the boy's look of admiration. He gazed at her now as if the fantastic animal at the zoo had put its paw through the bars and given him a loving poke. She thought he looked as if he wanted to kiss her again and she walked on before he had the chance.

"Ain't there somewheres we can sit down sometime?" he murmured, his voice softening toward the end of the sentence.

"In that barn," she said.

They made for it rapidly as if it might slide away like a train. It was a large two-story barn, cool and dark inside. The boy pointed up the ladder that led into the loft and said, "It's too bad we can't go up there."

"Why can't we?" she asked.

"Yer leg," he said reverently.

The girl gave him a contemptuous look and putting both hands on the ladder, she climbed it while he stood below, apparently awestruck. She pulled herself expertly through the opening and then looked down at him and said, "Well, come on if you're coming," and he began to climb the ladder, awkwardly bringing the suitcase with him.

"We won't need the Bible," she observed.

"You never can tell," he said, panting. After he had got into the loft, he was a few seconds catching his breath. She had sat down in a pile of straw. A wide sheath of sunlight, filled with dust particles, slanted over her. She lay back against a bale, her face turned away, looking out the front opening of the barn where hay was thrown from a wagon into the loft. The two pink-speckled hillsides lay back against a dark ridge of woods. The sky was cloudless and cold blue. The boy dropped down by her side and put one arm under her and the other over her and began methodically kissing her face, making little noises like a fish. He did not remove his hat but it was pushed far enough back not to interfere. When her glasses got in his way, he took them off of her and slipped them into his pocket.

The girl at first did not return any of the kisses but

presently she began to and after she had put several on his cheek, she reached his lips and remained there, kissing him again and again as if she were trying to draw all the breath out of him. His breath was clear and sweet like a child's and the kisses were sticky like a child's. He mumbled about loving her and about knowing when he first seen her that he loved her, but the mumbling was like the sleepy fretting of a child being put to sleep by his mother. Her mind, throughout this, never stopped or lost itself for a second to her feelings. "You ain't said you loved me none," he whispered finally, pulling back from her. "You got to say that."

She looked away from him off into the hollow sky and then down at a black ridge and then down farther into what appeared to be two green swelling lakes. She didn't realize he had taken her glasses but this landscape could not seem exceptional to her for she seldom paid any close attention to her surroundings.

"You got to say it," he repeated. "You got to say you love me."

She was always careful how she committed herself. "In a sense," she began, "if you use the word loosely, you might say that. But it's not a word I use. I don't have illusions. I'm one of those people who see *through* to nothing."

The boy was frowning. "You got to say it. I said it and you got to say it," he said.

The girl looked at him almost tenderly. "You poor baby," she murmured. "It's just as well you don't understand," and she pulled him by the neck, face-down, against her. "We are all damned," she said, "but some of us have taken off our blindfolds and see that there's nothing to see. It's a kind of salvation."

The boy's astonished eyes looked blankly through the ends of her hair. "Okay," he almost whined, "but do you love me or don'tcher?"

"Yes," she said and added, "in a sense. But I must tell

you something. There mustn't be anything dishonest between us." She lifted his head and looked him in the eye. "I am thirty years old," she said. "I have a number of degrees."

The boy's look was irritated but dogged. "I don't care," he said. "I don't care a thing about what all you done. I just want to know if you love me or don'tcher?" and he caught her to him and wildly planted her face with kisses until she said, "Yes, yes."

"Okay then," he said, letting her go. "Prove it."

She smiled, looking dreamily out on the shifty landscape. She had seduced him without even making up her mind to try. "How?" she asked, feeling that he should be delayed a little.

He leaned over and put his lips to her ear. "Show me where your wooden leg joins on," he whispered.

The girl uttered a sharp little cry and her face instantly drained of color. The obscenity of the suggestion was not what shocked her. As a child she had sometimes been subject to feelings of shame but education had removed the last traces of that as a good surgeon scrapes for cancer; she would no more have felt it over what he was asking than she would have believed in his Bible. But she was as sensitive about the artificial leg as a peacock about his tail. No one ever touched it but her. She took care of it as someone else would his soul, in private and almost with her own eyes turned away. "No," she said.

"I known it," he muttered, sitting up. "You're just playing me for a sucker."

"Oh no no!" she cried. "It joins on at the knee. Only at the knee. Why do you want to see it?"

The boy gave her a long penetrating look. "Because," he said, "it's what makes you different. You ain't like anybody else."

She sat staring at him. There was nothing about her face or her round freezing-blue eyes to indicate that this had moved her; but she felt as if her heart had stopped and left her mind to pump her blood. She decided that for the first time in her life she was face to face with real innocence. This boy, with an instinct that came from beyond wisdom, had touched the truth about her. When after a minute, she said in a hoarse high voice, "All right," it was like surrendering to him completely. It was like losing her own life and finding it again, miraculously, in his.

Very gently he began to roll the slack leg up. The artificial limb, in a white sock and brown flat shoe, was bound in a heavy material like canvas and ended in an ugly jointure where it was attached to the stump. The boy's face and his voice were entirely reverent as he uncovered it and said, "Now show me how to take it off and on."

She took it off for him and put it back on again and then he took it off himself, handling it as tenderly as if it were a real one. "See!" he said with a delighted child's face. "Now I can do it myself!"

"Put it back on," she said. She was thinking that she would run away with him and that every night he would take the leg off and every morning put it back on again. "Put it back on," she said.

"Not yet," he murmured, setting it on its foot out of her reach. "Leave it off for a while. You got me instead."

She gave a little cry of alarm but he pushed her down and began to kiss her again. Without the leg she felt entirely dependent on him. Her brain seemed to have stopped thinking altogether and to be about some other function that it was not very good at. Different expressions raced back and forth over her face. Every now and then the boy, his eyes like two steel spikes, would glance behind him where the leg stood. Finally she pushed him off and said, "Put it back on me now."

"Wait," he said. He leaned the other way and pulled the valise toward him and opened it. It had a pale blue spotted lining and there were only two Bibles in it. He took one of these out and opened the cover of it. It was hollow and contained a pocket flask of whiskey, a pack of cards, and a small blue box with printing on it. He laid these out in front of her one at a time in an evenly-spaced row, like one presenting offerings at the shrine of a goddess. He put the blue box in her hand. THIS PRODUCT TO BE USED ONLY FOR THE PREVENTION OF DISEASE, she read, and dropped it. The boy was unscrewing the top of the flask. He stopped and pointed, with a smile, to the deck of cards. It was not an ordinary deck but one with an obscene picture on the back of each card. "Take a swig," he said, offering her the bottle first. He held it in front of her, but like one mesmerized, she did not move.

Her voice when she spoke had an almost pleading sound. "Aren't you," she murmured, "aren't you just good country people?"

The boy cocked his head. He looked as if he were just beginning to understand that she might be trying to insult him. "Yeah," he said, curling his lip slightly, "but it ain't held me back none. I'm as good as you any day in the week."

"Give me my leg," she said.

He pushed it farther away with his foot. "Come on now, let's begin to have us a good time," he said coaxingly. "We ain't got to know one another good yet."

"Give me my leg!" she screamed and tried to lunge for it but he pushed her down easily.

"What's the matter with you all of a sudden?" he asked, frowning as he screwed the top on the flask and put it quickly back inside the Bible. "You just a while ago said you didn't believe in nothing. I thought you was some girl!"

Her face was almost purple. "You're a Christian!" she hissed. "You're a fine Christian! You're just like them all —say one thing and do another. You're a perfect Christian, you're . . ."

The boy's mouth was set angrily. "I hope you don't

think," he said in a lofty indignant tone, "that I believe in that crap! I may sell Bibles but I know which end is up and I wasn't born yesterday and I know where I'm going!"

"Give me my leg!" she screeched. He jumped up so quickly that she barely saw him sweep the cards and the blue box back into the Bible and throw the Bible into the valise. She saw him grab the leg and then she saw it for an instant slanted forlornly across the inside of the suitcase with a Bible at either side of its opposite ends. He slammed the lid shut and snatched up the valise and swung it down the hole and then stepped through himself.

When all of him had passed but his head, he turned and regarded her with a look that no longer had any admiration in it. "I've gotten a lot of interesting things," he said. "One time I got a woman's glass eye this way. And you needn't to think you'll catch me because Pointer ain't really my name. I use a different name at every house I call at and don't stay nowhere long. And I'll tell you another thing, Hulga," he said, using the name as if he didn't think much of it, "you ain't so smart. I been believing in nothing ever since I was born!" and then the toast-colored hat disappeared down the hole and the girl was left, sitting on the straw in the dusty sunlight. When she turned her churning face toward the opening, she saw his blue figure struggling successfully over the green speckled lake.

Mrs. Hopewell and Mrs. Freeman, who were in the back pasture, digging up onions, saw him emerge a little later from the woods and head across the meadow toward the highway. "Why, that looks like that nice dull young man that tried to sell me a Bible yesterday," Mrs. Hopewell said, squinting. "He must have been selling them to the Negroes back in there. He was so simple," she said, "but I guess the world would be better off if we were all that simple."

Mrs. Freeman's gaze drove forward and just touched him before he disappeared under the hill. Then she returned her attention to the evil-smelling onion shoot she was lifting from the ground. "Some can't be that simple," she said. "I know I never could."

THE DISPLACED PERSON

The peacock was following Mrs. Shortley up the road to the hill where she meant to stand. Moving one behind the other, they looked like a complete procession. Her arms were folded and as she mounted the prominence, she might have been the giant wife of the countryside, come out at some sign of danger to see what the trouble was. She stood on two tremendous legs, with the grand self-confidence of a mountain, and rose, up narrowing bulges of granite, to two icy blue points of light that pierced forward, surveying everything. She ignored the white afternoon sun which was creeping behind a ragged wall of cloud as if it pretended to be an intruder and cast her gaze down the red clay road that turned off from the highway.

The peacock stopped just behind her, his tail—glittering green-gold and blue in the sunlight—lifted just enough so that it would not touch the ground. It flowed out on either side like a floating train and his head on the long blue reed-like neck was drawn back as if his attention were fixed in the distance on something no one else could see.

Mrs. Shortley was watching a black car turn through the gate from the highway. Over by the toolshed, about fifteen feet away, the two Negroes, Astor and Sulk, had stopped work to watch. They were hidden by a mulberry tree but Mrs. Shortley knew they were there.

Mrs. McIntyre was coming down the steps of her house to meet the car. She had on her largest smile but Mrs. Shortley, even from her distance, could detect a nervous slide in it. These people who were coming were only hired help, like the Shortleys themselves or the Negroes. Yet here was the owner of the place out to welcome them. Here she was, wearing her best clothes and a string of beads, and now bounding forward with her mouth stretched.

The car stopped at the walk just as she did and the priest was the first to get out. He was a long-legged black-suited old man with a white hat on and a collar that he wore backwards, which, Mrs. Shortley knew, was what priests did who wanted to be known as priests. It was this priest who had arranged for these people to come here. He opened the back door of the car and out jumped two children, a boy and a girl, and then, stepping more slowly, a woman in brown, shaped like a peanut. Then the front door opened and out stepped the man, the Displaced Person. He was short and a little sway-backed and wore gold-rimmed spectacles.

Mrs. Shortley's vision narrowed on him and then widened to include the woman and the two children in a group picture. The first thing that struck her as very peculiar was that they looked like other people. Every time she had seen them in her imagination, the image she had got was of the three bears, walking single file, with wooden shoes on like Dutchmen and sailor hats and bright coats with a lot of buttons. But the woman had on a dress she might have worn herself and the children were dressed like anybody from around. The man had on khaki pants and a blue shirt. Suddenly, as Mrs. McIntyre held out her hand to him, he bobbed down from the waist and kissed it.

Mrs. Shortley jerked her own hand up toward her mouth and then after a second brought it down and rubbed it vigorously on her seat. If Mr. Shortley had tried to kiss her hand, Mrs. McIntyre would have knocked him into the middle of next week, but then Mr. Shortley wouldn't have kissed her hand anyway. He didn't have time to mess around.

She looked closer, squinting. The boy was in the center of the group, talking. He was supposed to speak the most English because he had learned some in Poland and so he was to listen to his father's Polish and say it in English and then listen to Mrs. McIntyre's English and say that in Polish. The priest had told Mrs. McIntyre his name was Rudolph and he was twelve and the girl's name was Sledgewig and she was nine. Sledgewig sounded to Mrs. Shortley like something you would name a bug, or vice versa, as if you named a boy Bollweevil. All of them's last name was something that only they themselves and the priest could pronounce. All she could make out of it was Gobblehook. She and Mrs. McIntyre had been calling them the Gobblehooks all week while they got ready for them.

There had been a great deal to do to get ready for them because they didn't have anything of their own, not a stick of furniture or a sheet or a dish, and everything had had to be scraped together out of things that Mrs. McIntyre couldn't use any more herself. They had collected a piece of odd furniture here and a piece there and they had taken some flowered chicken feed sacks and made curtains for the windows, two red and one green, because they had not had enough of the red sacks to go around. Mrs. McIntyre said she was not made of money and she could not afford to buy curtains. "They can't talk," Mrs. Shortley said. "You reckon they'll know what colors even is?" and Mrs. McIntyre had said that after what those people had been through, they should be grateful for anything they could get. She said to think how lucky they were to escape from over there and come to a place like this.

Mrs. Shortley recalled a newsreel she had seen once of a small room piled high with bodies of dead naked people all in a heap, their arms and legs tangled together, a head thrust in here, a head there, a foot, a knee, a part that should have been covered up sticking out, a hand raised clutching nothing. Before you could realize that it was real and take it into your head, the picture changed and a hollow-sounding voice was saying, "Time marches on!" This was the kind of thing that was happening every day in Europe where they had not advanced as in this country, and watching from her vantage point, Mrs. Shortley had the sudden intuition that the Gobblehooks, like rats with typhoid fleas, could have carried all those murderous ways over the water with them directly to this place. If they had come from where that kind of thing was done to them, who was to say they were not the kind that would also do it to others? The width and breadth of this question nearly shook her. Her stomach trembled as if there had been a slight quake in the heart of the mountain and automatically she moved down from her elevation and went forward to be introduced to them, as if she meant to find out at once what they were capable of.

She approached, stomach foremost, head back, arms folded, boots flopping gently against her large legs. About fifteen feet from the gesticulating group, she stopped and made her presence felt by training her gaze on the back of Mrs. McIntyre's neck. Mrs. McIntyre was a small woman of sixty with a round wrinkled face and red bangs that came almost down to two high orange-colored penciled eyebrows. She had a little doll's mouth and eyes that were a soft blue when she opened them wide but more like steel or granite when she narrowed them to inspect a milk can. She had buried one husband and divorced two and Mrs. Shortley respected her as a person nobody had put anything over on yet—except, ha, ha, perhaps the Shortleys. She held out her arm in Mrs. Shortley's direction and said to the Rudolph boy, "And this is Mrs. Shortley. Mr. Shortley is my dairyman. Where's Mr. Shortley?" she asked as his wife began to approach again, her arms still folded. "I want him to meet the Guizacs."

Now it was Guizac. She wasn't calling them Gobblehook to their face. "Chancey's at the barn," Mrs. Shortley said. "He don't have time to rest himself in the bushes like them niggers over there."

Her look first grazed the tops of the displaced people's heads and then revolved downwards slowly, the way a buzzard glides and drops in the air until it alights on the carcass. She stood far enough away so that the man would not be able to kiss her hand. He looked directly at her with little green eyes and gave her a broad grin that was toothless on one side. Mrs. Shortley, without smiling, turned her attention to the little girl who stood by the mother, swinging her shoulders from side to side. She had long braided hair in two looped pigtails and there was no denying she was a pretty child even if she did have a bug's name. She was better looking than either Annie Maude or Sarah Mae, Mrs. Shortley's two girls going on fifteen and seventeen but Annie Maude had never got her growth and Sarah Mae had a cast in her eye. She compared the foreign boy to her son, H. C., and H. C. came out far ahead. H. C. was twenty years old with her build and eye-glasses. He was going to Bible school now and when he finished he was going to start him a church. He had a strong sweet voice for hymns and could sell anything. Mrs. Shortley looked at the priest and was reminded that these people did not have an advanced religion. There was no telling what all they believed since none of the foolishness had been reformed out of it. Again she saw the room piled high with bodies.

The priest spoke in a foreign way himself, English but as if he had a throatful of hay. He had a big nose and a bald rectangular face and head. While she was observing him, his large mouth dropped open and with a stare behind her, he said, "Arrrrrr!" and pointed.

Mrs. Shortley spun around. The peacock was standing a few feet behind her, with his head slightly cocked.

"What a beauti-ful birdrrrd!" the priest murmured.

"Another mouth to feed," Mrs. McIntyre said, glancing in the peafowl's direction.

"And when does he raise his splendid tail?" asked the priest.

"Just when it suits him," she said. "There used to be twenty or thirty of those things on the place but I've let them die off. I don't like to hear them scream in the middle of the night."

"So beauti-ful," the priest said. "A tail full of suns," and he crept forward on tiptoe and looked down on the bird's back where the polished gold and green design began. The peacock stood still as if he had just come down from some sun-drenched height to be a vision for them all. The priest's homely red face hung over him, glowing with pleasure.

Mrs. Shortley's mouth had drawn acidly to one side. "Nothing but a peachicken," she muttered.

Mrs. McIntyre raised her orange eyebrows and exchanged a look with her to indicate that the old man was in his second childhood. "Well, we must show the Guizacs their new home," she said impatiently and she herded them into the car again. The peacock stepped off toward the mulberry tree where the two Negroes were hiding and the priest turned his absorbed face away and got in the car and drove the displaced people down to the shack they were to occupy.

Mrs. Shortley waited until the car was out of sight and then she made her way circuitously to the mulberry tree and stood about ten feet behind the two Negroes, one an old man holding a bucket half full of calf feed and the other a yellowish boy with a short woodchuck-like head pushed into a rounded felt hat. "Well," she said slowly, "yawl have looked long enough. What you think about them?"

The old man, Astor, raised himself. "We been watching," he said as if this would be news to her. "Who they now?"

"They come from over the water," Mrs. Shortley said with a wave of her arm. "They're what is called Displaced Persons."

"Displaced Persons," he said. "Well now. I declare. What do that mean?"

"It means they ain't where they were born at and there's

nowhere for them to go—like if you was run out of here and wouldn't nobody have you."

"It seem like they here, though," the old man said in a reflective voice. "If they here, they somewhere."

"Sho is," the other agreed. "They here."

The illogic of Negro-thinking always irked Mrs. Shortley. "They ain't where they belong to be at," she said. "They belong to be back over yonder where everything is still like they been used to. Over here it's more advanced than where they come from. But yawl better look out now," she said and nodded her head. "There's about ten million billion more just like them and I know what Mrs. McIntyre said."

"Say what?" the young one asked.

"Places are not easy to get nowadays, for white or black, but I reckon I heard what she stated to me," she said in a sing-song voice.

"You liable to hear most anything," the old man remarked, leaning forward as if he were about to walk off but holding himself suspended.

"I heard her say, 'This is going to put the Fear of the Lord into those shiftless niggers!'" Mrs. Shortley said in a ringing voice.

The old man started off. "She say something like that every now and then," he said. "Ha. Ha. Yes indeed."

"You better get on in that barn and help Mr. Shortley," she said to the other one. "What you reckon she pays you for?"

"He the one sont me out," the Negro muttered. "He the one gimme something else to do."

"Well you better get to doing it then," she said and stood there until he moved off. Then she stood a while longer, reflecting, her unseeing eyes directly in front of the peacock's tail. He had jumped into the tree and his tail hung in front of her, full of fierce planets with eyes that were each ringed in green and set against a sun that was gold in one second's light and salmon-colored in the next. She might have been looking at a map of the universe but she didn't notice it any more than she did the spots of sky that cracked the dull green of the tree. She was having an inner vision instead. She was seeing the ten million billion of them pushing their way into new places over here and herself, a giant angel with wings as wide as a house, telling the Negroes that they would have to find another place. She turned herself in the direction of the barn, musing on this, her expression lofty and satisfied.

She approached the barn from an oblique angle that allowed her a look in the door before she could be seen herself. Mr. Chancey Shortley was adjusting the last milking machine on a large black and white spotted cow near the entrance, squatting at her heels. There was about a half-inch of cigarette adhering to the center of his lower lip. Mrs. Shortley observed it minutely for half a second. "If she seen or heard of you smoking in this barn, she would blow a fuse," she said.

Mr. Shortley raised a sharply rutted face containing a washout under each cheek and two long crevices eaten down both sides of his blistered mouth. "You gonter be the one to tell her?" he asked.

"She's got a nose of her own," Mrs. Shortley said.

Mr. Shortley, without appearing to give the feat any consideration, lifted the cigarette stub with the sharp end of his tongue, drew it into his mouth, closed his lips tightly, rose, stepped out, gave his wife a good round appreciative stare, and spit the smoldering butt into the grass.

"Aw Chancey," she said, "haw haw," and she dug a little hole for it with her toe and covered it up. This trick of Mr. Shortley's was actually his way of making love to her. When he had done his courting, he had not brought a guitar to strum or anything pretty for her to keep, but had sat on her porch steps, not saying a word, imitating a paralyzed man propped up to enjoy a cigarette. When the cigarette got the proper size, he would turn his eyes to her and open his mouth and draw in the butt and then sit there as if he had swallowed it, looking at her with the most loving look anybody could imagine. It nearly drove her wild and every time he did it, she wanted to pull his hat down over his eyes and hug him to death.

"Well," she said, going into the barn after him, "the Gobblehooks have come and she wants you to meet them, says, 'Where's Mr. Shortley?' and I says, 'He don't have time . . .'"

"Tote up them weights," Mr. Shortley said, squatting to the cow again.

"You reckon he can drive a tractor when he don't know English?" she asked. "I don't think she's going to get her money's worth out of them. That boy can talk but he looks delicate. The one can work can't talk and the one can talk can't work. She ain't any better off than if she had more niggers."

"I rather have a nigger if it was me," Mr. Shortley said.

"She says it's ten million more like them, Displaced Persons, she says that there priest can get her all she wants."

"She better quit messin with that there priest," Mr. Shortley said.

"He don't look smart," Mrs. Shortley said, "–kind of foolish."

"I ain't going to have the Pope of Rome tell me how to run no dairy," Mr. Shortley said.

"They ain't Eye-talians, they're Poles," she said. "From Poland where all them bodies were stacked up at. You remember all them bodies?"

"I give them three weeks here," Mr. Shortley said.

Three weeks later Mrs. McIntyre and Mrs. Shortley drove to the cane bottom to see Mr. Guizac start to operate the silage cutter, a new machine that Mrs. McIntyre had just bought because she said, for the first time, she had somebody who could operate it. Mr. Guizac could drive a tractor, use the rotary hay-baler, the silage cutter, the combine, the letz mill, or any other machine she had on the place. He was an expert mechanic, a carpenter, and a mason. He was thrifty and energetic. Mrs. McIntyre said she figured he would save her twenty dollars a month on repair bills alone. She said getting him was the best day's work she had ever done in her life. He could work milking machines and he was scrupulously clean. He did not smoke.

She parked her car on the edge of the cane field and they got out. Sulk, the young Negro, was attaching the wagon to the cutter and Mr. Guizac was attaching the cutter to the tractor. He finished first and pushed the colored boy out of the way and attached the wagon to the cutter himself, gesticulating with a bright angry face when he wanted the hammer or the screwdriver. Nothing was done quick enough to suit him. The Negroes made him nervous.

The week before, he had come upon Sulk at the dinner hour, sneaking with a croker sack into the pen where the young turkeys were. He had watched him take a frying-size turkey from the lot and thrust it in the sack and put the sack under his coat. Then he had followed him around the barn, jumped on him, dragged him to Mrs. McIntyre's back door and had acted out the entire scene for her, while the Negro muttered and grumbled and said God might strike him dead if he had been stealing any turkey, he had only been taking it to put some black shoe polish on its head because it had the sorehead. God might strike him dead if that was not the truth before Jesus. Mrs. McIntyre told him to go put the turkey back and then she was a long time explaining to the Pole that all Negroes would steal. She finally had to call Rudolph and tell him in English and have him tell his father in Polish, and Mr. Guizac had gone off with a startled disappointed face.

Mrs. Shortley stood by hoping there would be trouble

with the silage machine but there was none. All of Mr. Guizac's motions were quick and accurate. He jumped on the tractor like a monkey and maneuvered the big orange cutter into the cane; in a second the silage was spurting in a green jet out of the pipe into the wagon. He went jolting down the row until he disappeared from sight and the noise became remote.

Mrs. McIntyre sighed with pleasure. "At last," she said, "I've got somebody I can depend on. For years I've been fooling with sorry people. Sorry people. Poor white trash and niggers," she muttered. "They've drained me dry. Before you all came I had Ringfields and Collins and Jarrells and Perkins and Pinkins and Herrins and God knows what all else and not a one of them left without taking something off this place that didn't belong to them. Not a one!"

Mrs. Shortley could listen to this with composure because she knew that if Mrs. McIntyre had considered her trash, they couldn't have talked about trashy people together. Neither of them approved of trash. Mrs. McIntyre continued with the monologue that Mrs. Shortley had heard oftentimes before. "I've been running this place for thirty years," she said, looking with a deep frown out over the field, "and always just barely making it. People think you're made of money. I have the taxes to pay. I have the insurance to keep up. I have the repair bills. I have the feed bills." It all gathered up and she stood with her chest lifted and her small hands gripped around her elbows. "Ever since the Judge died," she said, "I've barely been making ends meet and they all take something when they leave. The niggers don't leave—they stay and steal. A nigger thinks anybody is rich he can steal from and that white trash thinks anybody is rich who can afford to hire people as sorry as they are. And all I've got is the dirt under my feet!"

You hire and fire, Mrs. Shortley thought, but she didn't always say what she thought. She stood by and let Mrs.

McIntyre say it all out to the end but this time it didn't end as usual. "But at last I'm saved!" Mrs. McIntyre said. "One fellow's misery is the other fellow's gain. That man there," and she pointed where the Displaced Person had disappeared, "—he has to work! He wants to work!" She turned to Mrs. Shortley with her bright wrinkled face. "That man is my salvation!" she said.

Mrs. Shortley looked straight ahead as if her vision penetrated the cane and the hill and pierced through to the other side. "I would suspicion salvation got from the devil," she said in a slow detached way.

"Now what do you mean by that?" Mrs. McIntyre asked, looking at her sharply.

Mrs. Shortley wagged her head but would not say anything else. The fact was she had nothing else to say for this intuition had only at that instant come to her. She had never given much thought to the devil for she felt that religion was essentially for those people who didn't have the brains to avoid evil without it. For people like herself, for people of gumption, it was a social occasion providing the opportunity to sing; but if she had ever given it much thought, she would have considered the devil the head of it and God the hanger-on. With the coming of these displaced people, she was obliged to give new thought to a good many things.

"I know what Sledgewig told Annie Maude," she said, and when Mrs. McIntyre carefully did not ask her what but reached down and broke off a sprig of sassafras to chew, she continued in a way to indicate she was not telling all, "that they wouldn't be able to live long, the four of them, on seventy dollars a month."

"He's worth raising," Mrs. McIntyre said. "He saves me money."

This was as much as to say that Chancey had never saved her money. Chancey got up at four in the morning to milk her cows, in winter wind and summer heat, and he had been doing it for the last two years. They had been with her the longest she had ever had anybody. The gratitude they got was these hints that she hadn't been saved any money.

"Is Mr. Shortley feeling better today?" Mrs. McIntyre asked.

Mrs. Shortley thought it was about time she was asking that question. Mr. Shortley had been in bed two days with an attack. Mr. Guizac had taken his place in the dairy in addition to doing his own work. "No he ain't," she said. "That doctor said he was suffering from over-exhaustion."

"If Mr. Shortley is over-exhausted," Mrs. McIntyre said, "then he must have a second job on the side," and she looked at Mrs. Shortley with almost closed eyes as if she were examining the bottom of a milk can.

Mrs. Shortley did not say a word but her dark suspicion grew like a black thunder cloud. The fact was that Mr. Shortley did have a second job on the side and that, in a free country, this was none of Mrs. McIntyre's business. Mr. Shortley made whisky. He had a small still back in the farthest reaches of the place, on Mrs. McIntyre's land to be sure, but on land that she only owned and did not cultivate, on idle land that was not doing anybody any good. Mr. Shortley was not afraid of work. He got up at four in the morning and milked her cows and in the middle of the day when he was supposed to be resting, he was off attending to his still. Not every man would work like that. The Negroes knew about his still but he knew about theirs so there had never been any disagreeableness between them. But with foreigners on the place, with people who were all eyes and no understanding, who had come from a place continually fighting, where the religion had not been reformed—with this kind of people, you had to be on the lookout every minute. She thought there ought to be a law against them. There was no reason they couldn't stay over there and take the places of some of the people who had been killed in their wars and butcherings.

"What's furthermore," she said suddenly, "Sledgewig said as soon as her papa saved the money, he was going to buy him a used car. Once they get them a used car, they'll leave you."

"I can't pay him enough for him to save money," Mrs. McIntyre said. "I'm not worrying about that. Of course," she said then, "if Mr. Shortley got incapacitated, I would have to use Mr. Guizac in the dairy all the time and I would have to pay him more. He doesn't smoke," she said, and it was the fifth time within the week that she had pointed this out.

"It is no man," Mrs. Shortley said emphatically, "that works as hard as Chancey, or is as easy with a cow, or is more of a Christian," and she folded her arms and her gaze pierced the distance. The noise of the tractor and cutter increased and Mr. Guizac appeared coming around the other side of the cane row. "Which can not be said about everybody," she muttered. She wondered whether, if the Pole found Chancey's still, he would know what it was. The trouble with these people was, you couldn't tell what they knew. Every time Mr. Guizac smiled, Europe stretched out in Mrs. Shortley's imagination, mysterious and evil, the devil's experiment station.

The tractor, the cutter, the wagon passed, rattling and rumbling and grinding before them. "Think how long that would have taken with men and mules to do it," Mrs. McIntyre shouted. "We'll get this whole bottom cut within two days at this rate."

"Maybe," Mrs. Shortley muttered, "if don't no terrible accident occur." She thought how the tractor had made mules worthless. Nowadays you couldn't give away a mule. The next thing to go, she reminded herself, will be niggers.

In the afternoon she explained what was going to happen to them to Astor and Sulk who were in the cow lot, filling the manure spreader. She sat down next to the block of salt under a small shed, her stomach in her lap, her arms on top of it. "All you colored people better look out," she said. "You know how much you can get for a mule."

"Nothing, no indeed," the old man said, "not one thing."

"Before it was a tractor," she said, "it could be a mule. And before it was a Displaced Person, it could be a nigger. The time is going to come," she prophesied, "when it won't be no more occasion to speak of a nigger."

The old man laughed politely. "Yes indeed," he said. "Ha ha."

The young one didn't say anything. He only looked sullen but when she had gone in the house, he said, "Big Belly act like she know everything."

"Never mind," the old man said, "your place too low for anybody to dispute with you for it."

She didn't tell her fears about the still to Mr. Shortley until he was back on the job in the dairy. Then one night after they were in bed, she said, "That man prowls."

Mr. Shortley folded his hands on his bony chest and pretended he was a corpse.

"Prowls," she continued and gave him a sharp kick in the side with her knee. "Who's to say what they know and don't know? Who's to say if he found it he wouldn't go right to her and tell? How you know they don't make liquor in Europe? They drive tractors. They got them all kinds of machinery. Answer me."

"Don't worry me now," Mr. Shortley said. "I'm a dead man."

"It's them little eyes of his that's foreign," she muttered. "And that way he's got of shrugging." She drew her shoulders up and shrugged several times. "Howcome he's got anything to shrug about?" she asked.

"If everybody was as dead as I am, nobody would have no trouble," Mr. Shortley said.

"That priest," she muttered and was silent for a minute. Then she said, "In Europe they probably got some different way to make liquor but I reckon they know all the ways. They're full of crooked ways. They never have advanced or reformed. They got the same religion as a thousand years ago. It could only be the devil responsible for that. Always fighting amongst each other. Disputing. And then get us into it. Ain't they got us into it twict already and we ain't got no more sense than to go over there and settle it for them and then they come on back over here and snoop around and find your still and go straight to her. And liable to kiss her hand any minute. Do you hear me?"

"No," Mr. Shortley said.

"And I'll tell you another thing," she said. "I wouldn't be a tall surprised if he don't know everything you say, whether it be in English or not."

"I don't speak no other language," Mr. Shortley murmured.

"I suspect," she said, "that before long there won't be no more niggers on this place. And I tell you what. I'd rather have niggers than them Poles. And what's furthermore, I aim to take up for the niggers when the time comes. When Gobblehook first come here, you recollect how he shook their hands, like he didn't know the difference, like he might have been as black as them, but when it come to finding out Sulk was taking turkeys, he gone on and told her. I known he was taking turkeys. I could have told her myself."

Mr. Shortley was breathing softly as if he were asleep.

"A nigger don't know when he has a friend," she said. "And I'll tell you another thing. I get a heap out of Sledgewig. Sledgewig said that in Poland they lived in a brick house and one night a man come and told them to get out of it before daylight. Do you believe they ever lived in a brick house?

"Airs," she said. "That's just airs. A wooden house is good enough for me. Chancey," she said, "turn thisaway. I hate to see niggers mistreated and run out. I have a heap of pity for niggers and poor folks. Ain't I always had?" she asked. "I say ain't I always been a friend to niggers and poor folks?

"When the time comes," she said, "I'll stand up for the niggers and that's that. I ain't going to see that priest drive out all the niggers."

Mrs. McIntyre bought a new drag harrow and a tractor with a power lift because she said, for the first time, she had someone who could handle machinery. She and Mrs. Shortley had driven to the back field to inspect what he had harrowed the day before. "That's been done beautifully!" Mrs. McIntyre said, looking out over the red undulating ground.

Mrs. McIntyre had changed since the Displaced Person had been working for her and Mrs. Shortley had observed the change very closely: she had begun to act like somebody who was getting rich secretly and she didn't confide in Mrs. Shortley the way she used to. Mrs. Shortley suspected that the priest was at the bottom of the change. They were very slick. First he would get her into his Church and then he would get his hand in her pocketbook. Well, Mrs. Shortley thought, the more fool she! Mrs. Shortley had a secret herself. She knew something the Displaced Person was doing that would floor Mrs. McIntyre. "I still say he ain't going to work forever for seventy dollars a month," she murmured. She intended to keep her secret to herself and Mr. Shortley.

"Well," Mrs. McIntyre said, "I may have to get rid of some of this other help so I can pay him more."

Mrs. Shortley nodded to indicate she had known this for some time. "I'm not saying those niggers ain't had it coming," she said. "But they do the best they know how. You can always tell a nigger what to do and stand by until he does it."

"That's what the Judge said," Mrs. McIntyre said and looked at her with approval. The Judge was her first husband, the one who had left her the place. Mrs. Shortley had heard that she had married him when she was thirty and he was seventy-five, thinking she would be rich as soon as he died, but the old man was a scoundrel and when his estate was settled, they found he didn't have a nickel. All he left her were the fifty acres and the house. But she always spoke of him in a reverent way and quoted his sayings, such as, "One fellow's misery is the other fellow's gain," and "The devil you know is better than the devil you don't."

"However," Mrs. Shortley remarked, "the devil you know is better than the devil you don't," and she had to turn away so that Mrs. McIntyre would not see her smile. She had found out what the Displaced Person was up to through the old man, Astor, and she had not told anybody but Mr. Shortley. Mr. Shortley had risen straight up in bed like Lazarus from the tomb.

"Shut your mouth!" he had said.

"Yes," she had said.

"Naw!" Mr. Shortley had said.

"Yes," she had said.

Mr. Shortley had fallen back flat.

"The Pole don't know any better," Mrs. Shortley had said. "I reckon that priest is putting him up to it is all. I blame the priest."

The priest came frequently to see the Guizacs and he would always stop in and visit Mrs. McIntyre too and they would walk around the place and she would point out her improvements and listen to his rattling talk. It suddenly came to Mrs. Shortley that he was trying to persuade her to bring another Polish family onto the place. With two of them here, there would be almost nothing spoken but Polish! The Negroes would be gone and there would be the two families against Mr. Shortley and herself! She began to imagine a war of words, to see the Polish words and the English words coming at each other, stalking forward, not sentences, just words, gabble gabble gabble, flung out high and shrill and stalking forward and then grappling with each other. She saw the Polish words, dirty and all-knowing and unreformed, flinging mud on the clean English words until everything was equally dirty. She saw them all piled up in a room, all the dead dirty words, theirs and hers too, piled up like the naked bodies in the newsreel. God save me! she cried silently, from the stinking power of Satan! And she started from that day to read her Bible with a new attention. She pored over the Apocalypse and began to quote from the Prophets and before long she had come to a deeper understanding of her existence. She saw plainly that the meaning of the world was a mystery that had been planned and she was not surprised to suspect that she had a special part in the plan because she was strong. She saw that the Lord God Almighty had created the strong people to do what had to be done and she felt that she would be ready when she was called. Right now she felt that her business was to watch the priest.

His visits irked her more and more. On the last one, he went about picking up feathers off the ground. He found two peacock feathers and four or five turkey feathers and an old brown hen feather and took them off with him like a bouquet. This foolish-acting did not deceive Mrs. Shortley any. Here he was: leading foreigners over in hoards to places that were not theirs, to cause disputes, to uproot niggers, to plant the Whore of Babylon in the midst of the righteous! Whenever he came on the place, she hid herself behind something and watched until he left.

It was on a Sunday afternoon that she had her vision. She had gone to drive in the cows for Mr. Shortley who had a pain in his knee and she was walking slowly through the pasture, her arms folded, her eyes on the distant low-lying clouds that looked like rows and rows of white fish washed up on a great blue beach. She paused after an incline to heave a sigh of exhaustion for she had an immense weight to carry around and she was not as young as she used to be. At times she could feel her heart, like a child's fist, clenching and unclenching inside her chest, and when the feeling came, it stopped her thought altogether and she would go about like a large hull of herself, moving for no reason; but she gained this incline without a tremor and stood at the top of it, pleased with herself. Suddenly while she watched, the sky folded back in two pieces like the curtain to a stage and a gigantic figure stood facing her. It was the color of the sun in the early afternoon, white-gold. It was of no definite shape but there were fiery wheels with fierce dark eyes in them, spinning rapidly all around it. She was not able to tell if the figure was going forward or backward because its magnificence was so great. She shut her eyes in order to look at it and it turned blood-red and the wheels turned white. A voice, very resonant, said the one word, "Prophesy!"

She stood there, tottering slightly but still upright, her eyes shut tight and her fists clenched and her straw sun hat low on her forehead. "The children of wicked nations will be butchered," she said in a loud voice. "Legs where arms should be, foot to face, ear in the palm of hand. Who will remain whole? Who will remain whole? Who?"

Presently she opened her eyes. The sky was full of white fish carried lazily on their sides by some invisible current and pieces of the sun, submerged some distance beyond them, appeared from time to time as if they were being washed in the opposite direction. Woodenly she planted one foot in front of the other until she had crossed the pasture and reached the lot. She walked through the barn like one in a daze and did not speak to Mr. Shortley. She continued up the road until she saw the priest's car parked in front of Mrs. McIntyre's house. "Here again," she muttered. "Come to destroy."

Mrs. McIntyre and the priest were walking in the yard. In order not to meet them face to face, she turned to the left and entered the feed house, a single-room shack piled on one side with flowered sacks of scratch feed. There were spilled oyster shells in one corner and a few old dirty calendars on the wall, advertising calf feed and various patent medicine remedies. One showed a bearded gentleman in a frock coat, holding up a bottle, and beneath his feet was the inscription, "I have been made regular by this marvelous discovery!" Mrs. Shortley had always felt close to this man as if he were some distinguished person she was acquainted with but now her mind was on nothing but the dangerous presence of the priest. She stationed herself at a crack between two boards where she could look out and see him and Mrs. McIntyre strolling toward the turkey brooder, which was placed just outside the feed house.

"Arrrrr!" he said as they approached the brooder. "Look at the little biddies!" and he stooped and squinted through the wire.

Mrs. Shortley's mouth twisted.

"Do you think the Guizacs will want to leave me?" Mrs. McIntyre asked. "Do you think they'll go to Chicago or some place like that?"

"And why should they do that now?" asked the priest, wiggling his finger at a turkey, his big nose close to the wire.

"Money," Mrs. McIntyre said.

"Arrrr, give them some morrre then," he said indifferently. "They have to get along."

"So do I," Mrs. McIntyre muttered. "It means I'm going to have to get rid of some of these others."

"And arrre the Shortleys satisfactory?" he inquired, paying more attention to the turkeys than to her.

"Five times in the last month I've found Mr. Shortley smoking in the barn," Mrs. McIntyre said. "Five times."

"And arrre the Negroes any better?"

"They lie and steal and have to be watched all the time," she said.

"Tsk, tsk," he said. "Which will you discharge?"

"I've decided to give Mr. Shortley his month's notice tomorrow," Mrs. McIntyre said.

The priest scarcely seemed to hear her he was so busy wiggling his finger inside the wire. Mrs. Shortley sat down on an open sack of laying mash with a dead thump that sent feed dust clouding up around her. She found herself looking straight ahead at the opposite wall where the gentleman on the calendar was holding up his marvelous discovery but she didn't see him. She looked ahead as if she saw nothing whatsoever. Then she rose and ran to her house. Her face was an almost volcanic red.

She opened all the drawers and dragged out boxes and old battered suitcases from under the bed. She began to unload the drawers into the boxes, all the time without pause, without taking off the sunhat she had on her head. She set the two girls to doing the same. When Mr. Shortley came in, she did not even look at him but merely pointed one arm at him while she packed with the other. "Bring the car around to the back door," she said. "You ain't waiting to be fired!"

Mr. Shortley had never in his life doubted her omniscience. He perceived the entire situation in half a second and, with only a sour scowl, retreated out the door and went to drive the automobile around to the back.

They tied the two iron beds to the top of the car and the two rocking chairs inside the beds and rolled the two mattresses up between the rocking chairs. On top of this they tied a crate of chickens. They loaded the inside of the car with the old suitcases and boxes, leaving a small space for Annie Maude and Sarah Mae. It took them the rest of the afternoon and half the night to do this but Mrs. Shortley was determined that they would leave before four o'clock in the morning, that Mr. Shortley should not adjust another milking machine on this place. All the time she had been working, her face was changing rapidly from red to white and back again.

Just before dawn, as it began to drizzle rain, they were ready to leave. They all got in the car and sat there cramped up between boxes and bundles and rolls of bedding. The square black automobile moved off with more than its customary grinding noises as if it were protesting the load. In the back, the two long bony yellow-haired girls were sitting on a pile of boxes and there was a beagle hound puppy and a cat with two kittens somewhere under the blankets. The car moved slowly, like some overfreighted leaking ark, away from their shack and past the white house where Mrs. McIntyre was sleeping soundly —hardly guessing that her cows would not be milked by Mr. Shortley that morning—and past the Pole's shack on top of the hill and on down the road to the gate where the two Negroes were walking, one behind the other, on their way to help with the milking. They looked straight at the car and its occupants but even as the dim yellow headlights lit up their faces, they politely did not seem to see anything, or anyhow, to attach significance to what was there. The loaded car might have been passing mist in the early morning half-light. They continued up the road at the same even pace without looking back.

A dark yellow sun was beginning to rise in a sky that was the same slick dark gray as the highway. The fields stretched away, stiff and weedy, on either side. "Where we goin?" Mr. Shortley asked for the first time.

Mrs. Shortley sat with one foot on a packing box so that her knee was pushed into her stomach. Mr. Shortley's elbow was almost under her nose and Sarah Mae's bare left foot was sticking over the front seat, touching her ear.

"Where we goin?" Mr. Shortley repeated and when she didn't answer again, he turned and looked at her.

Fierce heat seemed to be swelling slowly and fully into her face as if it were welling up now for a final assault. She was sitting in an erect way in spite of the fact that one leg was twisted under her and one knee was almost into her neck, but there was a peculiar lack of light in her icy blue eyes. All the vision in them might have been turned around, looking inside her. She suddenly grabbed Mr. Shortley's elbow and Sarah Mae's foot at the same time and began to tug and pull on them as if she were trying to fit the two extra limbs onto herself.

Mr. Shortley began to curse and quickly stopped the car and Sarah Mae yelled to quit but Mrs. Shortley apparently intended to rearrange the whole car at once. She thrashed forward and backward, clutching at everything she could get her hands on and hugging it to herself, Mr. Shortley's head, Sarah Mae's leg, the cat, a wad of white bedding, her own big moon-like knee; then all at once her fierce expression faded into a look of astonishment and her grip on what she had loosened. One of her eyes drew near to the other and seemed to collapse quietly and she was still.

The two girls, who didn't know what had happened to her, began to say, "Where we goin, Ma? Where we goin?" They thought she was playing a joke and that their father, staring straight ahead at her, was imitating a dead man. They didn't know that she had had a great experience or ever been displaced in the world from all that belonged to her. They were frightened by the gray slick road before them and they kept repeating in higher and higher voices, "Where we goin, Ma? Where we goin?" while their mother, her huge body rolled back still against the seat and her eyes like blue-painted glass, seemed to contemplate for the first time the tremendous frontiers of her true country.

II

"Well," Mrs. McIntyre said to the old Negro, "we can get along without them. We've seen them come and seen them go—black and white." She was standing in the calf barn while he cleaned it and she held a rake in her hand and now and then pulled a corn cob from a corner or pointed to a soggy spot that he had missed. When she discovered the Shortleys were gone, she was delighted as it meant she wouldn't have to fire them. The people she hired always left her—because they were that kind of people. Of all the families she had had, the Shortleys were the best if she didn't count the Displaced Person. They had been not quite trash; Mrs. Shortley was a good woman, and she would miss her but as the Judge used to say, you couldn't have your pie and eat it too, and she was satisfied with the D. P. "We've seen them come and seen them go," she repeated with satisfaction.

"And me and you," the old man said, stooping to drag his hoe under a feed rack, "is still here."

She caught exactly what he meant her to catch in his tone. Bars of sunlight fell from the cracked ceiling across his back and cut him in three distinct parts. She watched his long hands clenched around the hoe and his crooked old profile pushed close to them. You might have been here *before* I was, she said to herself, but it's mighty likely I'll be here when you're gone. "I've spent half my life fooling with worthless people," she said in a severe voice, "but now I'm through."

"Black and white," he said, "is the same."

"I am through," she repeated and gave her dark smock that she had thrown over her shoulders like a cape a quick snatch at the neck. She had on a broad-brimmed black straw hat that had cost her twenty dollars twenty years ago and that she used now for a sunhat. "Money is the root of all evil," she said. "The Judge said so every day. He said he deplored money. He said the reason you niggers were so uppity was because there was so much money in circulation."

The old Negro had known the Judge. "Judge say he long for the day when he be too poor to pay a nigger to work," he said. "Say when that day come, the world be back on its feet."

She leaned forward, her hands on her hips and her neck

stretched and said, "Well that day has almost come around here and I'm telling each and every one of you: you better look sharp. I don't have to put up with foolishness any more. I have somebody now who *has* to work!"

The old man knew when to answer and when not. At length he said, "We seen them come and we seen them go."

"However, the Shortleys were not the worst by far," she said. "I well remember those Garrits."

"They was before them Collinses," he said.

"No, before the Ringfields."

"Sweet Lord, them Ringfields!" he murmured.

"None of that kind *want* to work," she said.

"We seen them come and we seen them go," he said as if this were a refrain. "But we ain't never had one before," he said, bending himself up until he faced her, "like what we got now." He was cinnamon-colored with eyes that were so blurred with age that they seemed to be hung behind cobwebs.

She gave him an intense stare and held it until, lowering his hands on the hoe, he bent down again and dragged a pile of shavings alongside the wheelbarrow. She said stiffly, "He can wash out that barn in the time it took Mr. Shortley to make up his mind he had to do it."

"He from Pole," the old man muttered.

"From Poland."

"In Pole it ain't like it is here," he said. "They got different ways of doing," and he began to mumble unintelligibly.

"What are you saying?" she said. "If you have anything to say about him, say it and say it aloud."

He was silent, bending his knees precariously and edging the rake along the underside of the trough.

"If you know anything he's done that he shouldn't, I expect you to report it to me," she said.

"It warn't like it was what he should ought or oughtn't," he muttered. "It was like what nobody else don't do."

"You don't have anything against him," she said shortly, "and he's here to stay."

"We ain't never had one like him before is all," he murmured and gave his polite laugh.

"Times are changing," she said. "Do you know what's happening to this world? It's swelling up. It's getting so full of people that only the smart thrifty energetic ones are going to survive," and she tapped the words, smart, thrifty, and energetic out on the palm of her hand. Through the far end of the stall she could see down the road to where the Displaced Person was standing in the open barn door with the green hose in his hand. There was a certain stiffness about his figure that seemed to make it necessary for her to approach him slowly, even in her thoughts. She had decided this was because she couldn't hold an easy conversation with him. Whenever she said anything to him, she found herself shouting and nodding extravagantly and she would be conscious that one of the Negroes was leaning behind the nearest shed, watching.

"No indeed!" she said, sitting down on one of the feed racks and folding her arms, "I've made up my mind that I've had enough trashy people on this place to last me a lifetime and I'm not going to spend my last years fooling with Shortleys and Ringfields and Collins when the world is full of people who *have* to work."

"Howcome they so many extra?" he asked.

"People are selfish," she said. "They have too many children. There's no sense in it any more."

He had picked up the wheelbarrow handles and was backing out the door and he paused, half in the sunlight and half out, and stood there chewing his gums as if he had forgotten which direction he wanted to move in.

"What you colored people don't realize," she said, "is that I'm the one around here who holds all the strings together. If you don't work, I don't make any money and I can't pay you. You're all dependent on me but you each and every one act like the shoe is on the other foot."

It was not possible to tell from his face if he heard her. Finally he backed out with the wheelbarrow. "Judge say the devil he know is better than the devil he don't," he said in a clear mutter and turned and trundled off.

She got up and followed him, a deep vertical pit appearing suddenly in the center of her forehead, just under the red bangs. "The Judge has long since ceased to pay the bills around here," she called in a piercing voice.

He was the only one of her Negroes who had known the Judge and he thought this gave him title. He had had a low opinion of Mr. Crooms and Mr. McIntyre, her other husbands, and in his veiled polite way, he had congratulated her after each of her divorces. When he thought it necessary, he would work under a window where he knew she was sitting and talk to himself, a careful roundabout discussion, question and answer and then refrain. Once she had got up silently and slammed the window down so hard that he had fallen backwards off his feet. Or occasionally he spoke with the peacock. The cock would follow him around the place, his steady eye on the ear of corn that stuck up from the old man's back pocket or he would sit near him and pick himself. Once from the open kitchen door, she had heard him say to the bird, "I remember when it was twenty of you walking about this place and now it's only you and two hens. Crooms it was twelve. McIntyre it was five. You and two hens now."

And that time she had stepped out of the door onto the porch and said, "MISTER Crooms and MISTER McIntyre! And I don't want to hear you call either of them anything else again. And you can understand this: when that peachicken dies there won't be any replacements."

She kept the peacock only out of a superstitious fear of annoying the Judge in his grave. He had liked to see them walking around the place for he said they made him feel rich. Of her three husbands, the Judge was the one most present to her although he was the only one she had buried. He was in the family graveyard, a little space fenced in the middle of the back cornfield, with his mother and father and grandfather and three great aunts and two infant cousins. Mr. Crooms, her second, was forty miles away in the state asylum and Mr. McIntyre, her last, was intoxicated, she supposed, in some hotel room in Florida. But the Judge, sunk in the cornfield with his family, was always at home.

She had married him when he was an old man and because of his money but there had been another reason that she would not admit then, even to herself: she had liked him. He was a dirty snuff-dipping Court House figure, famous all over the county for being rich, who wore high-top shoes, a string tie, a gray suit with a black stripe in it, and a yellowed panama hat, winter and summer. His teeth and hair were tobacco-colored and his face a clay pink pitted and tracked with mysterious prehistoric-looking marks as if he had been unearthed among fossils. There had been a peculiar odor about him of sweaty fondled bills but he never carried money on him or had a nickel to show. She was his secretary for a few months and the old man with his sharp eye had seen at once that here was a woman who admired him for himself. The three years that he lived after they married were the happiest and most prosperous of Mrs. McIntyre's life, but when he died his estate proved to be bankrupt. He left her a mortgaged house and fifty acres that he had managed to cut the timber off before he died. It was as if, as the final triumph of a successful life, he had been able to take everything with him.

But she had survived. She had survived a succession of tenant farmers and dairymen that the old man himself would have found hard to outdo, and she had been able to meet the constant drain of a tribe of moody unpredictable Negroes, and she had even managed to hold her own against the incidental bloodsuckers, the cattle dealers and lumber men and the buyers and sellers of anything who drove up in pieced-together trucks and honked in the yard.

She stood slightly reared back with her arms folded under her smock and a satisfied expression on her face as she watched the Displaced Person turn off the hose and disappear inside the barn. She was sorry that the poor man had been chased out of Poland and run across Europe and had had to take up in a tenant shack in a strange country, but she had not been responsible for any of this. She had had a hard time herself. She knew what it was to struggle. People ought to have to struggle. Mr. Guizac had probably had everything given to him all the way across Europe and over here. He had probably not had to struggle enough. She had given him a job. She didn't know if he was grateful or not. She didn't know anything about him except that he did the work. The truth was that he was not very real to her yet. He was a kind of miracle that she had seen happen and that she talked about but that she still didn't believe.

She watched as he came out of the barn and motioned to Sulk, who was coming around the back of the lot. He gesticulated and then took something out of his pocket and the two of them stood looking at it. She started down the lane toward them. The Negro's figure was slack and tall and he was craning his round head forward in his usual idiotic way. He was a little better than half-witted but when they were like that they were always good workers. The Judge had said always hire you a half-witted nigger because they don't have sense enough to stop working. The Pole was gesticulating rapidly. He left something with the colored boy and then walked off and before she rounded the turn in the lane, she heard the tractor crank up. He was on his way to the field. The Negro was still hanging there, gaping at whatever he had in his hand.

She entered the lot and walked through the barn, looking with approval at the wet spotless concrete floor. It was only nine-thirty and Mr. Shortley had never got anything washed until eleven. As she came out at the other end, she saw the Negro moving very slowly in a diagonal path across the road in front of her, his eyes still on what Mr. Guizac had given him. He didn't see her and he paused and dipped his knees and leaned over his hand, his tongue describing little circles. He had a photograph. He lifted one finger and traced it lightly over the surface of the picture. Then he looked up and saw her and seemed to freeze, his mouth in a half-grin, his finger lifted.

"Why haven't you gone to the field?" she asked.

He raised one foot and opened his mouth wider while the hand with the photograph edged toward his back pocket.

"What's that?" she said.

"It ain't nothin," he muttered and handed it to her automatically.

It was a photograph of a girl of about twelve in a white dress. She had blond hair with a wreath in it and she looked forward out of light eyes that were bland and composed. "Who is this child?" Mrs. McIntyre asked.

"She his cousin," the boy said in a high voice.

"Well what are you doing with it?" she asked.

"She going to mah me," he said in an even higher voice.

"Marry you!" she shrieked.

"I pays half to get her over here," he said. "I pays him three dollar a week. She bigger now. She his cousin. She don't care who she mah she so glad to get away from there." The high voice seemed to shoot up like a nervous jet of sound and then fall flat as he watched her face. Her eyes were the color of blue granite when the glare falls on it, but she was not looking at him. She was looking down the road where the distant sound of the tractor could be heard.

"I don't reckon she goin to come nohow," the boy murmured.

"I'll see that you get every cent of your money back," she said in a toneless voice and turned and walked off, holding the photograph bent in two. There was nothing about her small stiff figure to indicate that she was shaken.

As soon as she got in the house, she lay down on her bed and shut her eyes and pressed her hand over her heart as if she were trying to keep it in place. Her mouth opened and she made two or three dry little sounds. Then after a minute she sat up and said aloud, "They're all the same. It's always been like this," and she fell back flat again. "Twenty years of being beaten and done in and they even robbed his grave!" and remembering that, she began to cry quietly, wiping her eyes every now and then with the hem of her smock.

What she had thought of was the angel over the Judge's grave. This had been a naked granite cherub that the old man had seen in the city one day in a tombstone store window. He had been taken with it at once, partly because its face reminded him of his wife and partly because he wanted a genuine work of art over his grave. He had come home with it sitting on the green plush train seat beside him. Mrs. McIntyre had never noticed the resemblance to herself. She had always thought it hideous but when the Herrins stole it off the old man's grave, she was shocked and outraged. Mrs. Herrin had thought it very pretty and had walked to the graveyard frequently to see it, and when the Herrins left the angel left with them, all but its toes, for the ax old man Herrin had used to break it off with had struck slightly too high. Mrs. McIntyre had never been able to afford to have it replaced.

When she had cried all she could, she got up and went into the back hall, a closet-like space that was dark and quiet as a chapel and sat down on the edge of the Judge's black mechanical chair with her elbow on his desk. This was a giant roll-top piece of furniture pocked with pigeon holes full of dusty papers. Old bankbooks and ledgers were stacked in the half-open drawers and there was a small safe, empty but locked, set like a tabernacle in the center of it. She had left this part of the house unchanged since the old man's time. It was a kind of memorial to him, sacred because he had conducted his business here. With the slightest tilt one way or the other, the chair gave a rusty skeletal groan that sounded something like him when he had complained of his poverty. It had been his first principle to talk as if he were the poorest man in the world and she followed it, not only because he had but because it was true. When she sat with her intense constricted face turned toward the empty safe, she knew there was nobody poorer in the world than she was.

She sat motionless at the desk for ten or fifteen minutes and then as if she had gained some strength, she got up and got in her car and drove to the cornfield.

The road ran through a shadowy pine thicket and ended on top of a hill that rolled fan-wise down and up again in a broad expanse of tasseled green. Mr. Guizac was cutting from the outside of the field in a circular path to the center where the graveyard was all but hidden by the corn, and she could see him on the high far side of the slope, mounted on the tractor with the cutter and wagon behind him. From time to time, he had to get off the tractor and climb in the wagon to spread the silage because the Negro had not arrived. She watched impatiently, standing in front of her black coupe with her arms folded under her smock, while he progressed slowly around the rim of the field, gradually getting close enough for her to wave to him to get down. He stopped the machine and jumped off and came running forward, wiping his red jaw with a piece of grease rag.

"I want to talk to you," she said and beckoned him to the edge of the thicket where it was shady. He took off the cap and followed her, smiling, but his smile faded when she turned and faced him. Her eyebrows, thin and fierce as a spider's leg, had drawn together ominously and the deep vertical pit had plunged down from under the red bangs into the bridge of her nose. She removed the bent picture from her pocket and handed it to him silently. Then she stepped back and said, "Mr. Guizac! You would bring this poor innocent child over here and try to marry her to a half-witted thieving black stinking nigger! What kind of a monster are you!"

He took the photograph with a slowly returning smile. "My cousin," he said. "She twelve here. First Communion. Six-ten now."

Monster! she said to herself and looked at him as if she were seeing him for the first time. His forehead and skull were white where they had been protected by his cap but the rest of his face was red and bristled with short yellow hairs. His eyes were like two bright nails behind his gold-rimmed spectacles that had been mended over the nose with haywire. His whole face looked as if it might have been patched together out of several others. "Mr. Guizac," she said, beginning slowly and then speaking faster until she ended breathless in the middle of a word, "that nigger cannot have a white wife from Europe. You can't talk to a nigger that way. You'll excite him and besides it can't be done. Maybe it can be done in Poland but it can't be done here and you'll have to stop. It's all foolishness. That nigger don't have a grain of sense and you'll excite . . ."

"She in camp three year," he said.

"Your cousin," she said in a positive voice, "cannot come over here and marry one of my Negroes."

"She six-ten year," he said. "From Poland. Mamma die, pappa die. She wait in camp. Three camp." He pulled a wallet from his pocket and fingered through it and took out another picture of the same girl, a few years older, dressed in something dark and shapeless. She was standing against a wall with a short woman who apparently had no teeth. "She mamma," he said, pointing to the woman. "She die in two camp."

"Mr. Guizac," Mrs. McIntyre said, pushing the picture back at him, "I will not have my niggers upset. I cannot run this place without my niggers. I can run it without you but not without them and if you mention this girl to

Sulk again, you won't have a job with me. Do you understand?"

His face showed no comprehension. He seemed to be piecing all these words together in his mind to make a thought.

Mrs. McIntyre remembered Mrs. Shortley's words: "He understands everything, he only pretends he don't so as to do exactly as he pleases," and her face regained the look of shocked wrath she had begun with. "I cannot understand how a man who calls himself a Christian," she said, "could bring a poor innocent girl over here and marry her to something like that. I cannot understand it. I cannot!" and she shook her head and looked into the distance with a pained blue gaze.

After a second he shrugged and let his arms drop as if he were tired. "She no care black," he said. "She in camp three year."

Mrs. McIntyre felt a peculiar weakness behind her knees. "Mr. Guizac," she said, "I don't want to have to speak to you about this again. If I do, you'll have to find another place yourself. Do you understand?"

The patched face did not say. She had the impression that he didn't see her there. "This is my place," she said. "I say who will come here and who won't."

"Ya," he said and put back on his cap.

"I am not responsible for the world's misery," she said as an afterthought.

"Ya," he said.

"You have a good job. You should be grateful to be here," she added, "but I'm not sure you are."

"Ya," he said and gave his little shrug and turned back to the tractor.

She watched him get on and maneuver the machine into the corn again. When he had passed her and rounded the turn, she climbed to the top of the slope and stood with her arms folded and looked out grimly over the field.

"They're all the same," she muttered, "whether they come from Poland or Tennessee. I've handled Herrins and Ringfields and Shortleys and I can handle a Guizac," and she narrowed her gaze until it closed entirely around the diminishing figure on the tractor as if she were watching him through a gunsight. All her life she had been fighting the world's overflow and now she had it in the form of a Pole. "You're just like all the rest of them," she said, "—only smart and thrifty and energetic but so am I. And this is my place," and she stood there, a small black-hatted, black-smocked figure with an aging cherubic face, and folded her arms as if she were equal to anything. But her heart was beating as if some interior violence had already been done to her. She opened her eyes to include the whole field so that the figure on the tractor was no larger than a grasshopper in her widened view.

She stood there for some time. There was a slight breeze and the corn trembled in great waves on both sides of the slope. The big cutter, with its monotonous roar, continued to shoot it pulverized into the wagon in a steady spurt of fodder. By nightfall, the Displaced Person would have worked his way around and around until there would be nothing on either side of the two hills but the stubble, and down in the center, risen like a little island, the graveyard where the Judge lay grinning under his desecrated monument.

III

The priest, with his long bland face supported on one finger, had been talking for ten minutes about Purgatory while Mrs. McIntyre squinted furiously at him from an opposite chair. They were drinking ginger ale on her front porch and she had kept rattling the ice in her glass, rattling her beads, rattling her bracelet like an impatient pony jingling its harness. There is no moral obligation to keep him, she was saying under her breath, there is absolutely no moral obligation. Suddenly she lurched up and her voice fell across his brogue like a drill into a mechanical saw. "Listen!" she said, "I'm not theological. I'm practical! I want to talk to you about something practical!"

"Arrrrrr," he groaned, grating to a halt.

She had put at least a finger of whisky in her own ginger ale so that she would be able to endure his full-length visit and she sat down awkwardly, finding the chair closer to her than she had expected. "Mr. Guizac is not satisfactory," she said.

The old man raised his eyebrows in mock wonder.

"He's extra," she said. "He doesn't fit in. I have to have somebody who fits in."

The priest carefully turned his hat on his knees. He had a little trick of waiting a second silently and then swinging the conversation back into his own paths. He was about eighty. She had never known a priest until she had gone to see this one on the business of getting her the Displaced Person. After he had got her the Pole, he had used the business introduction to try to convert her—just as she had supposed he would.

"Give him time," the old man said. "He'll learn to fit in. Where is that beautiful birrrd of yours?" he asked and then said, "Arrrrr, I see him!" and stood up and looked out over the lawn where the peacock and the two hens were stepping at a strained attention, their long necks ruffled, the cock's violent blue and the hens' silver-green, glinting in the late afternoon sun.

"Mr. Guizac," Mrs. McIntyre continued, bearing down with a flat steady voice, "is very efficient. I'll admit that. But he doesn't understand how to get on with my niggers and they don't like him. I can't have my niggers run off. And I don't like his attitude. He's not in the least grateful for being here."

The priest had his hand on the screen door and he opened it, ready to make his escape. "Arrrr, I must be off," he murmured.

"I tell you if I had a white man who understood the Negroes, I'd have to let Mr. Guizac go," she said and stood up again.

He turned then and looked her in the face. "He has nowhere to go," he said. Then he said, "Dear lady, I know you well enough to know you wouldn't turn him out for a trifle!" and without waiting for an answer, he raised his hand and gave her his blessing in a rumbling voice.

She smiled angrily and said, "I didn't create his situation, of course."

The priest let his eyes wander toward the birds. They had reached the middle of the lawn. The cock stopped suddenly and curving his neck backwards, he raised his tail and spread it with a shimmering timbrous noise. Tiers of small pregnant suns floated in a green-gold haze over his head. The priest stood transfixed, his jaw slack. Mrs. McIntyre wondered where she had ever seen such an idiotic old man. "Christ will come like that!" he said in a loud gay voice and wiped his hand over his mouth and stood there, gaping.

Mrs. McIntyre's face assumed a set puritanical expression and she reddened. Christ in the conversation embarrassed her the way sex had her mother. "It is not my responsibility that Mr. Guizac has nowhere to go," she said. "I don't find myself responsible for all the extra people in the world."

The old man didn't seem to hear her. His attention was fixed on the cock who was taking minute steps backward, his head against the spread tail. "The Transfiguration," he murmured.

She had no idea what he was talking about. "Mr. Guizac didn't have to come here in the first place," she said, giving him a hard look.

The cock lowered his tail and began to pick grass.

"He didn't have to come in the first place," she repeated, emphasizing each word.

The old man smiled absently. "He came to redeem us," he said and blandly reached for her hand and shook it and said he must go.

If Mr. Shortley had not returned a few weeks later, she would have gone out looking for a new man to hire. She had not wanted him back but when she saw the familiar black automobile drive up the road and stop by the side of the house, she had the feeling that she was the one returning, after a long miserable trip, to her own place. She realized all at once that it was Mrs. Shortley she had been missing. She had had no one to talk to since Mrs. Shortley left, and she ran to the door, expecting to see her heaving herself up the steps.

Mr. Shortley stood there alone. He had on a black felt hat and a shirt with red and blue palm trees designed in it but the hollows in his long bitten blistered face were deeper than they had been a month ago.

"Well!" she said. "Where is Mrs. Shortley?"

Mr. Shortley didn't say anything. The change in his face seemed to have come from the inside; he looked like a man who had gone for a long time without water. "She was God's own angel," he said in a loud voice. "She was the sweetest woman in the world."

"Where is she?" Mrs. McIntyre murmured.

"Daid," he said. "She had herself a stroke on the day she left out of here." There was a corpse-like composure about his face. "I figure that Pole killed her," he said. "She seen through him from the first. She known he come from the devil. She told me so."

It took Mrs. McIntyre three days to get over Mrs. Shortley's death. She told herself that anyone would have thought they were kin. She rehired Mr. Shortley to do farm work though actually she didn't want him without his wife. She told him she was going to give thirty days' notice to the Displaced Person at the end of the month and that then he could have his job back in the dairy. Mr. Shortley preferred the dairy job but he was willing to wait. He said it would give him some satisfaction to see the Pole leave the place, and Mrs. McIntyre said it would give her a great deal of satisfaction. She confessed that she should have been content with the help she had in the first place and not have been reaching into other parts of the world for it. Mr. Shortley said he never had cared for foreigners since he had been in the first world's war and seen what they were like. He said he had seen all kinds then but that none of them were like us. He said he recalled the face of one man who had thrown a hand-grenade at him and that the man had had little round eye-glasses exactly like Mr. Guizac's.

"But Mr. Guizac is a Pole, he's not a German," Mrs. McIntyre said.

"It ain't a great deal of difference in them two kinds," Mr. Shortley had explained.

The Negroes were pleased to see Mr. Shortley back. The Displaced Person had expected them to work as hard as he worked himself, whereas Mr. Shortley recognized their limitations. He had never been a very good worker himself with Mrs. Shortley to keep him in line, but without her, he was even more forgetful and slow. The Pole worked as fiercely as ever and seemed to have no inkling that he was about to be fired. Mrs. McIntyre saw jobs done in a short time that she had thought would never get done at all. Still she was resolved to get rid of him. The sight of his small stiff figure moving quickly here and there had come to be the most irritating sight on the place for her, and she felt she had been tricked by the old priest. He had said there was no legal obligation for her to keep the Displaced Person if he was not satisfactory, but then he had brought up the moral one.

She meant to tell him that *her* moral obligation was to

her own people, to Mr. Shortley, who had fought in the world war for his country and not to Mr. Guizac who had merely arrived here to take advantage of whatever he could. She felt she must have this out with the priest before she fired the Displaced Person. When the first of the month came and the priest hadn't called, she put off giving the Pole notice for a little longer.

Mr. Shortley told himself that he should have known all along that no woman was going to do what she said she was when she said she was. He didn't know how long he could afford to put up with her shilly-shallying. He thought himself that she was going soft and was afraid to turn the Pole out for fear he would have a hard time getting another place. He could tell her the truth about this: that if she let him go, in three years he would own his own house and have a television aerial sitting on top of it. As a matter of policy, Mr. Shortley began to come to her back door every evening to put certain facts before her. "A white man sometimes don't get the consideration a nigger gets," he said, "but that don't matter because he's still white, but sometimes," and here he would pause and look off into the distance, "a man that's fought and bled and died in the service of his native land don't get the consideration of one of them like them he was fighting. I ast you: is that right?" When he asked her such questions he could watch her face and tell he was making an impression. She didn't look too well these days. He noticed lines around her eyes that hadn't been there when he and Mrs. Shortley had been the only white help on the place. Whenever he thought of Mrs. Shortley, he felt his heart go down like an old bucket into a dry well.

The old priest kept away as if he had been frightened by his last visit but finally, seeing that the Displaced Person had not been fired, he ventured to call again to take up giving Mrs. McIntyre instructions where he remembered leaving them off. She had not asked to be instructed but he instructed anyway, forcing a little definition of one of the sacraments or of some dogma into each conversation he had, no matter with whom. He sat on her porch, taking no notice of her partly mocking, partly outraged expression as she sat shaking her foot, waiting for an opportunity to drive a wedge into his talk. "For," he was saying, as if he spoke of something that had happened yesterday in town, "when God sent his Only Begotten Son, Jesus Christ Our Lord"—he slightly bowed his head—"as a Redeemer to mankind, He . . ."

"Father Flynn!" she said in a voice that made him jump. "I want to talk to you about something serious!"

The skin under the old man's right eye flinched.

"As far as I'm concerned," she said and glared at him fiercely, "Christ was just another D. P."

He raised his hands slightly and let them drop on his knees. "Arrrrr," he murmured as if he were considering this.

"I'm going to let that man go," she said. "I don't have any obligation to him. My obligation is to the people who've done something for their country, not to the ones who've just come over to take advantage of what they can get," and she began to talk rapidly, remembering all her arguments. The priest's attention seemed to retire to some private oratory to wait until she got through. Once or twice his gaze roved out onto the lawn as if he were hunting some means of escape but she didn't stop. She told him how she had been hanging onto this place for thirty years, always just barely making it against people who came from nowhere and were going nowhere, who didn't want anything but an automobile. She said she had found out they were the same whether they came from Poland or Tennessee. When the Guizacs got ready, she said, they would not hesitate to leave her. She told him how the people who looked rich were the poorest of all because they had the most to keep up. She asked him how he thought she paid her feed bills. She told him she would like to have her house done over but she couldn't afford it. She couldn't even afford to have the monument restored over her husband's grave. She asked him if he would like to guess what her insurance amounted to for the year. Finally she asked him if he thought she was made of money and the old man suddenly let out a great ugly bellow as if this were a comical question.

When the visit was over, she felt let down, though she had clearly triumphed over him. She made up her mind now that on the first of the month, she would give the Displaced Person his thirty days' notice and she told Mr. Shortley so.

Mr. Shortley didn't say anything. His wife had been the only woman he was ever acquainted with who was never scared off from doing what she said. She said the Pole had been sent by the devil and the priest. Mr. Shortley had no doubt that the priest had got some peculiar control over Mrs. McIntyre and that before long she would start attending his Masses. She looked as if something was wearing her down from the inside. She was thinner and more fidgety and not as sharp as she used to be. She would look at a milk can now and not see how dirty it was and he had seen her lips move when she was not talking. The Pole never did anything the wrong way but all the same he was very irritating to her. Mr. Shortley himself did things as he pleased—not always her way—but she didn't seem to notice. She had noticed though that the Pole and all his family were getting fat; she pointed out to Mr. Shortley that the hollows had come out of their cheeks and that they saved every cent they made. "Yes'm, and one of these days he'll be able to buy and sell you out," Mr. Shortley had ventured to say, and he could tell that the statement had shaken her.

"I'm just waiting for the first," she had said.

Mr. Shortley waited too and the first came and went and she didn't fire him. He could have told anybody how it would be. He was not a violent man but he hated to see a woman done in by a foreigner. He felt that that was one thing a man couldn't stand by and see happen.

There was no reason Mrs. McIntyre should not fire Mr. Guizac at once but she put it off from day to day. She was worried about her bills and about her health. She didn't sleep at night or when she did she dreamed about the Displaced Person. She had never discharged any one before; they had all left her. One night she dreamed that Mr. Guizac and his family were moving into her house and that she was moving in with Mr. Shortley. This was too much for her and she woke up and didn't sleep again for several nights; and one night she dreamed that the priest came to call and droned on and on, saying, "Dear lady, I know your tender heart won't suffer you to turn the porrrrr man out. Think of the thousands of them, think of the ovens and the boxcars and the camps and the sick children and Christ Our Lord."

"He's extra and he's upset the balance around here," she said, "and I'm a logical practical woman and there are no ovens here and no camps and no Christ Our Lord and when he leaves, he'll make more money. He'll work at the mill and buy a car and don't talk to me—all they want is a car."

"The ovens and the boxcars and the sick children," droned the priest, "and our dear Lord."

"Just one too many," she said.

The next morning, she made up her mind while she was eating her breakfast that she would give him his notice at once, and she stood up and walked out of the kitchen and down the road with her table napkin still in her hand. Mr. Guizac was spraying the barn, standing in his sway-backed way with one hand on his hip. He turned off the hose and gave her an impatient kind of attention as if she were interfering with his work. She had not thought of what she would say to him, she had merely come. She stood in the barn door, looking severely at the wet spotless floor and the dripping stanchions. "Ya goot?" he said.

"Mr. Guizac," she said, "I can barely meet my obligations now." Then she said in a louder, stronger voice, emphasizing each word, "I have bills to pay."

"I too," Mr. Guizac said. "Much bills, little money," and he shrugged.

At the other end of the barn, she saw a long beak-nosed shadow glide like a snake halfway up the sunlit open door and stop; and somewhere behind her, she was aware of a silence where the sound of the Negroes shoveling had come a minute before. "This is my place," she said angrily. "All of you are extra. Each and every one of you are extra!"

"Ya," Mr. Guizac said and turned on the hose again. She wiped her mouth with the napkin she had in her hand and walked off, as if she had accomplished what she came for.

Mr. Shortley's shadow withdrew from the door and he leaned against the side of the barn and lit half of a cigarette that he took out of his pocket. There was nothing for him to do now but wait on the hand of God to strike, but he knew one thing: he was not going to wait with his mouth shut.

Starting that morning, he began to complain and to state his side of the case to every person he saw, black or white. He complained in the grocery store and at the courthouse and on the street corner and directly to Mrs. McIntyre herself, for there was nothing underhanded about him. If the Pole could have understood what he had to say, he would have said it to him too. "All men was created free and equal," he said to Mrs. McIntyre, "and I risked my life and limb to prove it. Gone over there and fought and bled and died and come back on over here and find out who's got my job—just exactly who I been fighting. It was a hand-grenade come that near to killing me and I seen who throwed it—little man with eye-glasses just like his. Might have bought them at the same store. Small world," and he gave a bitter little laugh. Since he didn't have Mrs. Shortley to do the talking any more, he had started doing it himself and had found that he had a gift for it. He had the power of making other people see his logic. He talked a good deal to the Negroes.

"Whyn't you go back to Africa?" he asked Sulk one morning as they were cleaning out the silo. "That's your country, ain't it?"

"I ain't goin there," the boy said. "They might eat me up."

"Well, if you behave yourself it isn't any reason you can't stay here," Mr. Shortley said kindly. "Because you didn't run away from nowhere. Your granddaddy was brought. He didn't have a thing to do with coming. It's the people that run away from where they come from that I ain't got any use for."

"I never felt no need to travel," the Negro said.

"Well," Mr. Shortley said, "if I was going to travel again, it would be to either China or Africa. You go to either of them two places and you can tell right away what the difference is between you and them. You go to these other places and the only way you can tell is if they say something. And then you can't always tell because about half of them know the English language. That's where we make our mistake," he said, "–letting all them people onto English. There'd be a heap less trouble if everybody only knew his own language. My wife said knowing two languages was like having eyes in the back of your head. You couldn't put nothing over on her."

"You sho couldn't," the boy muttered, and then he added, "She was fine. She was sho fine. I never known a finer white woman than her."

Mr. Shortley turned in the opposite direction and worked silently for a while. After a few minutes he leaned up and tapped the colored boy on the shoulder with the handle of his shovel. For a second he only looked at him while a great deal of meaning gathered in his wet eyes. Then he said softly, "Revenge is mine, saith the Lord."

Mrs. McIntyre found that everybody in town knew

Mr. Shortley's version of her business and that everyone was critical of her conduct. She began to understand that she had a moral obligation to fire the Pole and that she was shirking it because she found it hard to do. She could not stand the increasing guilt any longer and on a cold Saturday morning, she started off after breakfast to fire him. She walked down to the machine shed where she heard him cranking up the tractor.

There was a heavy frost on the ground that made the fields look like the rough backs of sheep; the sun was almost silver and the woods stuck up like dry bristles on the sky line. The countryside seemed to be receding from the little circle of noise around the shed. Mr. Guizac was squatting on the ground beside the small tractor, putting in a part. Mrs. McIntyre hoped to get the fields turned over while he still had thirty days to work for her. The colored boy was standing by with some tools in his hand and Mr. Shortley was under the shed about to get up on the large tractor and back it out. She meant to wait until he and the Negro got out of the way before she began her unpleasant duty.

She stood watching Mr. Guizac, stamping her feet on the hard ground, for the cold was climbing like a paralysis up her feet and legs. She had on a heavy black coat and a red head-kerchief with her black hat pulled down on top of it to keep the glare out of her eyes. Under the black brim her face had an abstracted look and once or twice her lips moved silently. Mr. Guizac shouted over the noise of the tractor for the Negro to hand him a screwdriver and when he got it, he turned over on his back on the icy ground and reached up under the machine. She could not see his face, only his feet and legs and trunk sticking impudently out from the side of the tractor. He had on rubber boots that were cracked and splashed with mud. He raised one knee and then lowered it and turned himself slightly. Of all the things she resented about him, she resented most that he hadn't left of his own accord.

Mr. Shortley had got on the large tractor and was backing it out from under the shed. He seemed to be warmed by it as if its heat and strength sent impulses up through him that he obeyed instantly. He had headed it toward the small tractor but he braked it on a slight incline and jumped off and turned back toward the shed. Mrs. McIntryre was looking fixedly at Mr. Guizac's legs lying flat on the ground now. She heard the brake on the large tractor slip and, looking up, she saw it move forward, calculating its own path. Later she remembered that she had seen the Negro jump silently out of the way as if a spring in the earth had released him and that she had seen Mr. Shortley turn his head with incredible slowness and stare silently over his shoulder and that she had started to shout to the Displaced Person but that she had not. She had felt her eyes and Mr. Shortley's eyes and the Negro's eyes come together in one look that froze them in collusion forever, and she had heard the little noise the Pole made as the tractor wheel broke his backbone. The two men ran forward to help and she fainted.

She remembered, when she came to, running somewhere, perhaps into the house and out again but she could not remember what for or if she had fainted again when she got there. When she finally came back to where the tractors were, the ambulance had arrived. Mr. Guizac's body was covered with the bent bodies of his wife and two children and by a black one which hung over him, murmuring words she didn't understand. At first she thought this must be the doctor but then with a feeling of annoyance she recognized the priest, who had come with the ambulance and was slipping something into the crushed man's mouth. After a minute he stood up and she looked first at his bloody pants legs and then at his face which was not averted from her but was as withdrawn and expressionless as the rest of the countryside. She only stared at him for she was too shocked by her experience to be quite herself. Her mind was not taking hold of all that was happening. She felt she was in some foreign country where the people bent over the body were natives, and she watched like a stranger while the dead man was carried away in the ambulance.

That evening Mr. Shortley left without notice to look for a new position and the Negro, Sulk, was taken with a sudden desire to see more of the world and set off for the southern part of the state. The old man Astor could not work without company. Mrs. McIntyre hardly noticed that she had no help left for she came down with a nervous affliction and had to go to the hospital. When she came back, she saw that the place would be too much for her to run now and she turned her cows over to a professional auctioneer (who sold them at a loss) and retired to live on what she had, while she tried to save her declining health. A numbness developed in one of her legs and her hands and head began to jiggle and eventually she had to stay in bed all the time with only a colored woman to wait on her. Her eyesight grew steadily worse and she lost her voice altogether. Not many people remembered to come out to the country to see her except the old priest. He came regularly once a week with a bag of breadcrumbs and, after he had fed these to the peacock, he would come in and sit by the side of her bed and explain the doctrines of the Church.

OTHER IMAGE BOOKS

OUR LADY OF FATIMA – William Thomas Walsh (D1) – 95¢
THE SPIRIT OF CATHOLICISM – Karl Adam (D2) – 95¢
DAMIEN THE LEPER – John Farrow (D3) – 85¢
MR. BLUE – Myles Connolly. Modern classic about a contemporary St. Francis (D5) – 75¢
THE CHURCH SPEAKS TO THE MODERN WORLD – Edited by Étienne Gilson. Social teachings of Leo XIII. An Image Original (D7) – $1.25
PEACE OF SOUL – Fulton J. Sheen (D8) – 95¢
LIFT UP YOUR HEART – Fulton J. Sheen (D9) – 95¢
THE PERFECT JOY OF ST. FRANCIS – Felix Timmermans. Novel based on the saint's life (D11) – 95¢
SAINTS FOR OUR TIMES – Theodore Maynard. Eighteen significant biographies (D12) – 95¢
THE IMITATION OF CHRIST – Thomas à Kempis. Edited with an Introduction by Harold C. Gardiner, S.J. (D17) – 95¢
THE EVERLASTING MAN – G. K. Chesterton (D18) – 95¢
A GRAMMAR OF ASSENT – John Henry Cardinal Newman. Introduction by Étienne Gilson (D19) – $1.45
ST. FRANCIS OF ASSISI – Johannes Jorgensen (D22) – 95¢
ON THE TRUTH OF THE CATHOLIC FAITH (Summa Contra Gentiles) – St. Thomas Aquinas. An Original Image Series:
Book One: God – Translated by Anton C. Pegis (D26) – $1.25
THE SIGN OF JONAS – Thomas Merton (D31) – $1.25
PARENTS, CHILDREN, AND THE FACTS OF LIFE – Henry V. Sattler, C.SS.R. (D32) – 95¢
SAINT THOMAS AQUINAS – G. K. Chesterton (D36) – 95¢
A HANDBOOK OF THE CATHOLIC FAITH – Dr. N. G. M. Van Doornik, Rev. S. Jelsma, and Rev. De Lisdonk. Edited by Rev. John Greenwood (D38) – $1.65
MARIA CHAPDELAINE – by Louis Hemon. An epic of French-Canadian life (D40) – 75¢
THE STORY OF THE TRAPP FAMILY SINGERS – Maria Augusta Trapp (D46) – 95¢
ST. FRANCIS OF ASSISI – G. K. Chesterton (D50) – 85¢
VIPER'S TANGLE – François Mauriac. A novel of evil and redemption (D51) – 95¢
THE AUTOBIOGRAPHY OF ST. THÉRÈSE OF LISIEUX: The Story of a Soul – Translated by John Beevers. An Image Original (D56) – 85¢
THE GREATEST BIBLE STORIES: A Catholic Anthology from World Literature – Edited by Anne Fremantle (D58) – 85¢
THE CITY OF GOD – St. Augustine. Edited by Vernon J. Bourke. Introduction by Étienne Gilson. Specially abridged (D59) – $1.95

OTHER IMAGE BOOKS

CANA IS FOREVER – Charles Hugo Doyle. Catholic guide to dating, courtship, and marriage (D62) – 95¢

ASCENT OF MOUNT CARMEL – St. John of the Cross. Edited and translated by E. Allison Peers (D63) – $1.45

RELIGION AND THE RISE OF WESTERN CULTURE – Christopher Dawson (D64) – 95¢

PRINCE OF DARKNESS AND OTHER STORIES – J. F. Powers (D65) – 95¢

JESUS AND HIS TIMES (2 Volumes) – Henri Daniel-Rops (D67a, D67b) – $1.25 ea.

THE BELIEF OF CATHOLICS – Ronald Knox (D72) – 85¢

THE IDEA OF A UNIVERSITY – John Henry Cardinal Newman. Introduction by G. N. Shuster (D75) – $1.65

DARK NIGHT OF THE SOUL – St. John of the Cross. Edited and translated by E. Allison Peers (D78) – 85¢

TERESA OF AVILA – Marcelle Auclair. Translated by Kathleen Pond (D79) – $1.45

WOMAN OF THE PHARISEES – François Mauriac (D82) – 95¢

THE PILLAR OF FIRE – Karl Stern. A psychiatrist's spiritual journey from Judaism to Catholicism (D83) – 95¢

A POPULAR HISTORY OF THE REFORMATION – Philip Hughes (D92) – $1.25

THE CONFESSIONS OF ST. AUGUSTINE – Translated with an Introduction by John K. Ryan (D101) – $1.45

BABY GROWS IN AGE AND GRACE – Sister Mary de Lourdes. An invaluable practical guide for the physical, mental, and spiritual training of the preschool child (D104) – 95¢

THE THIRD REVOLUTION: A Study of Psychiatry and Religion – Dr. Karl Stern (D113) – 95¢

A WOMAN CLOTHED WITH THE SUN – Edited by John J. Delaney (D118) – $1.25

INTERIOR CASTLE – St. Teresa of Avila. Translated with an Introduction and Notes by E. Allison Peers (D120) – 95¢

THE GREATEST STORY EVER TOLD – Fulton Oursler (D121) – $1.25

THE MEANING OF MAN – Jean Mouroux. The significance of man and his relation to God (D122) – $1.25

WE AND OUR CHILDREN – Mary Reed Newland. Counsels for molding the child in Christian virtues (D123) – 95¢

SOUL OF THE APOSTOLATE – Jean-Baptiste Chautard, O.C.S.D. (D124) – 85¢

LATE HAVE I LOVED THEE – Ethel Mannin. A deeply moving novel of spiritual regeneration (D130) – $1.25

A HISTORY OF PHILOSOPHY: VOLUME 1 – GREECE AND ROME (2 Volumes) – Frederick Copleston, S.J. (D134a, D134b) – $1.45 ea.

A 70 – 2

OTHER IMAGE BOOKS

OTHER IMAGE BOOKS

THE CHURCH IN CRISIS: A History of the General Councils, 325–1870 – Philip Hughes (D168) – $1.25

ISRAEL AND THE ANCIENT WORLD – Henri Daniel-Rops (D169) – $1.55

THE SPIRITUAL EXERCISES OF ST. IGNATIUS – Translated by Anthony Mottola, Ph.D. Introduction by Robert W. Gleason, S.J. (D170) – 85¢

THESE ARE THE SACRAMENTS – Described by Fulton J. Sheen. Photos by Karsh (D174) – 95¢

THE WAY OF PERFECTION – St. Teresa of Avila. Translated and edited by E. Allison Peers (D176) – 85¢

THE CATHOLIC REFORMATION (2 Volumes) – Henri Daniel-Rops (D179a, D179b) – $1.25 ea.

WE HOLD THESE TRUTHS: Catholic Reflections on the American Proposition – John Courtney Murray, S.J. (D181) – $1.25

LIFE AND HOLINESS – Thomas Merton. Exposition of the principles of the spiritual life (D183) – 75¢

MY LIFE WITH CHRIST – Anthony J. Paone, S.J. (D185) – $1.25

A FAMILY ON WHEELS: Further Adventures of the Trapp Family Singers – Maria Augusta Trapp with Ruth T. Murdoch (D187) – 85¢

AMERICAN CATHOLICISM – John Tracy Ellis. A comprehensive survey of the American Church (D190) – 95¢

PARDON AND PEACE – Alfred Wilson, C.P. A complete explanation of the sacrament of penance (D196) – 95¢

THE CATHOLIC FAMILY HANDBOOK – Msgr. George A. Kelly. Foreword by Francis Cardinal Spellman. A complete guide to every aspect of Catholic life (D197) – 95¢

THE COUNCIL, REFORM AND REUNION – with a new Introduction by Fr. Hans Kung (D198) – 95¢

WITH GOD IN RUSSIA – Walter J. Ciszek, S.J., with Daniel L. Flaherty, S.J. (D200) – $1.25

CURRENT TRENDS IN THEOLOGY – Edited by Donald J. Wolf, S.J., and James V. Schall, S.J. (D202) – 95¢

A HOPKINS READER, Revised and Enlarged Edition – Edited with an Introduction by John Pick (D203) – $1.45

JOY – Bertrand Weaver, C.P. A series of meditations on the concept of joy (D211) – 75¢

THE TWO-EDGED SWORD – John L. McKenzie, S.J. Outstanding interpretation of the Old Testament (D215) – $1.35

MORTE D'URBAN – J. F. Powers. A brilliant, poignantly satiric portrait of a worldly priest (D218) – 95¢

OUR CHILDREN GROW UP – Mary Reed Newland. A common-sense guide for Catholic parents (D219) – 85¢

OTHER IMAGE BOOKS

THE INNER SEARCH – Dom Hubert van Zeller, O.S.B. Meditations with a refreshingly new approach (D220) – 95¢

STRANGERS IN THE HOUSE: Catholic Youth in America – Andrew M. Greeley (D221) – 95¢

THE DEPTHS OF THE SOUL: A Christian Approach to Psychoanalysis – Ignace Lepp (D222) – 95¢

THE LILIES OF THE FIELD – William E. Barrett (D225) – 95¢

LETTERS TO NANCY – from Andrew M. Greeley (D226) – 85¢

THE FAMILY AND THE BIBLE – Mary Reed Newland (D228) – $1.25

THE DIVIDING OF CHRISTENDOM – Christopher Dawson (D229) – 95¢

NO MAN IS AN ISLAND – Thomas Merton (D231) – $1.25

AND YOUNG MEN SHALL SEE VISIONS – Andrew M. Greeley. Letters to a young collegian on subjects of burning interest to young men today (D232) – 85¢

CONJECTURES OF A GUILTY BYSTANDER – Thomas Merton. A collection of notes, opinions, reflections (D234) – $1.45

THE POWER OF LOVE – Fulton J. Sheen (D235) – 75¢

THE STORY OF THOMAS MORE – John Farrow (D236) – 95¢

THE NOONDAY DEVIL: Spiritual Support in Middle Age – Bernard Basset, S.J. A funny-serious book of spiritual direction (D237) – 95¢

UNDERSTAND THE BIBLE – J. Holland Smith (D238) – $1.25

HEALTH OF MIND AND SOUL – Ignace Lepp (D239) – 95¢

RELIGION AND PERSONALITY – Adrian van Kaam, C.S.Sp. (D240) – $1.25

RELIGIONS OF THE WORLD (2 Volumes) – John A. Hardon, S.J. An account of the history, beliefs, and practices of the major religions of the world (D241a, D241b) – $1.45 ea.

THE RELIGION OF TEILHARD DE CHARDIN – Henri de Lubac, S.J. (D242) – $1.65

MOMENTS OF TRUTH – Edited by Dan Herr and Joel Wells. An anthology portraying crises of the human spirit by 16 great authors (D243) – 95¢

CHRISTIAN RENEWAL IN A CHANGING WORLD – Bernard Häring, C.SS.R. (D244) – $1.45

THE REED OF GOD – Caryll Houselander. Meditations on our Lady (D245) – 95¢

CHRISTIAN SACRAMENTS AND CHRISTIAN PERSONALITY – Bernard J. Cooke, S.J. (D246) – $1.25

THOUGHTS IN SOLITUDE – Thomas Merton (D247) – 85¢

WE NEUROTICS: A Handbook for the Half-Mad – Bernard Basset, S.J. (D248) – 95¢

POPE JOHN – Meriol Trevor (D249) – $1.25

OTHER IMAGE BOOKS

WHAT IS THE BIBLE? Revised Edition – Henri Daniel-Rops (D250) – 95¢

NEW TESTAMENT ESSAYS – Raymond E. Brown, S.S. (D251) – $1.35

TEILHARD DE CHARDIN AND THE MYSTERY OF CHRIST – Christopher Mooney, S.J. (D252) – $1.35

THE NEW TESTAMENT OF THE JERUSALEM BIBLE: Reader's Edition – Alexander Jones, General Editor (D253) – $1.65

THE HESITANT PILGRIM – American Catholicism After the Council – Andrew M. Greeley (D254) – $1.25

THE FOUR GOSPELS: AN INTRODUCTION (2 Volumes) – Bruce Vawter, C.M. (D255a, D255b) – $1.25 ea.

FACING GOD – William H. Quiery, S.J. (D256) – 95¢

PRAYERS AND DEVOTIONS FROM POPE JOHN XXIII – John P. Donnelly, Editor (D257) – $1.25

IN PURSUIT OF DIETRICH BONHOEFFER – William Kuhns (D258) – $1.35

THE PROTESTANT CHURCHES OF AMERICA – Revised Edition – John A. Hardon (D259) – $1.45

EXISTENTIAL FOUNDATIONS OF PSYCHOLOGY – Adrian van Kaam (D260) – $1.45

THE CATHOLIC EXPERIENCE – An Interpretation of the History of American Catholicism – Andrew M. Greeley (D261) – $1.25

PICNIC IN BABYLON – A Jesuit Priest's Journal – John L'Heureux (D262) – $1.25

SHALOM: PEACE – The Sacrament of Reconciliation – Revised Edition – Bernard Haring, C.SS.R. (D263) – $1.35

LOVE AND SEXUALITY: A CHRISTIAN APPROACH – Revised Edition – Mary Perkins Ryan and John Julian Ryan (D264) – 95¢

PAUL TILLICH IN CATHOLIC THOUGHT – Revised Edition – Thomas F. O'Meara and Donald M. Weisser, Editors (D265) – $1.45

MORALITY FOR OUR TIME – Marc Oraison (D266) – 95¢

THE ECUMENICAL REVOLUTION – Revised and Updated – Robert McAfee Brown (D267) – $1.45

THE WIT AND WISDOM OF BISHOP FULTON J. SHEEN – Edited by Bill Adler (D268) – 95¢

THE SECULAR JOURNAL OF THOMAS MERTON – The personal diary of the late Trappist monk (D269) – $1.25

SUMMA THEOLOGIAE – Thomas Aquinas – Thomas Gilby, O.P., General Editor

Volume 1: The Existence of God; Part One: Questions 1–13 (D270) – $1.45

Volume 2: The Mind and Power of God; Part One: Questions 14–26 (D271) – $1.45

A 70 – 6

OTHER IMAGE BOOKS

THE MIDDLE AGES: A POPULAR HISTORY – Joseph Dahmus (D274) – $1.95

HISTORY OF ETHICS (2 Volumes) – Vernon J. Bourke (D275a, D275b) – $1.45 ea.

THE GOSPELS AND THE JESUS OF HISTORY – Xavier Léon-Dufour, S.J. (D276) – $1.75

WE AGNOSTICS: On the Tightrope to Eternity – Bernard Basset, S.J. (D277) – 95¢

INTRODUCTION TO THE OLD TESTAMENT (2 Volumes) – André Robert and André Feuillet (D278a, D278b) – $1.95 ea.